PROVE IT: MU[illegible]

A Likable D[illegible]

Hannah R. Kurz

To my husband

Copyright © 2020 Hannah R. Kurz
All rights reserved.

CHAPTER 1

Skillful hands moved quickly and powerfully through yeasted dough – rolling, punching, folding, proving – until each mound achieved just the right bounce when prodded. Different spices speckled the workspace in turns before being cleared away, first cinnamon, then nutmeg, allspice, cloves, and a hint of cardamom. In the heat of the oven, the rolls ascended in glory before a necessary rest, their heady aroma rising to the apartments above.

The familiar smells first awoke Steph in apartment number two, being directly above the bakery, and bleary eyes blinked open for what seemed at least the fifth, and final, time.

"Mmm, cinnamon buns," she gauged. She never tired from this type of awakening, but she would have appreciated it more an hour or two later. She had no way of knowing she wouldn't taste another for weeks to come, or that tomorrow a different team would gather in the bakery, taking stock of fluids, fibers, and fingerprints. And the only thing leaving in a to-go bag was a corpse.

Steph roused herself from the armchair, careful not to wake her newborn daughter. She hoped she hadn't dozed off in there for too long. The pediatrician might not approve of their unconventional sleeping arrangement, but it had been mommy or bust last night.

2

Steph put the baby down and checked the clock. More than an hour had passed since she last recalled reading a neon-red "5:00." She said aloud, "I wonder if I have time to—" and a small cry pierced her thought.

The seven pound ten ounce, two-week-old bundle informed her, firstly, she was wet, and secondly, anything short of mom's body heat was unacceptable.

Steph tended to the little nursling as fast as unpracticed fingers could, putting her down again for a minute to change into her mom uniform of late. The high-waisted leggings were supportive, though they made her legs feel like sausages, while the long t-shirt hid what she wasn't ready for the world to see. She pulled on an oversized sweater for extra warmth and disguise. Sweater weather was her favorite. Like a wearable weighted blanket, nothing made her feel cozier or more secure than a heavy knit, and for half of the year upstate New York delivered the requisite cold, sometimes earlier than expected or desired. At least she didn't need galoshes, yet.

Contrary to expectations, living above a bakery hadn't made her gain excessively during pregnancy. Morning sickness had kept her appetite in check most days, but she still felt bloated and out of sorts. It would take time for her organs to settle back in properly after acquiescing to baby's frequent requests for more space. Her abs might never want to return.

She peered into the bottom half of the bathroom mirror for a minute, flattening flyaway strands of chestnut hair. Nowadays, kept up in a messy bun for convenience, in the past a perfectly sleek ponytail regularly swished back and forth, brushing her shoulders as then Stephanie Smit pivoted around future partner Henry Wu to complete another layup. He had later told her he was "Smit-ten" at first sight. There was no way he could have missed the shortest, and "cutest," girl on the basketball courts. She replied she was "smitten with Wu, too."

She picked up a tube of concealer, then set it back down. "Too dark," she told herself. She hadn't spent as much time out in the sun this past summer. Pregnancy and heat wave didn't mix.

Picking up her daughter, who appreciated her mother's pillowy parts, Steph then made her way to the kitchen where hot tea and scrambled eggs awaited her. She stood on her tiptoes to kiss her husband on his freshly-shaven jaw. She would have hugged him or run her fingers through his silky black hair, but she was afraid the baby's head would wobble.

Henry pulled both wife and child into a careful embrace. When they separated, Steph noticed her husband was dressed for work and remembered his paternity leave was over.

"Are-you-going-to-be-okay-by-yourself? Do-you-want-me-to-call-my-sister? I-can-come-back-during-lunch-and-give-you-a-break," Henry offered.

Steph was sure he didn't say that all in one breath, but in her semi-comatose state everything was racing past her. A minute later she replied, "No… I think I want to try to see if I can manage by myself today. Thanks." She flashed him a tired smile.

She wolfed down the food, then quickly added, "And thanks for the eggs." She scanned the kitchen, eager for more calories to inhale. Henry noticed her hungry look.

"These are from downstairs," her husband said, handing her a brown bag. "Everyone's hoping to get a glimpse of Madeline later. They said there's more waiting for you."

Salivary glands in suspense, Steph pulled out a massive cinnamon roll, generously frosted. God, she loved living here. She hadn't planned on staying so far north long-term, just for college, but the area, and her husband, had successfully wooed her.

She had moved in four years prior. She couldn't resist the FOR RENT sign in the window a few feet above a gorgeous display of jewel-toned macarons, the house specialty alongside anise and turmeric buns at the French-Lebanese bakery. Gilded lettering charmed while perfectly golden baked goods and sumptuous smells further enticed. Upstairs, the accommodations equally enchanted, with old glass windows, oak floors, and a generous bathtub.

Steph awoke every day to the smell of

breads, cakes, and spices, and since The Likable Daisy opened so early, it closed at dinnertime, a quiet, ideal neighbor. In addition, her popularity at work rose as high as the bakery's pumpkin brioche since she started bringing a fresh loaf every Friday.

When the question of where to live after getting married arose, it didn't take much more than a fresh hot cross bun to convince her husband-to-be this was the place to be. As soon as someone vacated the two-bedroom apartment on the second floor, they snatched that up like the last hot cookie on a plate.

Later, surprise, a honeymoon baby arrived, and Steph still didn't have the heart to leave. In fact, she fell more deeply in love with the historic wrought iron and brick and the picturesque views of the old downtown. Bashful pinks and youthful greens adorned its tree-lined avenues in spring, while ruby and amber reigned in autumn.

Soft furnishings and puffy pastries on demand further heightened the comfy-cozy atmosphere to which Steph aspired. Bringing a baby home here only made the feeling more complete.

And how could she forget her delightful neighbors, who were just as much a part of the building as its features. Rachel Park, a grad school violinist, played beautifully and at sensible hours in the studio on the third floor, which endeared her to everyone. Next door to Rachel, inhabiting Steph's old single bedroom apartment was recent college grad Greg Nowak and his mischievous husky

Alaska, who had also adopted the other humans in the building. Residents often bumped into each other downstairs, and the promise of a hot drink and fresh-out-of-the-oven goodness easily persuaded people to stay and chat.

Steph took a gulp of Earl Grey. Coffee could wait until later when she was conscious enough to make it properly. Last time, she forgot to add the beans and ended up with hot water. On second thought, maybe she should leave brewing to the professionals, who had much nicer equipment.

She straightened her husband's tie. After college he had traded his high tops and top knot for Windsor knots and QuickBooks. Then she kissed and thanked him generously for the food. One last cuddle with their daughter and he was off, leaving Steph by herself with the baby for the first time in two weeks.

What could she accomplish today, she wondered. Would Madeline be happy on her own, or would she need to wear her in a carrier the entire time? For the moment, she seemed content in her bouncer. Steph tried to appreciate each indulgent bite of cinnamon roll, but she knew she'd only have so much time before sticky fingers would be inconvenient.

Her roll devoured, Steph checked her list of things to do while on maternity leave. She attempted a few thank-you cards first. After three baby showers, plenty remained, but her hand cramped, and she kept getting interrupted. She resisted the urge to check her work e-mail.

Steph was a graphic designer at a local ad agency. Back in the day, she had double majored in painting and graphic design. However, upon graduating, she hadn't seen a career for herself as a full-time artist, at least, one that would pay off her student loans quickly. At the moment, she had three more weeks of maternity leave to figure out what she wanted to do when it ended.

Putting a pause on her existential crisis, Steph placed Madeline in a soft wrap carrier and set about fluffing cushions and catching up on British gardening shows instead. The baby dozed on her. After accomplishing some laundry folding, she convinced herself now was a good time for a break and headed to the bakery.

A bell above the door announced her entrance, and a wave of warmth and comforting scents washed over her. She could not only smell, but also see her sweet tooth's desire. The regulars quickly got up to welcome her and take a peek at the baby. "Isn't she just darling?" they all cooed.

"Welcome back," said Charlotte, the head baker, walking in toward the front from the kitchen. Tight curls attempted to escape a faded ball cap speckled with flour, while rolled up sleeves revealed a blooming orchid tattooed on one forearm and a spray of crocuses on the other. A smattering of freckles across her nose glistened from exertion. "I'll take care of this customer," she told John, who had been working the register and fulfilling simple orders. "You can take a short break."

"Yes, Charlotte." The broad-shouldered young man walked away to get himself a glass of water.

"New guy," Charlotte explained. "You know, I played football with his older brother years ago. Now that was a tight end." She winked. Charlotte had been a lineman, or so Steph remembered. Football wasn't her forte. "I don't recommend it though. I still get random headaches sometimes." She paused. "Is that sweet little Madeline? What an angel! I see she got momma's hair!"

Yes, Madeline had inherited Steph's brown locks, but everything else was all Daddy. There was no denying her paternity.

"What would you like? This one's on me." Charlotte was already reaching for a chocolate croissant.

"You know me." Steph laughed. Charlotte grabbed one and reached for a second.

"Are you still eating for two," Charlotte said with a smile. That had been Steph's excuse when she had previously indulged while pregnant.

"Nursing," she declared affirmatively. "It burns something like five hundred calories a day!" Charlotte put both pastries on a plate.

"I gotta get me one of those. Do you suppose I could borrow her after the holidays?" Charlotte joked, then added, "Do you want a cappuccino to go with it?"

"Could you make it a double, or a triple?"

Steph asked with a smile. "I think my brain is stuck in another time zone even though I've only traveled downstairs." Sure, she could make one herself at home, but this was one local business she always loved to support.

"Well, bon appétit, Madame. May this flaky pastry transport you hours ahead to chère Paris." Charlotte handed her the plate. "You know, I remember when I started doing the early shift at the bakery, making everything ready for the morning crowd. The first month or so was brutal. The first time I made sweet turmeric rolls, I gave one to Sameed to taste. He bit into it, spat it out, and almost cried with laughter, then asked, 'What did Jesus say about salt?' I shrugged. He said, 'I don't know either, but I don't recommend it as a substitute for sugar.' I could have died. Afterward, he made me an espresso and started on a fresh batch of dough, while I woke up a little more. But since then, I've grown to enjoy the quiet mornings."

"No way!" Steph laughed.

"Yep, but I learned my lesson and do regular taste checks now. So good luck, momma!" Charlotte saluted her.

"Thanks." Grabbing her plate, Steph chose a table by one of the displays, out of the way of normal foot traffic for her and Madeline. Indirect sunlight filtered through the wall of glass, and the bay window seemed to embrace them. Steph already felt a little more awake. What seemed like only a minute later, Charlotte brought over the cappuccino. She then traded places with the trainee and went back into the kitchen, while he stood at the counter.

The bakery had a gleaming, stainless steel coffee station behind the register. The top of the line Italian model sat boastfully on the counter, and the espresso it produced was exquisite. The delicious, tawny foam on top of a shot, which only a quality machine produces, added to the velvety texture. Steph was in heaven. The acidity of the coffee cut through the buttery pastry's flaky layers, while dark chocolate mingled decadently with both. She savored the experience every time.

"Steph! How wonderful to see you! How is that beautiful baby of yours?" A bright-smiling, clean-shaven figure in a pressed floral shirt, pants, and coordinating silk tie walked toward their table. Sameed Ishaaq Haddad, the owner of The Likeable Daisy, came out to greet one of his best and his newest customers. "Do you mind if I join you?" he asked Steph.

"Of course not," she replied. He pulled up a chair.

"So how are you doing?" Sameed was sincere. He had asked the same question about a thousand times when Steph was pregnant. So, Steph gave him an honest answer.

"Madeline's wonderful, but I'm exhausted."

"Can I get you another cappuccino?" he offered though her cup was still half full.

"Thanks, but Charlotte made this one a

triple. I should probably wait a few hours before I have another one of these." She flashed her pearly whites, hoping she didn't have any flakes stuck in between her teeth.

"Let me know when you need anything."

"Thank you." The bell rang again, and a middle-aged gentleman with a full, graying beard and dark clothing walked in. "Excuse me," Sameed said to Steph.

"Of course." He walked over to greet the taller, leaner man.

"Welcome, brother!"

"Salaam," said Ayman.

"What brings you in? Please." Sameed gestured toward an open table with two chairs a few feet from Steph. Both men sat down. "John, can you prepare two espressos?" His finger pointed down to where they were seated. John nodded. "Thanks."

"Well, since you never answer my calls or texts, this is the only way I can talk to you," Ayman answered. He lowered his voice. "I see you are not keeping halal." He pointed to Sameed's silk tie. "And hear you are seeing a –" Here, he used a word Steph didn't recognize. "Is this true? You know what our father would say."

"He's dead, and my dating life is none of your concern." Sameed matched his brother's tone and volume. John brought the espressos out. The small white cups each came accompanied by a packet of sugar and a tiny silver spoon. Both men ripped open the paper and poured.

"We're family, and whomever you marry becomes part of this family."

"As if family choosing for me worked so well the first time." They stirred aggressively.

"Maybe if you had tried, it would have." His brother took a breath. "Look. You should come to the mosque for evening prayer tonight. It would be good for you."

"I'm sorry. I have other plans. " By the look on his face, Steph thought Sameed expected another lecture. By the look on his brother's, it seemed one was coming. Steph felt as if she were watching a train wreck in progress. It was awkward, but she couldn't focus her attention anywhere else.

The elder switched to Arabic, setting down his spoon, while Sameed sipped his espresso. The two went back and forth. Sameed's curt responses contrasted his brother's longer diatribes. At one point, a finger pointed angrily at his chest before the hand slammed down on the table. A few heads turned. Sameed's brother switched back to English. "I should get going. Goodbye, brother." He stood up abruptly, leaving his espresso untouched.

"Goodbye." The younger man sighed as the other exited quickly. He checked his watch and cleared off the table himself, disappearing into the back.

When Sameed left, different neighbors and regulars joined Steph in turns for updates on "Little Maddie" and mom life, diffusing the tension.

"Hey Steph!" "Good to see you!" "How are you?" "How's the baby?"

"Great." "Tiring." "We're good." "Healthy." She was exhausted and sore, but that was to be expected. Overall, she was tremendously satisfied with things as they were at the moment.

Suddenly, Madeline's little face crumpled. It was time for another nap.

Steph drank her last cold sip of cappuccino and headed back upstairs, saying goodbye for now to everyone in the shop. Maybe now would be a good time to squeeze in a shower.

Bliss. She felt human again. The pounding heat soothed her back and sore body. She avoided looking down at the damage. Now was the time to show herself some compassion. Growing a human was hard work, and it took time to knit things back together. At least she could see her feet again.

Out of the shower, Steph brushed through straight, wet tangles, and wished for her mother's easy blond curls, though it was not something she could have inherited. Sadly, she wouldn't have time to blow dry. She checked her phone. She was expecting a friend to drop off a meal tonight. She was just finishing getting dressed when her doorbell rang.

"Hey, I'm here," said the intercom. She buzzed her friend Jane into the building. Once at the door, she greeted her friend with a hug.

"Hey! Thanks for coming! Ooh, this should keep the vamps away for *weeks*," Steph happily noted, smelling the heavy garlic before even checking out the chow.

"You can never be too careful now that the sun sets at five o'clock," A smart bobbed head replied, poking inside. "Where's the little one?"

"Snoozing. When's your next shift, or did you just get off?" Jane was wearing bumblebee scrubs. The loose-fitting work clothes hid a svelte body beneath. As a nurse, her fitness tracker only served as a timepiece and a reminder to check on patients. When off duty, Jane personified glamour and danced the night away.

"Aw. I have another hour or two before I need to be in." Jane worked at two different local hospitals. Because of her schedule, she often had afternoons free and usually spent them at Steph's place.

"Do you want to have dinner here first?"

"I'm sorry. I can't. I have some errands to run before work, but next time. I promise."

"Well, at least take this cinnamon roll," said Steph, offering the last one. Jane, ever the carb lover, graciously accepted before heading toward the door.

"You're the best," Jane exclaimed. "By the way, did you hear that Mick and Mara are dating? He broke up with Ashley, and she ended things with Brad. And your coworker Eliza is gonna have a baby in May." In one quick breath, Jane delivered four pieces of unpublished gossip. Steph was impressed.

"How do you know these things?"

"Give and you shall receive," Jane said sagely.

"And which is greater? I hope my life isn't juicy enough to merit sharing."

"Only the baby pictures you send," Jane promised, smiling. "How do I put this nicely… your life is drama deficient." And that was exactly how Steph liked it.

"Well, thanks again for the meal! Will I see you this Thursday?" Steph asked.

"I can do Thursday," her friend confirmed. "See you around lunchtime?"

"Perfect. Oh, and don't forget to ask off for next Saturday. Not this weekend, but the following. For my Halloween party." Other than having her in-laws over, it would be Steph's first attempt at hosting an event after baby.

"I wouldn't miss it for the world. I can't wait to see the costumes you three come up with, and I've already got mine picked out. Who else is coming again? Any single guys?"

"Great! So far there's you, Greg and Rachel from upstairs, Charlotte from downstairs, and Dennis, our landlord, though I don't think you'd go for him. Greg, maybe. We'll see. We might invite a few more people, but I'm really looking forward to it."

"Me too. See you later."

Back in the kitchen, Steph pulled her hair in a wet bun, warming the food on the stove and in the oven while she had the chance. Soon Henry would be home. She had officially survived a whole day by herself.

As soon as he was in doorway he said, "How was your day?" He led with his left side, obscuring the opposite arm behind his back. A bark from upstairs filtered through before the door closed.

"Thanks! It went pretty well. Did some laundry, showered, took some pictures…" Steph leaned to the side to try to peak around. "I can show you later. Do you have something there?" Steph's remembered the morning's treat with fondness.

"This is for you." He handed her a neatly wrapped package.

"Oh! What is it? Can I open it now?" She started to peel a corner. Something rolled inside. They weren't chocolates.

"Go ahead."

She tore into the paper, and her eyes lit up. "Thank you!" She exclaimed upon seeing a watercolor paint set. She appraised the box holding several gorgeous palettes. She couldn't wait to run her fingers over the paper and brushes. It had been some time since she had painted for pleasure. She hadn't wanted to take any risks pregnant.

"I thought you might like it." Henry set down his coat and keys.

"You are too sweet!" Steph hugged him, and Henry returned the embrace. "I can't wait to try it out." Henry smiled with satisfaction.

"How about after dinner?" he suggested.

"I'm starving." He sat down at the table.

"Of course. How was your day? Find any major accounting errors?" Steph plated two servings and took turns with Henry eating and holding Madeline, who woke up from her nap right at dinnertime.

"Fine. One woman tried to claim her chickens, and their eggs, as dependents, so her income wouldn't be taxable." Steph put down her spoon.

"You're kidding."

"Nope. I told her she couldn't deduct her chickens before they hatched, or after."

"How long have you been waiting to tell that joke, nine months?" She resumed eating.

"It's my right and duty as a father."

After finishing the meal Jane had kindly provided, Steph and Henry set to work on washing the few dirtied dishes in the sink. Madeline watched from her bouncer.

"So I was thinking about going back to work and—" *BAM!* A door slammed downstairs, a bowl shattered, and Madeline started crying.

"Shhhh! It's okay." Steph soothed. Startled, she had dropped her dish. "Sorry. That must be Sameed going home," she said to Henry. Steph picked up Madeline, while Henry swept up the ruined ceramic.

Afterward, the couple made themselves comfortable on the couch. Watching a mindless action movie with the volume on low sounded like a good plan. They assumed the baby couldn't tell what was going on as bullets rained on screen and another explosion went off. A second followed, but this one smelled. Henry offered to change her this time, pausing the film. The baby fed on and off for half an hour near the end, and once the film finished, they settled down for the night.

Steph changed into nursing pajamas, hating the feel of encased legs at bedtime. Her body still felt weird, so different from what it had been shape and function-wise less than a month ago, like a deflating dirigible devoid of its sole passenger.

She tiptoed into the bathroom to brush her teeth, squeezing past Henry.

"Sorry. Let me just get this… One second." Finally, she grasped her toothbrush. Having longer arms would have helped, or longer legs, or a longer torso.

"Are you going to be okay tomorrow by yourself? I could try to get off or take an early lunch," he suggested.

"I think I can handle it," Steph said with a little more confidence than she felt. She didn't want to be a bother and hoped she'd sleep better tonight. Little did she know of the challenges motherhood and mayhem would throw her way. After tomorrow, even Jane would agree the adjective "boring" ceased to apply to Steph's life.

CHAPTER 2

Steph was already semi-awake when the sirens came blaring down the street, but that wasn't unusual living downtown. What caught her off guard was the sound didn't continue down Greenway Avenue. Stray beams of flashing red and blue lights filtered through the crack where their blackout curtains met. Steph gently placed a finger in Madeline's tiny exposed ear.

For a second, panic pierced her heart, and she considered the possibility of a fire. However, the sirens shut off, and neither the wail of an oncoming fire engine, nor smoke alarm, was ever heard. Steph removed her finger and returned to cradling the newborn with both arms. Her daughter nursed blissfully unaware and unconscious.

A few hours later after the sun had risen and Henry had left, someone knocked on the door. Steph, still in last night's crinkled nursing gown and burping a baby, answered.

"Hello?" Steph spied through the peephole and got a glimpse of someone medium height dressed in a polo shirt and slacks.

"Hi, Steph. It's Dennis," her landlord, Dennis Kaplan, confirmed. She covered herself up with a long robe and opened the door to a familiar bespectacled face with salt and pepper hair.

"Good morning. Did I forget the rent check

this month? I could have sworn I dropped it off a day or two ago…" Steph tried to remember exactly when she paid him.

"No, it's not that. Unfortunately, Sameed was found dead early this morning."

"What?! No! How can that be possible?" If she hadn't been holding Madeline, Steph's hand would have slipped in disbelief.

"There was an accident in the kitchen. Charlotte found him."

"That's terrible! What happened?"

"I don't know. The police won't allow anyone near the scene, but from what I overheard, the detectives are pretty confident it was just an accident."

"I can't believe it," Steph said. Though Dennis wasn't the type to play cruel practical jokes, it almost seemed more plausible than the thought of Sameed being dead. "Poor Sameed… Does everyone else in the building already know?"

"Some do. A few already left, so I'll have to inform them tonight."

"I'm sorry it's your job to tell everyone. That can't be easy."

He shrugged.

"Well, I'll let you go," Steph suggested, not knowing what else to say and desirous of some privacy. The last thing she wanted was to get emotional in front of an audience.

She closed the door, and her breath hitched in her throat. She wondered how Sameed could be gone and what would become of the beloved bakery downstairs.

Difficult as it was with post-baby hormones, Steph suppressed the urge to cry because loud sounds upset Madeline. Steph sniffled and held her baby close instead. She would have to wait for Henry to come home and comfort her. She didn't have it in her to call him right now. Her throat was too tight for her to vocalize.

Steph wondered how it could be possible that her friend was gone. She had known him for four years. The Likable Daisy had hosted her wedding and baby showers. She wondered what would happen to that wonderful place he had built below. She hoped the bakery would find a way to continue. She ended her train of thought abruptly.

"Steph, what does it matter what happens to the bakery? Sameed is dead," she chastised. She sat on the couch for an hour or two, not marking the passage of time. Eventually, she realized she needed proper clothes and maybe a change of setting, and made her way back to her room. She put Madeline down to peruse her drawers, closet, and floor. Clean leggings were nowhere in sight, so she squeezed herself into a pair of pants. True, these were not her skinniest jeans, but she buttoned them feeling triumphant and the slightest bit distracted from her grief. Next, she slipped on something over her head that smelled clean and layered the baby carrier on top, placing in Madeline last.

Downstairs, she gazed sadly at the sign

flipped to CLOSED behind leaded glass, thinking her friend was truly gone. For the moment, she tried to banish the thought and jogged across the street into the arms of the competition. Black Coffee Bistro also offered hot drinks and small plates and had more in the way of lunch options, but their baked goods couldn't compare. Muffins, bagels, and loaves arrived by the truckload and were reheated on demand.

Steph recognized a few familiar faces inside, refugees like her, searching for a sugary sanctuary for the foreseeable future. Black Coffee Bistro was busier than ever. The restaurant predated The Likable Daisy, but the breakfast crowd had changed allegiance after the latter's arrival.

While waiting for her order, Steph scanned the people seated inside. Her neighbors and some of the other regulars downstairs formed a loose circle. A minute later, a barista called out "cappuccino" and handed her a disposable cup. Steph was immediately nostalgic for the porcelain ones across the street, and started to walk over toward the group.

"It's terrible isn't it," someone started, "what happened to Sameed?"

"Poor guy was only thirty-eight."

"No way."

"Really?"

"So young." Heads nodded in agreement. Steph wondered if it might be a mistake to join them.

"I heard he was strangled by his own tie," added another. "Wound by accident in a mixer." A collective "ugh" went through the small crowd. Steph gasped.

"Do you think he was working on a new recipe?" someone mused.

"At that hour? We'll never know now."

Steph absorbed this information drop by drop. She sipped her "cappuccino." It had too much milk for her liking. Her stomach might complain about that in a few hours. She sidled her way in.

"It's Steph and Maddie," they exclaimed, admiring the cute little baby with a full head of hair.

"You look well," exclaimed Rachel from upstairs. Well was pretty generous, thought Steph, with her red-rimmed eyes, but Rachel was always kind with her words.

"Thank you."

"How's life with the little one?" asked Caleb, a local retiree and former real estate agent. He still dressed sharply and had several grandchildren of his own. Steph considered how to put it accurately and succinctly.

"Amazing and tiring, so far," she admitted. "It's a marathon, really." She could say this with confidence, having experienced the swollen feet, trigger-happy bladder, and overall soreness that came with running 26.2 miles.

"We were talking about The Likable Daisy," Greg filled in after a lull, addressing the elephant in the room. He picked up his coffee, and a raven-haired beauty peeked out from beneath his long sleeve. "The rest of us are pretty unsettled."

"It's horrible," said Steph. "Poor Sameed. I can't believe he's gone. Do you think they'll close permanently?"

"No idea. Maybe Charlotte will take over," Greg suggested, taking a sip.

"Or maybe not, after that experience. Could you see yourself working in that place again after witnessing… you know," posed Rachel, ever the sympathetic one.

The group murmured its assent, then upon realizing they were gossiping about the competition, and perhaps a bit too loudly, switched to small talk.

Steph remained there for twenty minutes or so before heading back home. She dispensed of the remainder of her drink and cup on her way out. It was time for Madeline to take another nap. Back in her apartment and alone with her thoughts, she considered the things she had overheard. Confusion replaced some of her sadness.

Sameed, who usually didn't work in the kitchen, died there, baking sometime between closing and 4:00 AM.

He was wearing a tie, which was typical for him, but abnormal for anyone who got anywhere near the ovens.

He was ostensibly testing out a recipe, but was using the bakery's industrial mixer and doing so without his head baker.

None of it made any sense.

Something curdled in her gut, but it wasn't the excessively milky coffee she had imbibed earlier. More questions troubled her. When exactly did he die? Did he ever go home that night? Why make a large batch of something untested? She was wondering how and if she could find answers to them, when Henry turned the key in the door.

"How was your day," Henry asked, concerned by the look on Steph's face.

Where could she begin, she wondered. How did one go about saying, "Sameed is dead. He died in a freak baking accident, but I think he was killed?" Steph paused to assemble her thoughts.

"That bad, huh? Where's Maddie?"

"Sleeping in the bassinet."

"Do you want to order something tonight?" Henry suggested, noticing an empty stove and clear countertops.

"Oh. Sorry," Steph said. "I forgot about dinner. Does Greek food sound okay to you?" She could bring up the topic then.

"Yeah, order whatever you want. Just make sure there's extra," Henry replied.

"Sounds good." And within thirty minutes the aroma of floury pita, garlicky gyro meat, and tangy tzatziki sauce, among other luxurious smells, dominated the kitchen, another benefit of living downtown.

The pair dug in, forks and knives blazing. No entrée was left unscathed. While emotions tended to suppress her appetite, nursing was hungry work.

A few minutes into the meal, she mustered enough composure and courage to tell him the news and voice her crazy suspicion.

"Henry?"

"Yeah?"

"Did you hear about Sameed downstairs?"

"No, what about him?"

"He died. Charlotte found him in the bakery kitchen early this morning."

"Oh my God, that's horrible. What happened?"

"They say it looked like a freak accident with his tie and a mixer, but, Henry, look, I think something's not right."

"What do you mean?"

"I mean, things just don't add up. Why didn't Sameed go home for dinner? Didn't we hear him leave? If he did, why'd he come back in those clothes if he were going to bake? Why did he keep his tie on? Wouldn't it get dirty? Why was he using such a large mixer in the middle of the night after a long day? Wouldn't he know how to shut it off? I keep thinking about how unlike him it is to do any of those things."

"So," he said, chewing his words, "you think Sameed was murdered?" A peal from the bedroom announced Madeline had awoken.

"Well it sounds mad when you say it out loud, but nothing else makes sense," Steph replied, moving away from the table. "At the very least it seems suspicious, right?" She left Henry to ponder.

"Have you talked to anyone about it," he projected. "Are you going to mention anything to the police?"

"No," she said, coming back into the kitchen with the baby over her shoulder. "Do you think they'd believe me? I think maybe if I talk to Charlotte—"

"You want to interrogate the poor woman who found his body? Look, Steph, this is police business, and Charlotte has gone through enough as it is." He paused. "If you have a suspicion, talk to the police. Let them handle it."

She acquiesced and kept the knowledge of Sameed's argument with his brother to herself for the moment. The couple spent the remainder of the evening in quiet reverie, loving on the tiny little human they had created together, but in the back of her mind, the day's events twisted and turned. If Steph's suspicions were correct, then a monster lurked nearby.

CHAPTER 3

It was dark out when Steph awoke Thursday morning. However, the time on the clock convinced her going back to sleep made as much sense as decaf coffee. Yesterday she had spent in vain trying to get more shuteye, but Madeline and her grief wouldn't let her rest. So, she thought she would try the opposite approach today.

She slipped out of bed and made her way to the kitchen. As espresso brewed, her thoughts percolated. She suspected she didn't have enough evidence to substantiate her fears. What if they were only sleep deprivation-fueled hallucinations? Maybe the regulars would have new information to share in the form of gossip. The sound of splashing interrupted her thought.

"Oh no, not again," she cried, trying to quickly find a suitable cup to catch the remaining brew. She looked down ruefully at the tablespoon of dark liquid and forgotten espresso cup. Desperate, she poured the contents of the drip tray, passing it through the filter once more. Now, she had almost two shots worth. She reset the machine. "Let's make it four."

Steph frothed milk and added it to her cup, cradling the hot mug with both hands. She drank before it cooled, thinking she didn't have time to sip. The clock read, "6:30." As it remained quiet,

Steph made breakfast for herself and Henry, who had just walked into the kitchen. The heavy scent of sizzling bacon filled the air. For a moment, both forgot about the lack of smells coming from downstairs.

"You're up early," he noted.

"Mmhm."

"Any plans for today?"

"Maybe a walk to the park if the weather's nice."

"That sounds nice." They stopped to eat breakfast. Madeline awoke. Henry, the faster eater, went to pick her up.

"Hello, baby girl. Daddy's got you," he soothed. Madeline tried to suck on Henry's shoulder, leaving a wet mark.

"Oh, someone's hungry. I can take her," Steph said, shoveling down the last bite of eggs and toast with chocolate sprinkles. The Smits had passed on their love of the Dutch treat, as well as Gouda, herring, and French fries with mayo.

The couple traded goodbyes, and Steph sat down with Madeline on the couch. It was too cold to venture out this early, so they watched a gardening show. This made Steph the slightest bit envious of a yard. After the mercury climbed a few more degrees, they headed outside for a walk around the neighborhood.

The air was brisk for October, but the two had bundled up. Steph couldn't resist the matching mommy and me knitted hats. Madeline's little face peered up at her from the stroller. Cold as it was, she was well insulated on all sides and didn't seem to mind her accommodations.

Steph walked down Greenway Ave, appreciating the succession of colorful displays. Clothing boutiques with elegant mannequins, fancy oil and vinegar shops with gleaming bottles, restaurants with cozy chair gatherings, and more filled the rows of historic buildings. Steph wondered how many different lives and businesses had occupied them over the last hundred years, and still they breathed new life. It seemed almost every week she was hearing about a new place to try.

She stopped to sit on a bench in front of a nice little park and catch her breath. Her OB had warned her not to push herself too much. A bike path meandered through the middle of the still green lawn and disheveled trees, and two bistros sandwiched the plot. She considered getting a bite to eat. Soup would be nice on a day like today.

Steph gazed up at the sky but didn't like the look of the clouds. She checked her watch. She had best be heading back. Jane was supposed to hang out with her around noon. About a block away from her apartment, Steph noticed a woman in numerous layers of baggy clothes across the street. She walked slowly as if in pain, her gate uneven. She carried a rickety cane, but its length didn't seem right for her.

"I wonder where she's going," Steph thought when a sudden sprinkling announced the arrival of storm clouds. Thankfully, she had an umbrella stowed under the stroller for this very occasion, but it appeared the woman across the street had none. Steph felt sorry for her. She watched the woman for a moment before determining she seemed harmless and crossed the street to see if there was something she could do.

"Hi," Steph said, sheltering the other woman with part of her umbrella. "I couldn't help but notice you in the rain without an umbrella. If I had another, I'd give it to you. Can I help you get a ride somewhere? I could call my husband." Henry was at work, but he could take lunch early.

"No, that's sweet of you. If I could just borrow your phone, I can call my aunt and she can pick me up." Up close, exhaustion was written across the deep lines of the woman's pale, gaunt face, and a few straggly strands of hair wisped around her ears, poking out from under a loose beanie. She didn't seem quite as old as Steph's grandmother, Omi, but appeared to have lived a harder life.

"Sure, of course. Go ahead." Steph pulled out her cell. After two minutes, the woman hung up the phone and handed it back to Steph.

"She said she can be here in fifteen minutes."

"Okay, I can wait with you until then." Steph noticed the woman clutched a zippered bag in one hand. "Are you headed somewhere?" She felt silly for not knowing a better way to initiate a conversation.

"Nowhere in particular." The woman started

rambling about her life, how she grew up in this area, how she discovered she was allergic to heroin, how she lost her last job. A few missing teeth garbled her speech. Steph wondered how long she had been living like this, and how she survived.

At one point the woman commented, "Your baby is cute. Her daddy take care of you two?"

"Yes," Steph answered, then reminded, "My *husband* is at work today."

"That's good. Mine didn't stick around." Steph wasn't sure if the woman meant her father or a former partner, but she felt more sorry for her.

A neat, compact car pulled up and out walked a prim woman with graying hair pulled back in a tight bun. She looked to be wearing her Sunday best.

"Hi, Aunt Lucy," greeted the woman. When Steph had first heard "Aunt," she assumed an elderly woman hunched over and wearing bifocals. Lucy couldn't have been more than fifty-five. Steph suddenly realized her companion must be much younger than her original estimation.

"Get in the car," the older woman ordered, ushering her in. Steph got the impression this wasn't the first time her niece had called her. The aunt turned toward Steph. "Thank you, you didn't have to do that." The aunt assessed Steph's youthfulness. "You know, she's probably not much older than you," she reflected.

"I'm so sorry." Steph didn't know what else to say.

"It wasn't your doing. God bless." And two women drove off.

"Wow!" Steph thought. She hadn't realized drugs could age someone so dramatically.

She walked the rest of the way home a little shaken, but the experience gave her an idea. As she stopped in front of her building she noticed a figure moving behind the bakery displays. It was Charlotte. Charlotte noticed her too.

"Steph," she exclaimed a little less brightly than usual.

"Charlotte," Steph echoed with equal enthusiasm.

"How good to see you and little Maddie. How are you?"

"Well. How are you? I see you're taking down the displays." Steph pointed out the obvious to strike up a conversation.

"The pastries go bad pretty quickly. I think the cleaners assumed they were fake and forgot to toss them out, but they've gotta go too. It's a shame. It's quite a waste."

"Yeah, that's too bad. I do miss the pastries from here."

"Thanks. Maybe I can make something for you and the baby soon," Charlotte said with a smile. "Oh, and speaking of the cleaners, are you missing a diamond earring? They found one."

"No, I don't own a pair."

"Huh. Maybe belongs to a customer. No one on staff claimed it."

"You should probably hold onto it in case someone comes back here looking for it," Steph suggested.

"You're probably right." Then, the corners of Charlotte's mouth turned down a little. "That's if we ever open again. I'm not sure what will happen to this place," she confessed.

"I'm sorry." It was all Steph could think to say. She knew how much this place meant to Charlotte.

"I could have sworn no one was in the building," Charlotte started out of the blue. "All of the aprons were hanging up, and the place was freezing cold like it always is before we turn on the ovens. Everything was so normal, and then… to find Sameed like *that*…" Tears rolled down her face. Steph moved in to embrace her. Charlotte typically hefted fifty-pound bags of flour with ease, but now struggled to stay upright. As small as Steph was, it was her petite frame that supported the larger, stronger woman. "It was so awful, Steph. Why was he there all alone?"

"I'm so sorry, Charlotte. I'm so sorry you experienced that. I can't even imagine…" Steph trailed. Contrary to her words, Steph's mind did try to picture the quiet, dark kitchen and the surprise horror that awaited. "Would you like to come upstairs? I can make you something."

"No, it's alright. Thank you," Charlotte said, drying her tears with a sleeve.

"Anytime, please. You're always welcome to

come over. If you need to talk to someone, I'm here, or maybe you should go see someone, professionally," Steph said, doubting her ability to handle deep trauma.

"You might be right. Thanks. I need to finish cleaning, then go meet with Sameed's lawyer… I'll see you around. Take care of that sweet little baby for me."

"I will. Take care, Charlotte," Steph said, before the two parted ways, Charlotte back into the bakery to finish her work, and Steph up the stairs to her apartment.

As she turned the key in the door, Steph tried to remember that night. She didn't remember hearing any screaming, but they were pretty well insulated from noise. She briefly considered the implications of Charlotte's words, "Why was he there all alone? Was he there all alone?" before jumping into tidying up as best she could. Jane was going to be over soon, and her apartment was a disaster.

Jane's visit mostly coincided with Madeline's nap, and Steph was grateful. They took turns eating while the baby was awake, but she went down soon after that, giving her mom much needed time to sort out her thoughts aloud and with company.

"I keep going over things in my head," Steph confided. "The weird timing, the lack of kitchen prep… it could still be just a horrible accident, but it doesn't feel like it."

"You know, I was just talking with Deanna, she does shifts with me sometimes. Well, she's friends with Sameed's girlfriend's roommate, Laura," Jane relayed. "So, Laura drove Sharon, the girlfriend, to the hospital after she found out. Her car was in rough shape, and so was she. Poor thing was suffering from shock." Steph made a sympathetic sound. "Yeah... Laura told De she was floored. The two of them had dinner plans that evening, and he never showed up. She tried calling and even drove to the bakery, knocking on the door for some time. His car was still there, so she thought he had forgotten and turned his phone off. The roommate said she was pretty ticked he did that, but later she was beating herself up for being mad at him and not calling the police."

"How awful. There's no way she could have known," Steph sympathized. Her inner sleuth spoke up, "Did she mention around what time she drove by the bakery?"

"De told me they had a reservation at 5:30, so it must have been sometime after that." The bakery closed at 5:00, so he would have had plenty of time to meet her at any one of the nearby restaurants. Their street was lined with them and, like her building, many housed artistic types like her neighbors, who were attracted to the urban setting, walkability, and rent prices.

"Why would he start baking at the end of work, when the kitchen's all clean, minutes before a planned dinner with his girlfriend? That makes no sense," Steph declared.

"Maybe he wanted to surprise her," Jane suggested.

"Then he didn't start early enough, and the ovens weren't even on—," countered Steph before relaying what she had learned from Charlotte.

"Poor time management?" Steph recalled Sameed's personality and ever-present watch. She dismissed the idea and continued.

"I don't think so. And why didn't he answer his phone? No, Jane, it sounds all wrong."

"Steph, what are you getting at?"

Conscious she was talking a bit too loud and might wake the baby, Steph hushed herself. "I think he was murdered, Jane, I really do. He even had a massive argument with his brother that very morning. I'm going to call the police and tell them."

"Oh my God, Steph. Really? If you're right, and there is a killer still out there... Are you worried?"

The thought hadn't even occurred to Steph that *she* might be in danger. Her eyes darted to the nursery.

"No, I'm not," she replied, looking back mostly convinced. "This is a safe neighborhood, but if Sameed were murdered, then he deserves justice." Still, Jane was visibly ill at ease. "We're fine, Jane, I promise," Steph added.

"I'm sure you are." Jane weighed her words. "Just... be careful, Steph," she advised. "And call me if you need anything. I can pick you and Madeline up in a heartbeat if you need me." Steph and Henry shared a car, but he took it to work. She saved the offer for later.

"Thanks, Jane. I know I can always count on you." A lull in the conversation followed, while both pondered new, lighter topics to discuss.

"I watched this Ingmar Berman film yesterday," Jane said.

"Oh, I love her. Old Hollywood actresses seem so classy."

"No, not Ingrid Bergman," Jane corrected. "Ingmar Bergman. He's a director. Anyways, Seventh Seal, I'd recommend it, but you probably wouldn't like it."

"Oh, why?"

"Too much death, but Henry might enjoy the film since it's about chess."

"Thanks. I'll let him know about it."

A while later, they said their goodbyes and separated.

Steph closed the door and made up her mind. "I'll talk to Henry, tell him what I've learned and how I fell about it, and then I'll call the police." She was determined. Now, she just had to put those thoughts aside for a few hours and focus on surviving the afternoon. A nap sounded good.

For once, Steph awoke feeling refreshed, or at the very least half charged. She gazed in appreciation at the tiny human nestled in a bassinet a few feet away from the bed. It wasn't quite 5:00 PM, so Steph had time to do some meal prep and save a frozen meal or takeout for a rainier day.

As it turned out, fresh ingredients were somewhat sparse, but she realized she could cobble together a Cobb salad and try to undo all the donated desserts of late. Henry walked through the door around 5:30, finding a pensive Steph and alert baby.

"Hi," he greeted his wife.

"Did you have a good day?" he asked, assessing the table. "No new deaths, I presume. Want to tell me about it?"

"Yes." Her voice dropped to a more serious note. "Actually, I learned some things today from Charlotte and Jane. Before you start, no, I didn't pester her into describing anything. She wanted, needed, to talk to someone."

"Okay, what did you find out?" He sat down and started eating.

"Sameed wasn't even wearing an apron, and the ovens were off. If he were going to bake, shouldn't they have been pre-heating? And Jane told me her coworker told her that his girlfriend said—"

"That's quite a bit of telephone there," he interrupted.

"Let me finish. His girlfriend said he missed dinner, and they had had *reservations*," she emphasized. "Who starts baking right before a fancy date? Don't you think that's suspicious?" Henry chewed thoughtfully.

"Maybe he was going to surprise her and lost track of time, or perhaps there was a last minute order. It's unlikely, but it's possible."

"Sameed, lose track of time? I don't think so. He kept that fancy watch on at all times, remember? As for who would kill him, I don't know, a competitor or a crazy ex? How many professional bakers are killed by their own mixers?"

"And how many are mysteriously murdered?" Calmly as ever he added, "You should try calling the police. Even if they're not sure it's murder, it might be enough to open an investigation."

"I know. I'm going to, planning to. I just need to write everything down and get my thoughts in order before I call." Steph quickly stuffed in a bite.

"That's a good idea. Do you want to do it tonight while I'm here? I can watch Madeline while you're on the phone." She considered his offer.

"I was thinking of doing it in the morning, but you're probably right. It's better to do it while you're here. I'll eat, write some notes, and then call, okay?"

"Yeah. Do it." Henry was eager for his wife to get the idea of murder out of her system. Hopefully, calling the police would help.

Steph and Henry finished the rest of their salads in silence with a few audible crunches on the harder vegetables she included. For the moment,

Madeline was content to look up at her parents from her bouncer while they put away the dirty dishes and discussed the stronger points to bring up with the police.

After finishing, Henry cradled Madeline on the couch, while Steph walked into the bedroom for privacy. She could think more clearly without distractions.

Back in the living room, Henry heard his wife pacing. It was a habit of hers while on the phone. She was probably talking with her hands too. He brushed Madeline's cheek and elicited what looked like a smile. He returned it, wondering if her grin were real or reflexive.

Minutes later, Steph exited the bedroom, phone and crumpled list in hand. Henry tried to read her face.

"What did they say?" he asked.

"The person I talked to said she would pass on the information I gave. If they think there's something worth pursuing, they'll send someone to take statements from people in the building and nearby."

"That's good, right?" Henry hoped she would leave the rest to the police.

"I guess, I mean, I hope so. What if they don't take my tip seriously? What if they're too busy with other cases? I don't know, Henry. I wonder if there's something more I could be doing." Steph always wondered if there were something more she could be doing.

"Steph, you have enough on your plate as it is, remember? Leave the solving of crimes, or possible crimes, to the police," he urged, then after quickly changing Madeline and handing her over, added, "I'm going to take the trash out. Be right back."

Sure enough he returned within a few minutes, which was long enough for Steph and Madeline to require a fresh change of clothes. Madeline had overeaten and overflowed.

"The trash bins were full again," he said. "I had to put our bag beside it."

"Really? Didn't they pick it up this morning? Or was that yesterday? Either way, is it because of all our diapers?" she guessed, feeling a little guilty. Maybe she should have at least tried to use cloth ones, but she had zero experience and confidence with them.

"I don't think it's us," Henry said. "It's been a problem for a while. I think I'm only noticing it now because we are making more frequent trips. I'll send a message to Dennis about it."

"Maybe it's the display food from earlier that Charlotte was throwing out," Steph suggested.

"Could be," he agreed before relaxing into his personal indentation on the couch. "So, what do you want to watch tonight, a true crime show, a detective film, a how-to on catching murderers?"

"How about a docu-series on when women snap," Steph dryly replied.

"Romantic comedy it is then!"

Steph accepted, but before the movie started she turned to her husband.

"Henry?"

"Yeah?"

"Earlier today, I forgot to mention I ran into a homeless woman, not far from here. Well, it started to rain, and she didn't have an umbrella, so I went over to share mine. I asked her if I could call her a ride. She looked so tired, Henry, just completely worn out. She called her aunt." Henry looked at his wife bewildered, wondering how she could feel so comfortable approaching complete strangers.

"Did the aunt show up? You weren't out in the rain for long, were you?"

"She did. And no, I didn't have to wait long for it, but I was shocked when she arrived. They looked about the same age. I suppose that can happen, but I think it was drug use that had really aged her." Steph paused. "It got me thinking. How well did we really know Sameed? I mean, sure we knew him, and he invited us to his party every year, but did we really know him? What if he was into some shady business?"

Henry didn't want to pursue the murder avenue once again. "I don't think that's very likely. Sameed might not have been a practicing Muslim, but he was more straight-laced than most people we know. Sometimes terrible things just happen to good people." Odd as it was, Steph took comfort in the assertion of Sameed's goodness and didn't pursue the thought any longer. Henry started the movie.

They made it through about half before calling it quits for the night. Somewhere around two-thirds or three-quarters of the way through most rom-coms, some unnecessary drama would arise to briefly separate the would-be lovers. Steph generally found this part of the plot the most contrived and didn't mind missing it.

Slipping into bed, she felt a little more at ease, anticipating the police would get involved, but she didn't feel entirely ready to let go either. Hopefully, sleep would bring her some needed peace of mind. However, she would soon find out Sameed had secrets too, and they weren't his grandmother's recipes.

CHAPTER 4

The following morning, Steph ran into Rachel on her way to class, or so she assumed. Rachel wore anything from collegiate sweats to floor-length ball gowns depending on whether she was headed to school or a concert. Today, she sported her alma mater and a number of bags.

"Hi, Rachel."

"Hey, Steph, and hello little one." Rachel shifted her violin case and set down her lunch to fumble for the door. What looked like a heavy backpack slid with each movement.

"Here, let me help you," Steph offered as Rachel stabilized her belongings.

"You have a baby," she protested. "I should be helping you."

"It's fine. My hands are free thanks to whoever invented these." Steph gestured toward the baby carrier. "Are you headed to class?"

"I am. Thanks. I wish I could stay for a quick bite, but…" she trailed off, gesturing toward the CLOSED sign. The two ladies lingered near the doorway.

"Yeah, it's a shame. I miss coming here every morning."

"Me too. I miss the smells especially," Rachel added. "Whatever chemical they used to clean the kitchen must have been strong because I can still smell it every now and then."

"Really? That's too bad. I imagine it should clear out soon." Lately, Steph's nose had been distracted by regular number twos and diaper rash cream.

"I hope so. I've been lighting vanilla sugar cookie candles, but they just make me even hungrier."

"I'm getting hungry just thinking about it. Well, have a good day!"

"Thanks. You too!" Rachel then walked in the direction of the nearest bus stop, while Steph headed toward Black Coffee Bistro. It had been a few days since her last visit, and even though it wasn't The Likable Daisy, it was something. And she desired the sharp tang of espresso coupled with sugar saturated carbohydrates and familiar faces. Black Coffee Bistro did not disappoint, and it was clearly doing good business in the absence of its closest competitor.

Steph scanned the layout for a good spot for her and Madeline, and lo and behold, there, in the corner was Greg at a computer. He looked to be working, but glanced up for a moment and saw Steph.

"Hi, Steph."

"Hi, Greg. How are you?" He was dressed casually, but neatly. Most of the time she ran into him, he was wearing a black t-shirt and jeans. However, today was colder, so he sported long sleeves and slung a leather jacket over the back of his chair.

"Doing well, and you?"

"Pretty good today… so, I heard you were a photographer."

"Where'd you hear that?" He cocked head to the side, curious. His hair brushed his shoulders.

"Dennis told me you had turned my old room into a dark room. I used to live in your apartment."

"Oh, I see. Yes, I am."

"Do you do portraits? I was thinking of having Madeline's picture taken. Would you be available this weekend sometime?"

"Sorry. I'm busy this weekend with another job, but I'll get back to you some other time."

"Okay. Sure. Thanks." Steph wasn't entirely sure she needed to thank him, but it was a habit of hers.

"No problem." And with that, Steph left Greg alone and perused the blackboard menu while standing in line. She had originally planned on getting a muffin, but as her stomach rumbled she realized she was far hungrier.

"I'd like a steak sandwich with provolone. On ciabatta. Thanks. Oh, and can you add a sparkling water? Thanks." She swiped her card and waited at a table, giving Madeline a toy to gum. In retrospect, maybe she should have brought the car seat. Madeline was too little for a high chair. Steph went back up to the counter to ask that her order be made to go. This way she could put the baby in a bouncer at home and eat without dropping steak, peppers, and onions on her head.

Within a few short minutes, Steph had her sandwich and drink, and she and Madeline were back in their cozy apartment. Even though they hadn't stayed, it was nice to have run into Greg. Hopefully, his schedule would open up soon. It would be convenient to have pictures done right in the apartment, and maybe as her neighbor, he'd offer her a discount.

Later that afternoon during one of Madeline's naps, Steph heard an unexpected ringing. She ran to answer quickly. The screen showed a number she didn't recognize.

"Stephanie Wu?" a tenor voice asked. The incongruity of Steph's European looks and Asian last name often resulted in deliverymen and pharmacists double-checking her identity, not that the person on the phone would notice.

"Yes."

"Hi, this is Detective Harris with the local police department. You called last night about your neighbor's death?" Steph envisioned a young, fit man in a blue uniform, probably with close-cropped or buzzed hair and maybe ever so slightly still baby faced.

"Yes, I did."

"Now, I understand you have some concerns about how your neighbor died. Can you talk me through them?"

"Yes, so you see, Sameed, it was unusual for him to be baking."

"Unusual for a baker to be baking. Can you explain?" Steph heard some scribbling on the other end.

"The bakery opens early, so it was abnormal for him to stay late. Also, he usually leaves the baking, especially the creation of new recipes, to Charlotte. Charlotte Jeffords," she specified. "She's the head baker. He mostly manages and stays out of the kitchen."

"Was there anything else that made it unusual?"

"Yes, I heard from a friend of mine he had dinner plans with his girlfriend that night. It doesn't make sense that he would start baking after everything was cleaned up and so close to when he'd need to leave to keep his reservation."

"Who's this friend of yours?"

"Her name's Jane. Jane Moynihan. She works at the hospital. A friend of hers from work, or a friend of a friend, treated his girlfriend for shock, and she told her the whole story." Steph could hear Harris writing something down, assuming it was Jane's name. She continued with her suspicions. "Also, Sameed got caught in an industrial mixer. That's a lot of whatever he was planning to make, if he was planning to make anything. Was there even a recipe set out?"

"I can't answer that, Mrs. Wu. Now do you

have any other reasons for suspecting this wasn't an accident?" Steph strained to remember her other points.

"He wasn't wearing an apron, and the ovens weren't even on." Then, just in case Detective Harris didn't bake much, she added, "Most people pre-heat the oven first."

"How do you know he wasn't wearing an apron and the ovens weren't on?" Steph's pulse quickened, as the thought occurred to her that she could be a suspect. The detective might even think she was goading him.

"Charlotte told me," she insisted.

"The baker?"

"Yes."

"Have you told Charlotte you suspect her boss was murdered?" Steph wondered if she should have for a moment before remembering how much Charlotte had needed comforting at the time.

"No. We're friends. She just happened to tell me about the accident, what it was like finding him and how surprised she was he was there." Madeline made her presence in the other room known, and Steph went to get her. "Excuse me a moment. I'm going to put you on speakerphone if that's alright." She set the phone down to gather the squirmy baby. "Back."

"Ma'am, I understand your concern." Detective Harris' voice had audibly softened. Steph relaxed. "Is there anyone you suspect? Any motives you can think of?"

"Well, no, I hadn't thought that far. It had only occurred to me Sameed's death was suspicious, and I thought the police should know."

"We appreciate it. Is there anything else you want to tell me at this time?" Steph couldn't think of anything, forgetting the argument between brothers.

"No, officer. Thank you for your time."

"Thank you for calling last night. If you have any other concerns, don't hesitate to call again," Detective Harris advised.

"I will. Thanks." Steph hung up the phone, then sat back down feeling she had failed to convince him. Maybe the facts she had found so persuasive were just coincidences, she mused. Maybe her sleep-deprived brain had invented this horrific take on a cut and dry case. She looked at the clock and waited for Henry to come home. Having him here would make her feel better.

Steph felt she had loads to tell Henry as soon as he walked through the door.

"I talked to the police. They called me. The officer I spoke to listened, but I don't think he took me seriously. When he asked if I suspected anyone or any particular motive, I couldn't think of anything! He probably just thinks it was an accident and I'm being overanxious."

"Well, if the coroner ruled it an accident, then he's probably going to agree with their assessment, especially if there are no suspects."

"What do you think?" There was a small, plaintive cry, and Henry started toward it first.

"What?" Henry called from the other room, carrying Madeline.

"Who do you think would want to kill Sameed, and why?"

Sameed Ishaaq Haddad had been a pleasant, hardworking man, who considered cleanliness next to godliness. He had worked at several upscale restaurants to gain management experience and even interned in Paris before opening his own place. However, inspired by childhood trips to Beirut and his grandmother's kitchen, his dream had been to open a French-style patisserie with traditional Lebanese offerings. The Likable Daisy, named after his grandmother Dasia, was born.

Sameed had also dressed fashionably, treated employees fairly, and warmly greeted customers by name when he was out in front. Every year, he invited the neighbors to join in Eid al-Fitr, a celebration of the end of Ramadan. A broad table filled with towering cakes and emanating such scents as anise, mahleb, orange blossom, and rose water lined the longest wall. It was a spectacle. It didn't make sense for such a generous and wonderful person to die in such a horrible way, and Steph strongly felt that personal tragedies demanded closure.

Henry didn't answer. Steph continued brainstorming. "Did he have any exes? Hmm, now that's a question for Jane."

"I don't think a woman would be able to strangle him," Henry contradicted, skeptical.

"Sameed wasn't a big guy," Steph argued, which was true. It was one of the reasons why he had butted heads with Dennis, who had offered assistance with lifting on more than one occasion, to the shorter baker's chagrin, in addition to their disagreements over foreign policy.

"Still, for it to be a woman, she'd have to be quite strong."

"What about Tony from across the street? The opening of The Likable Daisy has certainly hurt his business," Steph suggested. Tony Russo, whose longstanding local family had a history of small businesses in the area, owned Black Coffee Bistro.

"They have a pretty decent lunch crowd, and I haven't heard anything about them being close to bankruptcy." A new angle came to Steph.

"Maybe the motive isn't personal, unless there's something deep and dark in Sameed's background we don't know about. To me, it looks staged, which suggests someone close. I don't think a random killer would bother. So, who had access?"

"Well, there's Dennis," Henry answered, slowly. "He has the keys to all the doors in the building. "

"Okay, anyone else?"

"Charlotte. She opens the bakery," he reminded her.

"How could you suggest Charlotte," Steph

exclaimed. "What reason could she possibly have?"

"I didn't say she had a motive, just a set of keys. Anyway, she's not the only one who could have locked up. "

"Oh, what if Sameed *let* someone in, someone he knew, you mean. Then after this mystery person does him in, they use his keys to lock. But who could that be? Who would seem friendly enough to let in, but also secretly be plotting murder? And where'd the keys end up?"

"I don't know. I'm not really a fan of accusing people we know of murder." Henry was ready to end the speculating. "It probably was just an accident."

"You're right. I'm stumped, and hungry," she added. "Do you mind frozen pizza for dinner?"

"That's fine." Henry passed a peckish Madeline to her mummy and got to work preheating the oven and removing the pizza from its packaging.

"Can you add some extra cheese and maybe some spinach or something to it?" Steph asked. "Whatever cheese we have. Sometimes they're stingy on the cheese. Oh, and I think we have a jar of sun-dried tomatoes in the pantry. Third shelf, far left." Sure enough, there they were, and they too made it onto the now more appetizing pre-made pizza.

Twenty minutes later the two had burn-your-mouth hot slices ready for the time-honored custom of blowing on scorching food while it sits on the tongue before ingesting. Waiting simply wouldn't do.

They split the pizza fifty-fifty and moved from one extreme to the other, breaking out the ice cream. It was Friday after all, and alcohol wasn't an option for Steph.

"So, how do you feel about this week?" Henry asked as they sat down on the couch together. "I mean, being alone with Madeline and not having anyone around to help."

"Pretty good. Tired, I guess."

"Do you want me to try to change my schedule for next week? Because I can," he offered.

"Thanks, but I think I'll be okay. I'll try to get a few things ready over the weekend for meals next week." Steph wanted to be able to handle things by herself. How well she could accomplish that, she'd find out.

"Okay." Henry and Steph relished the cool relief and borderline brain-freeze the sweet, chocolate treat offered. Steph, trying to balance her bowl with one pinned arm, dropped a dark splotch on her shirt. She almost lamented the loss before realizing it was not the first stain of the day.

"My shirt is starting to look like a Jackson Pollock," she commented. An artist herself, Steph felt conflicted about modernism. Liberation from the traditional boundaries of figures and mediums had birthed some objects that inspired wonder and introspection, as well as others lacking in both purpose and beauty. After putting Madeline down,

Steph changed out of her soiled tee before bed, rinsing off what she could. She looked over at Henry as he brushed his teeth. His shirt hadn't survived unscathed either.

Minutes later they turned toward each other in bed, exchanging goodnights. Steph was exhausted, but she couldn't easily forget the trouble of figuring out a killer and a motive. She tried to consider instead the delicious feeling of slipping between cool sheets and how her pillow gave just the right amount of give. However, the more she thought about her need and desire for sleep, the more it eluded and frustrated her. An angry hour passed. Her mind raced with incoherent ideas, jumping from subject to subject. She closed her eyes, willing herself to unconsciousness.

The front door creaked open. Steph could have sworn she had locked it. Heavy steps walked purposefully through the front rooms. Steph lifted her head from the pillow to hear better, her ears attuned to every sound. Would they turn left or right, she wondered, breaking a sweat. Her hand grasped around the nightstand for anything substantial. A knob turned. A dark figure edged into the widening door, and Steph screamed.

CHAPTER 5

A cry pierced through the darkness. Steph slid the comforter off her body and shivered when cold air hit the sweat on her arms and back. "It was just a dream," she told herself, though her heart continued at a manic speed. The unknown killer lurking in her imagination had stalked her in her sleep. She let Henry remain blissfully unconscious a while longer by occupying Madeline in the living room. Steph appreciated British broadcasting, while Madeline enjoyed the endless snuggles. Once Henry was awake, however, Steph handed him the baby, so she could take a much-needed shower. How many days had it been since her last, she wondered. Prior to motherhood she had never used dry shampoo, and now she survived on it.

After regaining her sense of humanity and fully enrobed in terry cloth, Steph wandered into the kitchen, wet hair wrapped into a loose bun. Towels were inconvenient.

"How'd you sleep?" Steph and Henry asked simultaneously. Henry answered first.

"Pretty good. You?"

"Pretty terrible." Steph debated telling Henry about her dream, but determined it would likely stress him out to hear her unconscious fears. And, he'd advise against her snooping even more strongly.

"I'm sorry. Do you want to go somewhere this morning?"

"Staying here is fine with me. Let me make coffee first, and I can handle breakfast. How do pancakes sound?" She needed syrup after last night.

"Great." The machine hissed at her. Steph had forgotten water this time. "What next?" A few minutes later, after caffeine started to work its magic, Steph flipped flapjack after flapjack until they both had a decent stack. Steph generously scraped butter over hers before pouring on the maple miracle. Table set, the two enjoyed a hearty breakfast together, one of the benefits of the weekend.

Steph and Henry played several rounds of pass the baby, taking turns tackling chores and getting dressed. "I can take out the trash this time," Steph offered, wanting to get a sense of what kind of day it was outside.

Using her muscles for lifting rather than cuddling felt different, but good. Hopefully, her OB would clear her to start exercising again soon. At the back of the building, tenants shared a dumpster and recycling bins. The Likable Daisy tried to be good about donating uneaten pastries at the end of the day instead of seeing them go to waste, but as a bakery they had their fair share of trash.

A narrow strip of struggling grass and stained concrete lined the alleyway. Steph assumed Dennis didn't care about landscaping on this side of the building. While depositing her trash in the reeking receptacle, Steph looked up and away reflexively and her eyes landed one of the windows in her old bedroom, now Greg's apartment. She wondered what kind of pictures he was developing inside. She thought maybe birds or dilapidated architecture.

She could also hear Rachel playing a melancholy tune she didn't recognize. Steph lingered a moment more despite the stench. As she was about to head back in, the thought occurred to her that maybe something incriminating remained in the trash. The police hadn't suspected murder, and maybe the killer himself – "or herself," she reminded – had needed to quickly dispose of evidence. Henry was upstairs with Madeline, so she'd be okay for a few minutes at least. Steph dove in. The smell intensified.

Steph sifted through bags of trash and loose garbage, not knowing exactly what she was looking for. Things squished, crunched, clanked, and even sloshed, dripping onto her clothes. "Dear God, please don't let there be bugs," she prayed. She'd take a rusty fork over a cockroach any day. *Clang.* Her toe stumbled across hollow metal. She brushed away some sad looking macarons and heaved aside a hefty black bag. Saturated diapers weighed a ton. It was just a can of paint thinner. She looked closer. There were a couple cans actually. Steph wondered who could have been painting recently. Maybe Rachel or Greg redid their apartment. Dennis certainly hadn't painted the common areas. She would have noticed, or so she thought. Perhaps, it had been the professional cleaners, she considered, thinking maybe they had needed to repaint the entire kitchen after stripping it.

She sifted through the dumpster for a few more minutes, coming across some cleaning supplies and more smooshed pastries, but no shredded documents, blood stained clothes, or smoking guns appeared. She decided to head back upstairs when Dennis showed up, peering down at her over his glasses.

"Steph, what the heck are you doing in there?" Steph popped her head out with a look of "who me?" on her face.

"Oh, I thought I accidentally threw away Maddie's favorite… panda lovey." Dennis wondered what a lovey could possibly be, and Steph knew for a fact that small stuff animal was in the middle of her living room floor.

"Couldn't you just buy a new one?" Surely, whatever this lovey was, it couldn't be *that* expensive, he thought.

"Yeah," Steph laughed awkwardly. "I just hate losing stuff," she explained, which was true.

"Well, good luck. Do you want any help?" His tone suggested he'd rather not, and the last thing Steph wanted was to inconvenience someone else by looking for an imaginary lost toy.

"No, no, it's fine. I'm done trying to find it here. Like you said, I can just buy a new one." Dennis slowly walked away toward the basement, where the finicky laundry machines were kept. Steph had successfully passed herself off as a harebrained parent.

She pulled herself out, using what upper body strength she had. Her still recovering abs struggled, but she made it. She looked down at her smeared outfit and wondered how she would explain what had happened. She determined instead to try to sneak in and race to the shower again if possible.

Steph walked around the corner and onto Greenway Ave. Of course before she made it safely inside she passed a rather confused and affronted-looking pedestrian who veered away from her. Steph hugged the wall and slipped inside as quickly as she could. She raced up the stairs before she bumped into anyone else. Opening her front door, she peaked her head through first to check for Henry. Not seeing him, she slipped off her disgusting shoes and made a beeline for the shower. Henry called out from the nursery after hearing the door close, while Madeline complained about her diaper change.

"Steph, is that you?"

"Yeah, I'm just gonna go to the bathroom real quick. Is that okay?" Silently, she begged, "Please don't come out."

"Go for it," Henry said behind the still closed door.

"Yes!" her mind screamed.

Steph stripped off the mucky clothes,

carefully peeling her shirt away from her face. She shampooed and washed as quickly as possible in scalding water. "Should I exfoliate too?" she asked herself, but looking at her red skin, decided against it. She'd done enough, and she didn't have the time.

"Did you change?" Henry asked after she emerged.

"Yeah, Maddie spat up on me earlier, and I wanted something clean," she fibbed. Henry raised an eyebrow.

"Your pants too?"

"Yeah, funny how it can get everywhere."

Steph collected Madeline and put her down for her first nap.

"Sorry," the young mom apologized privately. "That time wasn't your fault." Baby asleep, Steph determined now might be a good time to check in with Jane if she weren't working. Sometimes she worked on Saturdays. The prolonged ringing turned into voicemail.

"Hey, Jane. It's Steph. I was wondering if you knew anything about a crazy ex Sameed might have had. Thanks. Catch you later." *Boop*. Message sent.

Steph set the cell phone down. She'd have to wait to— A text message flashed. "I can ask around." Knowing Jane, it wouldn't be long before she had at least one suspect, if not twelve.

Steph twiddled her fingers. "What to do?" she wondered. Until Madeline awoke, it was best to stay put. Henry, too, was taking a nap, so she seriously considered his two suggested suspects who had easy access to the bakery, Charlotte and Dennis. Deducing by herself might be easier. Her mind set to work defending Charlotte first.

"Charlotte is too sweet," her mind protested, but an inner voice told her sweetness could be artificial. "But Sameed invited her to join him at the bakery. They were former coworkers. Wouldn't she be grateful?" Perhaps, she resented not being made a partner after all this time, or maybe she didn't have the creative flexibility she desired, the inner voice countered. "That's not a good enough motive," Steph told herself convincingly. If anything, her career prospects were probably injured by his loss. Moreover, as the first person on the scene, Charlotte might be the only person who could help catch Sameed's killer, assuming the murder was personal and not random. The fact that it appeared to be staged as an accident suggested the former. Steph moved onto Dennis.

Dennis was a good landlord, perhaps a little awkward, but never malicious. Was it possible he and Sameed had some much larger disagreement in private, she wondered, then asked, "What kind of disagreement could motivate someone to kill?" She couldn't think of one. It seemed unnecessary in this kind of business relationship. If Dennis had wanted Sameed out as a tenant, he could do so legally. There were even slightly more dubious ways that didn't require murdering him, like sabotaging a health inspection.

With no further information, Dennis seemed

unlikely. Steph considered the possibility of a silent partner. Maybe there was one more person who had keys to the bakery. "But who could it be?" she asked, "And how can I find out who they are?" Either Dennis or Charlotte might be able to help her here. Checking the clock, Steph determined now was a good time to rouse her husband and attempt lunch. She would let Madeline sleep longer. Steph still wasn't quite sure about how to schedule her baby's intermittent naps.

Grilled sandwiches in the making, Steph filled Henry in on her musings.

"Given what we know, I still don't think it makes sense for either Charlotte or Dennis to have killed Sameed even though they would have had the most opportunity to."

"How much do we not know?" Henry asked her, a valid question. "That said, given what we know, I agree with you."

"Great, but they are still not necessarily the only ones who had access to the bakery. What if there was a silent partner? Sameed was in his early thirties when he opened The Likable Daisy. Perhaps, he had a backer, someone we've never met. It might explain why Charlotte hasn't been become a partner in the business."

"That's possible, but I don't see what their motive would be." Undeterred, she continued.

"I was thinking of asking Dennis or Charlotte."

"Don't go snooping around," Henry

implored. "It could be dangerous."

"I don't think talking to Charlotte or Dennis is dangerous—" Steph started.

"But you don't *know*," he interjected. "And that makes a difference. If someone did murder Sameed, then they can murder again, and you're not putting just your life at risk by playing detective," he reminded her. He paused to collect his thoughts, while Steph considered her husband's feelings. "If you *happen* to find out something, whether you hear it from Jane or someone else, call the police again. Maybe they'll change their minds. Can you do that for me?"

"Yes, I can do that," she acquiesced, and the two ate their delightfully crunchy and perfectly cheesy paninis in peace, until Madeline decided she wanted to join them.

Unfortunately, the weather was not agreeable that afternoon, so the family went to an art museum for the afternoon to stretch their legs. While they were meandering through impressionist paintings and crisp, white walls, Steph received a call. It was from Jane. She gestured to Henry she was going to take it outside, passing several stunning pieces she would want to revisit. Even the gilded frames, rich in detail, merited a closer look. The short heel of her flats clicked on the marble floor, and she turned a corner.

"Hey, Jane. Sorry I couldn't pick up right

away. We were in a museum. How are you?"

"Good. Hey, so I was just calling you back about earlier. I asked a few people and found out Sameed had been married for a few years, but he and his wife Abila were getting a divorce."

"Really? So did he cheat on his wife with the girlfriend? What was her name again?"

"Sharon Andrews, and, no, it sounds like Sharon came along after they legally separated. Apparently, Sameed really wanted to start having kids, and Abila didn't."

"Do you know why?"

"Not sure. I think she was a bit younger, not ready maybe."

"That's... sad, but understandable." Sameed had always loved when children came to the bakery. Thinking through the idea of Sameed being married, Steph thought to ask, "Do you know if they ever finalized the divorce?"

"Unsure. If they did, it must have been really recent." Otherwise, she'd have heard about it, was the implication.

"Thanks, Jane. You've given me a lot to think about."

"Anytime."

"Are you at work right now?"

"No, I just got off. I'm driving home."

"I see. Are you free sometime during the week this next week? I can feed you, or we can go over to Black Coffee Bistro. I don't think their coffee is as good as The Likable Daisy's, but they make good sandwiches."

"That sounds great. I'll check my schedule when I get home, but I should be off at least one weekday next week."

"Great, I'll see you later then."

Steph walk backed into the exhibit.

"That was Jane," she said.

"And?"

"And she found out Sameed was married, or had been married. He had a wife named Abila, and they were getting a divorce because she didn't want kids. It makes things interesting, doesn't it," she asked.

"Doesn't what?"

"The fact they were divorcing but possibly not quite yet divorced."

"Spell it out for me," Henry requested.

"Maybe she didn't want the divorce to begin with, and she's still bitter."

"Maybe she did. Maybe it was mutual. Sameed had already moved on, since he had a girlfriend. Perhaps, his ex did too."

"Or... maybe he had a huge life insurance policy, and she wasn't going to get much or anything from him after a divorce."

"It's possible, but it's unlikely she could have overpowered her ex-husband. Granted, I've never seen this lady. So, maybe she's built like a body builder, but I doubt it."

"Well, *maybe* she hired someone," Steph suggested, "and if she were to drop by the bakery, he would probably let her in, wouldn't he? This mystery hit man could sneak up behind while she's distracting him."

"This is not a movie," he retorted. "How common do you think hiring a hit man is?" He looked around after his remark, careful to see if anyone had registered it.

"It could happen," Steph said. "All I'm saying is we have a lead. Before, we had none. If someone can place her at The Likable Daisy last Monday night, then we have a suspect with a motive."

"A potential motive. You have no idea if he had a life insurance policy, and how do you propose to place her at the bakery," Henry asked.

"I'm…not sure," Steph admitted. "Perhaps, Black Coffee Bistro will have security tapes, or someone saw a lady enter the bakery after hours. At least it's a start."

"I doubt they'll let you look at security tapes unless the police are involved," he reminded her. Steph blew air through her lips.

"Pfft." She tried to think of another idea. She felt like she was forgetting something. "Oh, the girlfriend's name was Sharon."

"You think she's a suspect?"

"No, but maybe her family wasn't too thrilled about her dating Sameed."

"That's possible, but it doesn't feel like a strong motive. You would have to know more about the family, more about her." Getting a little frustrated, he added, "Can we just enjoy the art?"

"But it's a lead," she insisted. Her mind raced with possibilities.

"Even so, it's not safe for you, or Jane, to be snooping around." Steph paused. She hadn't considered Jane being at risk and felt a little guilty for her carelessness.

Steph and Henry resumed their tour of the exhibit and upon finishing headed home to start dinner. As they were opening the outside door to the apartment building, they noticed a blond woman laying a bouquet of daisies down by a growing memorial. They had the same question, "is that her?" Steph tarried a moment outside instead of heading in, waiting for the woman to turn around.

"Excuse me," Steph started, "but are you Sharon?" The attractive young woman, though red-eyed and sniffling, looked at Steph surprised. She couldn't have been more than thirty, twenty-five even.

"Yes, excuse me. Do I know you?"

"Hi, I'm Steph," she introduced, "and this is my husband Henry and our daughter Madeline. We live above the bakery. We've known, we knew, Sameed for several years." Sharon assumed this meant he had told them about her.

"You did? He was such a wonderful man, wasn't he? So kind and so good with kids. You know, I think I remember you. Were you at his Eid party this year?" Steph could have kicked herself for forgetting.

"Yes, you probably saw me and my round belly hovering by the buffet table," Steph said, then paused. "We are so sorry for your loss."

"Sameed was a good man," Henry added. "He will be greatly missed."

"Yes, he will be… you know, we hadn't dated for very long, but we had already talked about getting married. We clicked. We just knew, and now he's gone." She held back tears. "What am I going to do?" Steph put her hand on Sharon's arm.

"Do you want to come upstairs?" Steph offered. Henry looked at her alarmed. "I can make you some tea, tell you some stories about Sameed."

"That sounds wonderful, but I need to get going. I'm supposed to meet my parents for dinner tonight. They feel terrible about what happened. It's a shame they weren't more understanding when he was alive," she said, looking down and sounding a little bitter. Steph and Henry quickly flashed their eyes toward each other. "I really would love to hear more about Sameed. Do you mind? I can give you my phone number."

"Not at all," Steph said, taking out her cell. "And these days I'm usually home, so almost any time is good." Sharon recited her digits and bid them a good evening.

"It was really nice meeting you," she said.

"It was a pleasure. I hope I see you again soon."

"Me too."

Steph took Madeline into her arms, and

Henry collapsed the stroller. They walked through the entrance and up the stairs in pensive silence. The creak of the opening, then closing front door to their apartment broke it.

"Steph," Henry began. "That woman was a stranger, and you invited her into our home. What if she's not who she says she is?"

"What motive would she have to lie? Anyway, assuming that was the real Sharon, and I'm sure it was, I can see why her family might not have been too keen on Sameed. At least ten years his junior and…"

"You can't be too careful," Henry interrupted. "And you basically told her you're here, alone, most of the time. Might as well make her a copy of our key." Steph didn't hear him.

"… she wasn't wearing a headscarf, which explains why Sameed's older brother didn't like her. He was in the bakery on Monday," Steph explained. "They were arguing about something. I'm pretty sure he mentioned a girlfriend, but it seemed like there was more to it. I couldn't catch everything because they switched to Arabic." Henry sighed. His wife's one-track mind could not be derailed.

"Why didn't you tell me this before?" He resigned himself to further suppositions.

"I wasn't sure it was important at the time. Do you think it is?"

"Maybe, maybe not. How often have you argued with someone in your family?" Though infrequent, it was often enough to make Steph reconsider.

"Okay, so it might not be enough to motivate him to kill, but maybe it was an accident," she suggested. "Sameed's brother, Sharon's father, or likely some other male relative got into a heated argument, lost his temper, and accidentally killed Sameed, then made it look like a work accident. Anyway, I'll try to find out more from Sharon when she visits."

"When?" Henry was trying to recall them setting a specific time.

"It's only a matter of time," Steph asserted confidently. She was certain of the other woman's desire to learn more about her late love. Henry was none too enthused, but perhaps this woman was as harmless as Steph saw her. He considered it futile to protest further. Instead, he watched his wife set Madeline down in a bouncer.

Changing the topic, Henry asked, "What's the plan for tomorrow night?"

"Tomorrow?"

"My parents are coming over for dinner, remember? Do we need to pick up anything?"

"Uh." Steph froze. The week's events had completely erased the upcoming dinner from her memory.

"We could order something, or my mom might even be willing to bring—"

"No, I'll think of something," She wanted to prove to her mother-in-law that she was a capable wife and mother herself. "If we go grocery shopping, I can make something Chinese."

"You don't have to," Henry said.

"I want to," she insisted.

"Okay then. What do you want to do tonight? Do we have anything in the fridge to eat?" Steph perused the shelves, checking the freezer as well.

"There's a frozen casserole someone made for us in here. Can you wait forty-five minutes or so?"

"Yeah, that's fine."

At dinner, since their brains had enough to digest, they focused only on chewing their food, and for the rest of the evening, Steph let her unconscious mind stew over the things she had learned that day. However, as the evening winded down and her mind moved on to planning the next day, dread began to rise in the pit of her stomach as she thought about dinner with her in-laws.

CHAPTER 6

Sunday morning Steph regained consciousness before Henry and gazed at his peaceful, sleeping face. Careful not to wake him, she traced the lines of his strong jaw and full lips with her eyes. It should have been a sin for a man to have such long lashes, but it was something he had passed onto their daughter as well. So, Steph forgave her husband. She tried to roll out from under the covers quietly, but the movement roused him.

"Good morning." How was it possible that someone who had been sleeping until a second ago could look so bright eyed and alert, Steph wondered, then figured it might have something to do with actually getting sleep. She considered again what a wonderful privilege it was to wake up beside him and felt sorrow over Sharon's loss.

The thought occurred to Steph that maybe they should try to attend church today. They hadn't gone since Madeline had been born, being too battle-weary to consider it, and Steph had figured Jesus would understand. However, she felt rather okay this morning, and guilt would get to her if she didn't attend. Also, Henry's parents would probably ask and disapprove if they answered in the negative.

"Black for you," she said, offering him coffee

a few minutes later. Henry, lover of Russians novels and Chinese cinema, appreciated the bitter things in life. Steph added milk to hers. She would concede not everything needed to be saccharine sweet, except pop music for long drives, but it didn't hurt to take the edge off either.

After eating, the three bundled up for a short drive to their church. Once through the front doors they were warmly welcomed and congratulated before the service commenced. Steph and Henry chose a pew near the back in case they needed a quick exit before Madeline's requests for food interrupted. The sky was overcast, so soft light fell from clear glass panes, shining down on the old wooden pews that had been smoothed by years of standing, sitting, and sliding over.

Steph managed to listen to two minutes of the sermon before Madeline decided she had heard enough and wanted to break for refreshments. Steph had gathered that the topic was the Garden of Eden, man's fall from grace, and the consequences of sin. Steph felt Eve's subsequent punishment, i.e., labor pains, was a little unfair. "Why should all womankind suffer for one person's mistake?" she asked internally.

Seated in a library armchair, surrounded by books on theology, Steph pondered generational sin and wondered how Eden applied in modern life.

"Why do I get to nurse a healthy baby, while another God-fearing woman struggles in the NICU, or worse?" If anything, Steph's past suggested she should be the one to suffer. Perhaps, one of the tomes on the musty built-in shelves contained the answer to that question, if there was one. Steph nursed Madeline and focused instead on feeling grateful.

Henry came looking for them in the church library, it being the quietest and most likely place, as soon as the congregation broke for coffee and conversation. It was one of the reasons why they liked their church, that and potlucks. Steph appreciated the built-in socialization.

"How was the sermon?" Steph asked.

"Good," Henry answered. Steph waited for details. None came. "Do you want to stay any longer to talk with people?" It was a tempting idea.

"I'd like to, but I think we should get going before Madeline falls asleep."

Driving back home after church, Steph asked, "Why does it seem that some people get an unequal share of suffering?"

"What do you mean?"

"Why should my life be so good, so, blessed, while someone like Sameed, his ends so abruptly?"

"I don't think there's a good answer for that." Henry stopped to think what his wife needed to hear. "Right now, all we can do is be thankful for what we have and be generous to others less fortunate."

The two put aside their musings when they walked up to the door, instead planning what to eat and how to prepare for dinner with his parents.

Steph made a list and sent Henry to the nearest Asian grocery store, while she stayed behind to put Madeline down. While seated, the thought occurred to Steph that no matter how much she prepared, she would never meet her in-laws' standards, and it was disheartening.

After Henry returned, the couple cleaned and tidied such things as throw pillow covers and dusty floor trim.

"Do you think I should wash the cushions too?" Steph asked.

"No, they're fine," Henry answered. "And I don't think we have the time."

It was the little things that counted, and any oversight could be another demerit for Steph. Once naptime concluded, Steph checked the clock and decided to switch to meal prep.

In the past, Steph had learned to make several different Chinese dishes in an attempt to impress her future in-laws. She had since taken her mother-in-law's "feedback" seriously. She purchased a better wok and chopsticks for cooking, proper baskets for steaming, and more appropriate dinnerware. She then carefully sourced her ingredients from approved grocers and triple-tested recipes using ones Henry translated for her. It was a labor of love.

Steph spared herself the agony of working on her dumpling skins and started on the fillings first. Pork and chive was a personal favorite. However, distracted by the future, arduous task of making uniform wrappers, pre-made would incur shame, her hand slipped while cutting the chives. Steph hissed as the blade made a paper-thin cut on her left pointer finger.

"Are you alright," Henry called out.

"I'm fine. It's nothing." He came into the kitchen.

"Do you want me to finish the chopping?" he supplied.

"I finished already, but you can make and fill the wrappers. Your dumplings always look better than mine anyway." Steph was losing her patience quickly, imagining the criticism that awaited, and needed to move on with the next dish. She started dough for steamed buns. She pounded her frustration into it and kneaded aggressively.

"There, that's one thing done." Already feeling better, she returned to her dumplings. Well-practiced, Henry had already enveloped half of the pork filling in perfect half-moons.

"How did you do that so quickly?" she asked, astonished.

"We had extra in the freezer from the last time you made them, remember?" Henry answered. Steph hoped the once frozen dough would taste good enough. She helped stuff the rest before punching down the risen dough one last time. Eventually, the fried buns would be dessert with sweetened condensed milk for a dipping sauce.

For a healthy starter, Steph went vegetarian. She actually enjoyed making egg drop soup.

Gossamer strands of egg swirled like an impressionist field of grain, and the simple heartiness of the soup always satisfied. However, king mushroom in garlic sauce would serve as the main attraction. Steph didn't know a vegetable could be so meaty until she tried it, and it was a dish she felt she could execute after practicing it on Henry a few times. Anything with deep-frying or double frying felt risky at best.

Feeling less alarmed by the state of her home and dinner, Steph sat down for a moment and fed Madeline while her husband watched the soup and the kettle. Her in-laws arrived at 6:30. Her mother-in-law, an attractive, older woman, with a pixie cut and customary red coat speckled with dog hair flanked her husband. Steph's father-in-law sported a dark wool coat and Syracuse orange scarf. She rarely saw him without something that color and knew he was the reason why Henry had played basketball.

"*Son,*" Li Ming warmly exclaimed in Chinese, "*and little Maddie.*" She smiled. "Steph." Li Ming tossed a curt nod to her daughter-in-law. Dutifully, Steph ignored the slight. She knew well-enough not to return the greeting with a hug after her then future mother-in-law had gone stiff as a board the first time they had met. She served both in-laws tea.

"How's Mei Mei?" Steph asked politely, making sure to say "may-may." Mei Mei was Li Ming's prize Chow Chow, the offspring of her previous dog and another purebred. After working hard as a groomer for years, supporting her family while he husband went to med school in the US, Li Ming had gone into breeding Chow Chows, the well-known Chinese canine.

"Mei Mei has an excellent disposition. I'm sure she'll make a great mother." Steph was a little jealous of the approbation.

"How's Syracuse looking this season?" Steph asked, turning to Wu Peng. While her husband's name followed Western tradition, her in-laws went by their last names first.

"The roster's looking pretty good. Lots of their good players are still around, and I like their new center. The season doesn't start for another two weeks though, so I guess we'll have to wait and see how well they work as a team."

"It looks like the trash needs to be taken out," Li Ming pointed out, somehow having found more things on the counter to toss. Cooking for four adults had resulted in an accumulation in the previously half-filled bag.

"I'll do it," Steph cheerfully claimed. Taking out the trash after a successful home-cooked meal would hopefully demonstrate to her mother-in-law what an excellent wife she was. She miscalculated.

"Likes to do everything herself, does she," Li Ming commented, as if Steph making dinner and cleaning up after was a patented rejection of the grandma's, Nai Nai's, obligation to help. Steph tried not to appear exasperated. In reality, Steph was only too eager to escape her mother-in-law for a few minutes.

"She spoils me," Henry defended, taking Madeline from his wife. He gave her a sympathetic look. "What do you have there?" Henry asked his father.

"Just a little something to celebrate," he said, offering his son a bottle of single-malt whiskey.

"*Give her to Nai Nai,*" Li Ming said, referring to Madeline. Steph denied herself the satisfaction of hearing her daughter cry in alarm by exiting the room quickly. However, she took her time going down the stairs and around the corner. It was already dark out, but light streaming from Greenway Ave illuminated enough of the path. Most shops were closed Sunday night, so there was little in the way of traffic sounds. As she turned to the back of the building, she noticed a slumped figure.

"Hello?" she called out. There was no answer. Steph inched a little closer. The silhouette suggested a homeless woman, perhaps sleeping. Steph felt sorry for her. It was dangerous for her to be so exposed. "Dennis will want to know about this," she said to herself. To give the woman a chance before cops were called on her, Steph tried again to rouse her, raising her voice. "Excuse me. Are you alright?"

Once again, there was no response. Steph used her phone as a flashlight. Keeping a safe distance, dim light panned up from grubby pants to purplish hands. Steph started to get a sick feeling in her stomach before she even reached the face. She raised her phone and revealed a sickly pallor and slack jaw. Heavy-lidded eyes pointed downward to a worn cane at her side. Steph knew this woman.

The lines of her face were softer, but she remembered the crow's feet, the wrinkles around the mouth. Something was terribly wrong. Steph dropped the trash and came closer. First she put two fingers to the woman's stiff wrist.

"Maybe, her pulse is too weak," she told herself when that didn't work. Her hand hovered over the woman's neck. She pressed her fingertips to the cold skin.

"Oh my God." Steph's phone clattered to the ground, and she clutched at her abdomen. Once she felt she could trust her empty stomach to stay put, Steph picked her phone back up with her clean hand and called the police, then Dennis, who lived nearby.

"Dennis, you need to come to the building. There's a woman here. Homeless. I think, I think she's dead." Steph waited outside. Her mind was a total whiteout. A figured crossed the street, heading her way. Steph hardly saw or heard anything, until she felt a hand on her shoulder.

"Steph?"

"Ah!" It was Dennis. The glare of the streetlamp on his glasses made it hard for Steph to read his eyes.

"Sorry. I didn't mean to scare you. You can go back upstairs now." Steph looked down and noticed she had missed a few texts from Henry.

"He's probably worried," Steph realized, feeling a little guilty, then responded, "Oh. Okay. D'you think?"

"I'm afraid so. Probably an overdose or alcohol poisoning," Dennis stated matter-of-factly. Steph wondered how much of this he'd seen before. For someone who had witnessed two deaths on his property in one week, Steph thought he seemed rather unfazed, but perhaps he was like Henry and kept his emotions to himself.

"How awful. I guess I'll go back home then. Do you think the police will want to talk to me?"

"Probably not. I'll call you if they do. I hope you have a better evening. Thanks for calling."

"Of course. You too."

Hurrying back to the front door, she wondered, "What am I going to tell Henry? When am I going to tell Henry?" His mother already disapproved of them living in the city instead of their cushy suburb with top-rated schools, even though Madeline was just a baby. "No, I won't say anything until after they've gone," she decided. "But how will I explain my absence?" Steph had been gone at least fifteen or twenty minutes, and her in-laws would consider that excessive, if not negligent, as a host.

As she walked back up the stairs, Steph recognized the red and blue lights of a police vehicle slowing as it reached the end of the street and turning. She opened the door and noticed Li

Ming standing over the stove, watching baskets steam.

"Where have you been?" Li Ming chastised. "We're all hungry, waiting for you."

"The neighbor's cat got out again, and it took me a while to coax her back inside," Steph fibbed, washing her hands furiously.

"You could have called," her mother-in-law replied. Steph closed the blinds overlooking the rear of the building to avoid providing more fodder for argumentation. "Well, let's eat." Henry and his parents sat down, while Steph took Madeline back from her husband.

"I'm going to go put her down. Start without me," Steph offered with little energy. Again, she took her time soothing the tired baby, but it wasn't to avoid her in-laws. She tried to process what had happened downstairs. "That woman was dead... I touched a dead person."

It sunk in that she had known her, however briefly, and now she was gone. Minutes slipped away as Madeline snoozed on her mother. Steph didn't mind until she realized that the lack of her company was likely being judged.

"Finally," Li Ming stated upon her return. "Next time, let me put the baby to sleep. When you go back to work, I can take care of Maddie for you. Here, eat." She thrust a bowl toward Steph. Steph took a sip. She tried to eat. She knew she should, but the evening's excitement and anxiety churned inside. "How can you feed that baby if you don't have dinner? *Son*, get your wife to eat."

"Li Ming." The tone of her husband's voice silenced her. It was obvious to everyone that Steph was unwell.

"Steph, maybe you should lie down. You must be tired," Henry suggested, helping Steph to her feet and toward their room. Once inside, he asked, "Are you okay? Is my mother being too much?"

"No." She sat down on their bed.

"Then, what's going on? And why did you lie about our neighbors having a cat?"

"There was a body," Steph replied quietly.

"What!" Henry's voice was hushed but emphatic. He sat down beside her.

"As I was taking down the trash, I saw a woman hunched over by the dumpster. I called out to her, but she didn't answer. I checked her pulse. Henry, she, it was the homeless woman I met earlier. She was dead. I didn't want your parents to find out. I know they already want us to move."

"*Darling*. I'm so sorry. It'll be okay. Did you call the police?" She nodded. "Do you want me to get you anything? Aspirin? Water?"

"I'm fine. I think I'll just go to sleep, if that's okay. Apologize to your parents for me."

"There's no need to. Go to sleep. I will join you in a little while." Henry left the room, turning off the light when he did. Steph ripped off her clothes, feeling contaminated. She scrubbed herself raw from her elbows to her fingertips over the sink before slipping on clean pajamas and passing out on the bed. She could faintly make out some of the conversation in the kitchen, *"wife… older sister… doctor… move… baby…"* Though her Chinese remained rudimentary, Steph could guess at their conversation, though calling it a lecture would be more accurate.

"You really should get a handle on your wife," his mother likely chastised. *"Why can't you be more like your older sister and become a doctor? It's not too late to go to med school."* At this point, Henry would probably rub the bridge of his nose. While her mother-in-law believed Henry's not pursuing med school had been Steph's fault, in reality, he had discovered he was not cut out for the sights and smells, not to mention the hours, of a career in medicine after his stint as an EMT.

The arguments likely continued. *"You would make more money. You could move, get a real house. Our suburb has great schools and is much safer. Think about what's best for the baby."* It was nothing the couple hadn't heard before, but after tonight, the last suggestion hit home.

"Perhaps you're right," he replied, stunning them.

"Maybe they are right," agreed Steph, quietly. Exhausted in every way, she was completely unconscious by the time her husband returned. In the dark, Henry draped a blanket over his wife, hoping she would get the sleep she so desperately needed.

CHAPTER 7

With the sun rose Henry, who needed to get ready for work once again. Steph merely stirred. She thought at one point she wished him a good morning or goodbye, but she couldn't be sure. The baby had decided to go back to sleep after her "breakfast," so Steph did too, awakening for the day after her husband had already left, or so she thought. She stepped outside her bedroom into the open living and dining space to find breakfast on the table and Madeline in Henry's arms.

"What are you doing here? Don't you have work," Steph asked. "Is this for me?" She pointed at the plate of eggs and toast. The sight made her realize how roaringly hungry she was. A proper, large mug full of tea also invited her to sit down.

"Yes, those are for you," he said, answering the last question first, so his wife would start eating. "I called and told them I was coming in late this morning. I can skip my lunch, or I can take the whole day off if you want me to."

"That's so sweet. Thank you." If Steph hadn't been stuffing her face at that moment, she could have kissed him. She buttered her toast generously and considered his offer. She took a sip of tea. Her cup had a splash of milk added and nothing more, just the way she liked it.

"So, what are you thinking? Do you want me

to stay all morning, all day? I thought after last night… I didn't know if you wanted to talk." Steph tried to rationalize what had happened and her feelings. She took a bite of toast and chewed.

"I don't think I improved your parents' opinion of me," she reflected. "Although, that much was to be expected, but they seemed to like Maddie."

"Of course they did, and don't worry about my parents. If anything, I think you found yourself an ally in my dad, but that doesn't matter. How are you after…?" He wasn't sure if it were better or worse to mention the body out loud.

"I…" She tried to find the words. "I'm okay. I feel sorry for that woman. The last time I saw her she looked so tired. Maybe now she can rest in peace." Steph took a deep breath. "These things happen, I guess. At least, I hear about it in the news, but perhaps your parents are right. Maybe we should move."

"You heard that?" He wondered what else she had caught.

"Yeah, what do you think?" Steph started on her second piece of toast.

"Eventually this place will feel too small for us, and we've talked about wanting a yard and some space."

"Can we afford that right now?" She wondered how that would be possible if she quit her job.

"Don't worry about it." Henry looked at the

clock. "Do you want me to stay longer?"

"I think I'll be fine for the rest of the day. Thanks for offering."

"Call me if you change your mind, okay?"

"Okay." She smiled. Henry handed over Madeline, grabbing his coat and lunch on his way to the door. Steph stopped him for a kiss goodbye first. "Thanks," she repeated.

After Henry left, Steph pulled out a pen and notepad. She wanted comfort food for dinner and not takeout or leftovers. They'd eat last night's leftovers some other time if Henry hadn't already packed it for lunch. She also had more laundry to do, but that was never-ending. Both she and Madeline changed clothes at least once or twice a day. Depending on the severity of the spew, Steph would try to salvage their outfits, but no one liked to feel wet.

In the middle of her musings, the phone rang.

"Hello? Who is this?"

"Hi, it's Sharon, Sameed's girlfriend?" Steph put a face to the voice.

"Hi, Sharon. How are you?"

"Empty. You?" Her honest response startled Steph.

"Um, fine. What's up?"

"I was wondering if I could come over this afternoon. I'm not scheduled for work today, and I'd love to hear some of your stories about Sameed, if you're not busy."

"Of course. I don't have any plans today."

"Is there a time that works best for you?" Sharon asked. Steph figured she should build in time for a shower.

"2 o'clock? Does that work?"

"I can do 2:00."

"Great. I'll see you then."

"Thanks, I look forward to it," Sharon said.

Steph said "bye," hung up the phone, and started cranking the can opener for chili. She loved the idea of fresh cornbread and a mountain of shredded cheese.

The morning's early burst of productivity satisfied her, and she settled onto the couch with Madeline in her arms to catch up on the landscape design challenges of tiny gardens. They were unspeakably quaint, but also crazy expensive.

When Madeline went down for her nap, Steph jumped into the shower. Mornings naps could be short, so it was lather, rinse, and go. Brief as it was, Steph still gloried in the sensation of being clean, especially after last night, and just as she was putting on her robe, Madeline woke up. Steph congratulated herself on her timing. She brought the baby into her bedroom with her to pick out and put on something that said, "relaxed mom, but not too relaxed, still actually trying to look put together." A nice knit went a long way.

A quick lunch, some hurried tidying up, and a check-up on the chili later, Steph heard the intercom buzz. Thankfully, Madeline, who had gone back to sleep, hadn't heard it.

"Hi, it's Sharon."

"Come on up." A minute later, Sharon was up the stairs at the door. She knocked, and Steph opened.

"Hi."

"Hi, come on in. You can put your things on the kitchen table if you like," offered Steph. "Do you want tea or coffee? I was gonna make something."

"Tea would be great. Do you have chamomile? Or something else caffeine-free?" Sharon laid a coat and messenger bag on the table.

"I have chamomile. I'll make a pot for both of us." Steph started heating up the kettle.

"Where's the baby?"

"She's taking a nap right now, but she'll probably be up in a few minutes."

"Good, I was hoping to see her too. By the way, thanks for having me over. I don't know many of Sameed's friends. Although he and his wife had been separated for much more than a year, since his divorce wasn't finalized, he didn't feel comfortable introducing me to people as his girlfriend. Not that he was ashamed of me, but he wanted to spare me their judgment. He was thoughtful like that."

Information flowed freely from Sharon's lips, all news to Steph, and the thought occurred to her that she had invited a stranger into her home. For all she knew, Sharon could be a baby snatcher, or maybe she had killed Sameed in a jealous rage and was only coming to probe Steph. They both smiled at each other, feeling a little awkward about the newness of their relationship. Sharon pushed a lock of hair behind one ear.

"Oh, wow, that's gorgeous," Steph exclaimed, pointing at a gold drop earring anchored to what looked like a sizable rock.

"She has a large, diamond earring," her mind whispered.

"This?" Sharon fingered the sparkling end. "It was a gift from Sameed for our six-month anniversary. It's the first time I've worn them, actually. I know it's a bit much..."

"No, they're beautiful, and that reminds me of one of the stories I wanted to tell you. Sameed was so excited for us when we found out we were expecting. He was the first to know we were having a girl, since we ordered a dozen pink-filled cupcakes from him. He was just thrilled for us, and he never let me go hungry while I was pregnant. After Madeline was born, he gave her a beautiful little bracelet. It's so precious. Let me show you." Steph went into the other room to take the gift out of its keepsake box. "Here. He was so generous." She pulled out a tiny gold bangle.

"That's so sweet. I'm not surprised. He absolutely spoiled his two nephews." Sharon took a sip of tea. "I wish I'd had a chance to meet them. I only know them from his stories. Poor things lost their mother two years ago." Sharon changed the subject to Steph. "What about you? Do you have any nieces or nephews?"

"I have three on my side of the family, but none on Henry's side yet."

"What are your in-laws like?" Sharon was curious, since Steph had married into a different culture. Steph debated how much to share, and Sharon read the pause accurately. "Not very welcoming?"

"Sadly, no. Henry once told me he could be a doctor, a lawyer, or a failure. I thought he was kidding until I met them. They weren't too thrilled that he had chosen the latter and married me."

"I'm sorry. Maybe things will be better now that you've given them a grandchild."

"I hope so."

"It's what I was hoping for too, actually." A bell rang in Steph's mind. "I haven't told anyone yet, but I'm expecting. Not even my family knows. I was going to tell Sameed last week, but then…"

"Heavens above, this poor woman," thought Steph.

"Now he'll never know," Sharon continued, sniffling. "It was the one thing he wanted more than anything, to be a father, and now I have to raise his child without him. How am I going to do this?"

"Oh, Sharon. I'm so sorry." And she was sorry for her. Steph was practically a stranger, and Sharon was pouring her heart out. She must not have anyone else to talk to, Steph surmised.

"I don't know what to tell my family, or when. They never liked him. They couldn't see past our differences." Steph could imagine how age, religion, and marital status likely played into their position, but she had sympathy for Sharon. "But we had so much more in common, and I was the one who convinced him we were a good match, and we were."

"I am so sorry," Steph reiterated. "I can't imagine... Do you mind if I ask how far along you are?"

"Only a few weeks. I wasn't sure until a week ago. I wanted to surprise him in some special way, which is why we were supposed to go out to dinner that night." Her throat constricted, and she stopped talking for a moment. Steph wasn't sure what to do other than feel gutted for her.

After Sharon visibly calmed down, Steph asked, "Will there be a funeral for Sameed?"

"His family already buried him," Sharon replied.

"What? So soon?"

"Yes, it's done as quickly as possible for religious reasons, but his mother is hosting a reception in his honor at her home tomorrow night." Sharon got an idea. "Could you come with me? I don't think I can manage by myself. It would be a great help."

"I'd be honored to. Do I need to dress a certain way?" Steph genuinely wanted the chance to grieve her friend.

"I don't think it's any different from how you'd dress for any other funeral, but I'll ask."

"Thanks. I'll write it down on my calendar

now and ask if Henry thinks he can manage Madeline for an evening."

"Thank you so much."

"Of course." Madeline stirred. "Would you like to hold her?" Steph asked.

"Please, I would love to," Sharon replied. Steph picked up the tiny babe and nestled her in Sharon's arms, before remembering she didn't know the woman well, but the happy baby gave a gummy smile. Reflex or not, it was adorable and exactly what Sharon needed to see. She smiled back.

"See, you're a natural," Steph praised.

"What a beautiful little baby you are," Sharon cooed. "Your mommy and daddy are so lucky to have you." The weight and warmth of the infant soothed her like a hot water bottle, and Sharon breathed deeply, then handed her back, relieving Steph.

The rest of Sharon's visit went smoothly. Steph found her to be open and gregarious. Steph laughed as Sharon recounted the time Sameed came to visit with marker on his face after visiting his nephews, which he called his "nibbles." They had been trying to give their uncle a "proper" beard. Sharon awwed when Steph told her about the time when Sameed rescued a litter of orphaned kittens found behind the bakery.

"They were so darling with their little paws and their tiny whiskered noses and itty-bitty pink tongues lapping up cream. It was adorable. If my husband weren't such a dog-lover, I would have been tempted," said Steph.

"That's the cutest thing I've ever heard."

"And the best part? The poor guy was red-eyed and sneezing every day he came into work, but he was willing to suffer until he found good homes for all of them. Near the end, his eyes were so puffy, we wondered how well he could see, but he was determined."

"Oh my goodness."

"He was a total sweetheart."

"Yeah, he was." Sharon looked at the clock. "I should probably be heading back to my apartment now, but thank you so much for having me. It was lovely being here."

"It was my pleasure. You are welcome to come back anytime."

"Thank you so much. I really appreciate it. I'll come and see you - and *you* - again." She directed her second "you" at Madeline and gathered her things. "Have a good rest of your day."

"You too."

Steph closed the door after her. She had so much to digest before Henry came home. A mindless task like washing dishes would be perfect, but not long after she started, her phone rang. It was Sharon.

"Hello?"

"Hey, Steph. It's Sharon. I'm just outside across the street. My car won't start. Do you have any cables?"

"No, sorry. My husband has them in the car, and he took it to work. Do you want to come back inside and wait while you call someone else?"

"Sure. Thanks. I'll call my brother."

Steph put Madeline in the carrier and let Sharon back inside the building. Sharon quickly dialed, speaking a few lines into the phone, then hung up.

"He can be here in ten minutes."

"So, you have a brother?" Steph asked.

"Yes, older." The way Sharon said 'older' suggested somewhat overbearing. Steph laughed.

"I know what that's like. Is he local?"

"He is for now until he's reassigned," she answered, then explained. "He's a Navy SEAL."

"Oh. Wow. Did he come back recently?"

"A week ago." Sharon kept an eye outside through the door in front of the stairwell.

"Do you want to go back upstairs?" Steph offered. "You could sit down."

"No, he should be here any minute. You don't have to wait with me."

"I don't mind." Steph was curious, anyhow. "What's his name?"

"David."

"Did you get along well as kids?" The look on Sharon's face suggested yes and no.

"He was a pretty cool older brother, but every now and then he got on my nerves, telling me what to do. When we were kids, he always made sure my skates were tightly laced before going out on the ice, but he ended a guy's hockey season after he hit on me."

"Older siblings," Steph replied, conspiratorially. "If it had been up to my brothers, they would have picked my prom date for me." Sharon giggled.

"Oh my gosh, yes! Actually, if it had been up to David, I would have never gone to prom with anybody." A pickup truck pulled up next to what must have been Sharon's elderly Volkswagen. "That's him. Thanks again, Steph. See you tomorrow!"

"Bye, Sharon!" As Steph waved, she peered through the door. She saw a bearded man with fair, shaggy hair standing beside a pickup, his massive forearms crossed, and he seemed tall, taller than her husband and much broader. She didn't wave for too long for fear of seeming awkward. By the time she was back in her apartment, she could hear the purr of Sharon's car engine and the roar of her brother's truck. She had even more to think about now.

When Henry returned home, the scent of chili filled the apartment, and Steph immediately began to ladle some for both of them with a large dollop of sour cream.

"How was your day?" he asked.

"Good," Steph replied. "Sharon came over today."

"Where's Madeline?"

"Sleeping in the nursery."

"So, what did you two talk about?"

"We talked about Sameed. There's going to be a reception at his mother's home tomorrow night. Sharon wants me to come with her. Do you think you'll be alright if I leave Madeline with you? I'll try not to stay for more than an hour."

"An hour should be fine."

"Great. Thanks. I should probably pick up a card and some flowers," said Steph, thinking aloud as she handed out bowls.

"I can do that later tonight if you want," Henry offered, stirring his chili.

"Perfect." Henry and Steph both started to eat their chili when it occurred to Steph the important details she had neglected to mention.

"Oh, Henry. I forgot to tell you – I don't think she'll mind if I tell you – Sharon is pregnant. Her family doesn't know, and she doesn't want them to know because of how much they disapproved of Sameed."

"How awful. I feel sorry for her."

"Me too. I can't imagine having a baby without you or my family's support. Do you think there's something we can do to help?"

"I'm sure there is. She's probably not ready to start getting baby stuff, but maybe when she is you can plan a shower for her." It was a lot to ask of a new friend, but it was the kind of thing Henry knew his wife would love to do.

"What a great idea! I knew there was a

reason why I married you." There were many, actually, and now that she had seen him be a father to their daughter, she had even more reasons, but words of affirmation were not Henry's love language. Instead, she asked, "Do you want more chili," taking his bowl.

"Yes, thanks." Going through his stomach was the more effective route.

"You know, I was thinking…" Steph started.

"What?"

"I was thinking about Madeline. I know your mom offered to watch her, but I'm not so sure I want to go back to my job in two weeks." Steph knew that it was asking a lot to make him the sole breadwinner. Henry's college had been taken care of, but they still had a car payment, doctor's visits, and her student loans to consider.

"That's up to you," Henry said before shoveling in another bite.

"Are you sure? Can we afford it?" His spoon paused for a moment.

"If it's what you really want, we'll make it work." Henry went back to eating. Steph was somewhat in awe of how calmly he could dismiss what seemed like a massive question mark.

"Thanks, I mean, I'm not totally decided yet. Maybe there's a way I could work from home for a while, so it's not such a huge financial leap. Or, maybe I'll feel differently in a few weeks. I don't know."

"You don't have to decide right this second,"

Henry reassured. "But when you're ready to make a decision, it's yours. I want you to be happy." Steph wished she knew which would make her happy, but his support pacified her.

"You're wonderful. Thank you. I'll look into a few options, see what the company is willing to offer." She smiled at him.

"Do you think you'll want to try painting again? Have Madeline sleep in our room and use the nursery as a studio?" It had been their original plan for the layout of their apartment.

"Maybe." Steph hadn't really put work into developing her own art since starting as a graphic designer. She had committed to overtime at the office instead, but she began to wonder if those had been hours well spent. She wasn't sure she knew who she was as an artist anymore.

"You could paint tonight while I watch Maddie," Henry suggested, hearing their daughter stir.

"I'd rather do something together, if that's okay." She wasn't feeling inspired at the moment.

"Of course. So, what do you want to do tonight?"

"I was thinking maybe a board game if Madeline will let us play one."

"Sounds good. Did you have a particular one in mind?"

"Well, we have one someone gave us as a wedding gift." The pair had run out of household items to request and added games to the list.

Surprisingly, their guests had obliged.

"Sure, let's try it." Steph and Henry cleared the table. Cleanup was a breeze, since the only pot she dirtied was the slow cooker. Steph hunkered down with Madeline and the instructions, getting in snuggles now, so she might be able to put her down for a length of time during the game. Henry popped out miniature pirate ships and treasure chests from their cardboard prisons.

Steph appreciated the design of the board, and Henry had a mind for math. Maybe one day they could come up with a game of their own.

Swashbuckling pirates skirted dangerous waters and enemy fire in search of buried treasure and glory. While fair winds blew ships toward friendly shores, powder, and rations, a bad storm could maroon them, or worse, send them to port where high taxes awaited.

Thankfully, like her pirate persona, Steph could play this with one hand, and they finished relatively quickly.

"That was pretty fun," Steph declared. "What did you think?"

"I liked it. The game could have been a little more strategic, but it was a nice change of pace from staring at a screen."

"Agreed. Let's do it again sometime." Happy to have found another option for evening entertainment, Steph and Henry settled down for the night. Steph put Madeline to sleep first, then joined Henry in their bedroom after brushing her teeth.

"What are you listening to?" Henry had his headphones plugged in.

"Math rock." It was Henry's favorite musical genre. "You know Asians and math," he joked. It was a style of rock Steph had been unfamiliar with before meeting Henry, but had since learned to recognize its almost jazz-like sound with unique chord progressions and calculated time signatures.

"Anything I would like?"

"Probably not. It's all instrumental." Henry knew how much Steph enjoyed singing along. He had heard her in the shower regularly.

"Gotcha." Back in the day, Henry had actually been in a band called Tiger Mom on lead guitar. His hair had been longer then. Once they drove six hours to play for five people. The headliner had rescheduled, but nobody told them. After the show, they gave everyone a tee shirt and a CD and shared pizza and beer together. Henry still considered it one of his favorite gigs.

To Steph's knowledge, only one of his band mates had attempted a career in music after college. She wasn't sure to what degree of success. The others became dentists or bank managers and the like. Following a passion took more than having talent. It seemed most people made an economical choice in the end. She slid into bed. "You know, I really appreciate you," she said, scooting closer.

"I appreciate you too," he replied. They held onto each other for a few minutes before separating to fall asleep. It was all Steph's postpartum body would allow her for the time being. "Goodnight."

"Goodnight." Falling asleep, Steph was sorry for her new friend, who had no partner to comfort her. Tomorrow, she would discover just how much an outsider Sharon really felt and see first-hand how much or how little others mourned Sameed's loss.

CHAPTER 8

On Tuesday morning, the sun was shining, the sky was clear, and the slightest breeze rustled fallen leaves along the sidewalk. The oddly delightful smell of natural decay mingled in the air. It was Steph's favorite weather, and she determined to make the most of it. She hadn't gone out at all Monday, and spent the better part of Sunday preparing for a disastrous dinner, which had started with a barrage of nit picking and ended with a dead body.

Steph had Madeline in the carrier and the stroller in hand again when she ran into Rachel in the stairwell.

"Have fun at class!" Steph called out. Rachel was further down the stairs in jeans, an oversized sweater, and a rather long scarf wrapped several times around, which seemed unnecessary until she turned around. Rachel also sported a surgical mask.

"Thanks. It's a rehearsal, actually, but please stay away. I think I have a cold, and I don't want to get you or the baby sick." Rachel coughed.

"Thanks," Steph said, taking a few steps back. "Is it really flu season already? I'm sorry you're not feeling well."

"Yeah, I hope I can survive the next two hours." Steph could imagine being surrounded by a hundred other instruments wasn't going to help.

"Good luck," Steph sympathized. "You don't need me to tell you to drink lots of water. Hopefully, some fresh air will do you good."

"I hope so. Thanks. See you around."

"See ya."

Steph let Rachel go through the door first, then opened it with her sleeve over the handle. She thought about which direction to go in and realized she and Henry had been so busy playing a game last night they had forgotten to buy flowers for Sameed's mother. Since the reception was tonight, Steph walked in the direction of the nearest flower shop.

Bells jingled when she walked through the front door of More Flower To You, and the heady scent of a hundred perfumes washed over her. Bouquets of cut flowers abounded, their final destination unknown. Playfully pink, those would do for a first date, and joyous bursts of yellow would brighten any hospital room. As much as she appreciated the beautiful displays, Steph didn't think she could maneuver around them with the stroller, so she put it aside.

Every flower spoke something different to Steph. Red roses whispered, "Romance," while forget-me-nots said, "Think of me." However, to her in-laws, orchids better demonstrated love, and thorny stems promised only pain and unhappiness. A kindly-looking woman with gray hair and a green apron asked, "Can I help you find something?"

"Yes," said Steph. "I'm attending a memorial

tonight for a friend at his mother's house. I was wondering which flowers I should get. He was Muslim. I don't know if that makes a difference."

"People often buy lilies or other white flowers for funerals, but you might want to check with the family."

"I will. Thanks." Steph turned away to call Sharon.

"Hi, Sharon? This is Steph. Um, I was wondering what kind of flower I should bring? I've never been to a Muslim funeral before."

"Hi, Steph. Flowers aren't actually very common. I had to look it up myself, but I'm sure Sameed's mother Leyla would appreciate a card from you. There's also a charity you could donate to in Sameed's honor if you want. I can send you the information in a little bit. I'm sorry I forgot to tell you yesterday."

"It's fine. Also, I was wondering if you heard anything about a dress code?"

"No, I haven't. I'm going to wear all black."

"Okay. Thanks, Sharon. By the way, what time do you want to meet?"

"It starts at 6 o'clock, so 5:45?"

"I'll be ready to meet you at 5:45 then. See you in a few hours."

"See you then." Steph hung up the phone, then looked around at all the flowers before turning her eyes back on the shopkeeper. She felt awkward.

"Excuse me," she started. "Do you have any sympathy cards?"

"Yes, we do. They're over by the register. Take your time." Steph read the headers quietly aloud.

"Get Well Soon. Birthday. Wedding. Anniversary... Sympathy." She reached out.

The first she selected for review had elegant gold calligraphy and plenty of space for writing, jackpot. Card chosen, she brought it to the register. The shopkeeper rang it up, and Steph swiped down payment.

"Do you want a bag for this?" the shopkeeper asked. Steph looked at her stroller. She didn't want to risk crumpling it.

"Yes, please."

"What an adorable baby you have, by the way." Steph smiled at the compliment. "Did you adopt her?" The smile took more effort.

"Thank you. No, she looks like my husband." Steph knew she shouldn't feel too disappointed. It was obvious Madeline took after Henry more than her, or at least appeared to for now. She told herself she should be prepared to hear that question more often in the future.

"Oh. Have a nice day!" Steph collected her purchase and walked toward the door. The shopkeeper was kind enough to hold it open for her while she shimmied out. Madeline dozed in the stroller on the way home.

After the baby's nap and Steph's long walk, both were famished. Once sufficiently supped, Steph took the opportunity to work on the card for

Leyla. She tried to think of something personal about Sameed, some previously unknown kindness about her son to ease her sorrow even the slightest.

She decided to write about the things she had told Sharon the other day, how Sameed had been so sweet to her during her pregnancy and a few other anecdotes. It was a lot to try to fit into one card. While she needed to be succinct, she wanted to do the stories justice. However, what she *really* wanted was justice for Sameed. She scowled. She wished she felt closer to achieving it.

Steph tried her best to pour out her heart onto the paper because she knew she wouldn't be able to say it well in person. She signed and sealed the card. She checked the clock and realized she had used up an entire hour. She sighed. It was a shame she couldn't write more quickly or elegantly.

For the rest of the afternoon, Steph slowly prepped for the evening, first changing, then styling her hair in a simple up-do, and lastly putting on a hint of makeup, so she wouldn't look as tired as she was. In between each stage, she fed, burped, changed, or entertained Madeline. Steph was grateful to her baby for pulling her mind back to the more joyful circumstances of the present, ignoring for the moment her frustration over the mystery of Sameed's death. She couldn't put into words why she felt so personally responsible for solving the crime, but it didn't seem fair to her that another person had been ripped from her life.

When Henry walked through the door, Steph

was stirring a pot of boiling water and spaghetti noodles. She wasn't sure if there would be food at the reception, and Henry often came home already hungry anyway.

"Hi, dinner will be ready in 10 minutes," she said.

"Great. I'll get changed then." Henry came back out in one hundred percent cotton, perfect for absorbing anything Madeline would throw at him later.

"Ready." Steph placed two plates of spaghetti with meat sauce on the table. She convinced herself that the tomatoes in the sauce counted as a sufficient serving of vegetables. The two dug in while Madeline watched from her bouncer.

"Hey." A thought occurred to Henry. "Is there a bottle ready for Maddie in case she gets hungry while you're gone?" He started clearing away the plates and loading the few new dishes in the dishwasher.

"No, I'll go pump in a minute. I'm almost done eating." Steph quickly ate the last of the pasta on her plate.

"How's Daddy's little dumpling?" Steph overheard when she left the kitchen. In the nursery, it took her some time to set up the electric pump. She hadn't used it yet, so she needed to first rinse all the pieces. After that, she sat down in an armchair and tried to make sure nothing popped off on accident and spilled the precious liquid. Madeline wouldn't be the only one to cry if Steph did. Madeline detested formula, so no milk meant one hangry baby.

While she waited, she looked with satisfaction at the nursery décor. Inspired by minimalism and a desire not to open a can of paint while pregnant, Steph kept the walls white, but brightened them with botanical artwork and bold furnishings. She and Henry had found Chinese watercolor paintings of flowers and married them with delft blue floral accents. Outside the pop of blue, rose pink and soft green added further color and a feminine touch to the armchair, curtains, and bedding.

After she had what seemed like enough, she came back out and handed the bottle to Henry.

"Do I need to refrigerate it," he asked.

"No, it's stays good at room temperature for a few hours. Call me if you need anything. I'm sure Sharon will understand if I need to go back early."

"We'll be fine. It's 5:40. You should probably start heading downstairs."

"Okay. Bye. Thank you. Bye my sweet little angel. Be good for Daddy. Mommy will be back soon." Steph hadn't spoken in the third person before having Madeline, but now it was a habit. She grabbed her purse with her phone, keys, checkbook, and the card inside.

Sharon pulled up in front just as Steph was walking out the front door of the building.

"Hi, thanks for picking me up," Steph said.

"Not a problem. Thanks for coming with me." Steph hopped in the passenger seat.

"Is it far away?" she asked, doing a last minute check of her makeup and outfit. To her dismay, a splotch of spit-up on her shoulder had escaped her notice earlier. Sharon responded.

"No, but I wasn't sure what the parking situation would be like with so many other people coming." Steph wet a tissue from her purse and rubbed at the spot. While willing it to go away, she noticed the fruit basket.

"Is that for Leyla? Was I supposed to bring some kind of food?" Thankfully, a patch of wetness on black wasn't very noticeable. Steph hoped it dried looking normal. Putting the used tissue back in her purse, she looked again toward the ground. This time her eyes were drawn to a small rolling bottle. She picked it up and placed it in a cup holder. She couldn't help noticing it was a prescription for lithium.

"Oh no, you're fine," Sharon reassured, slightly turning her neck. "And thanks. I forgot those were in here. I stopped taking them sometime before I got pregnant." Steph herself wasn't unfamiliar with antidepressants, though she had been off them for a decade. She took a good look at her new friend to see how she was doing. At the moment, she seemed pretty composed. Sharon wore a black turtleneck sweater, skirt, and tights. She too had her hair pulled back neatly in a bun.

"Are you alright?" Steph gently posed,

banishing the thought of Sharon's mental health having anything to do with Sameed's death. It was a gross, irresponsible theory.

"No." Sharon throat hitched slightly. "I'm just hoping to get through tonight. The funeral was just a family affair, so I didn't get to attend."

"But you *are* family," Steph insisted, then added, "Leyla doesn't know about the baby, does she?"

"No, she doesn't. I *will* tell her," Sharon promised. "I'm just not ready to yet, so please don't mention it."

"I won't. I promise." Steph paused. "I did tell Henry though. I hope that's okay."

"That's fine. I just don't want anyone else finding out."

"Does anyone else know?"

"My roommate and the nurse who treated me at the hospital, but that's it. It's still really early, so I don't feel comfortable letting everyone know."

"I understand," Steph said. "I waited until I was three months pregnant to tell anyone other than Henry…" Steph changed the subject. "So, what's it going to be like at Leyla's house?" She wondered if there were any clues or insights to be gathered.

"I couldn't say for sure," Sharon responded. "I guess we'll find out together." They drove up to the house. The driveway was packed with cars and others lined the street in both directions. "Family probably arrived a little early." Sharon and Steph parked a few houses down.

They walked up to the door and knocked. A stranger dressed in white answered. A glimpse inside showed more women in light hijabs and suggested they maybe had the correct address, but there was only one way to be sure.

"Is this Leyla's house?" Sharon posed. The woman asked them a question in Arabic, then French when they didn't respond. The second was so quick and unexpected that Steph struggled to catch it. The woman walked away, leaving them alone on the doorstep waiting. Steph watched her weave through a sea of similarly dressed people, remembering that in China too white was the color of mourning, not black. She wished she had thought to check earlier. Eventually, the attention of another woman in conversation turned to them. Steph wondered if it really were all right to be here. Maybe this was just supposed to be for family. Sharon tightened her grip on the gift for Leyla.

For a few minutes, they stood awkwardly to the side, closing the door to keep out the cold. Sharon struggled to place faces based on pictures and Sameed's descriptions. The two friends sensed a dozen pairs of eyes on them, and Steph considered doing some sleuthing while they were at the house to distract herself from the awkwardness.

"I want to say something to Ayman," Sharon informed her, upon spotting him. They moved in his direction. Others moved out of their way, whispering in Arabic. Sharon knew him from pictures. As uncomfortable as it was approaching someone who had refused to meet her, she still felt it appropriate to offer him condolences. Steph wondered if she'd see the face of a guilty man, would his eyes betray him, and would she even know what to look for.

"My deepest sympathies to you and your family." Up close, Steph hardly recognized Ayman as the man who had come in for espresso and a few choice words the day Sameed died. Steph thought he resembled his younger brother more than she had first thought. Their noses were identical, and Ayman quite possibly had the same jaw, though obscured by a beard. However, his eyes were hollow and cheeks sunken, emphasizing his relatively gaunt frame. Conviction gripped her. It was inappropriate to do anything other than grieve and console tonight.

"Thank you," he said, full of emotion. He looked at Steph. She felt like an interloper with the depth of his grief so painfully evident. There stood a man broken. Guilt gripped her for her earlier supposition.

Onlookers wondered at Sharon and her potential role in Sameed's failed marriage. She bore their judgment quietly.

"This is Steph. She was Sameed's neighbor and friend," Sharon quickly explained.

"He was a wonderful person. I'm so sorry for your loss," Steph reiterated.

"Thank you," Ayman replied curtly.

"Where can I put this?" Sharon asked,

gesturing to the fruit basket.

"In the kitchen, to your left." Accompanied by Steph, Sharon headed into the kitchen where a countertop of dishes and table full of baskets suggested others had thought the same. Once out of sight, the weight of everyone's stares dissipated. Steph spied a place for cards and set hers down.

"Hey, Sharon? You wouldn't happen to have an extra envelope in your purse, would you? I forgot to put the check for the charity in the card before I sealed it."

"No, sorry, but you can probably hand it to Leyla. We can walk back that way and look for her." They passed Ayman again as he welcomed a relative with a kiss, warmly thanking them for coming. He avoided making eye contact a second time. As they walked back toward the front door they heard a young female voice behind them complain about the inconvenient timing of the reception.

"There were several relatives who couldn't make it last week," Ayman explained to the thirty-something year old woman dressed in a headscarf with an exquisite gold hijab pin and red-soled shoes. Dr. Abila Khoury, Sameed's ex-wife, spent the majority of her time in a white coat and trainers as a doctor, having recently completed her residency. Any time she had off and wasn't working on her car, as Steph would later learn, Abila took the opportunity to dress up.

Despite her black clothes and lack of

religious covering, Steph's wedding band marked her as a person of no interest. However, Abila saw Sharon and put two and two together, noticing the long legs, youthful face, and bright blond hair. Her head might as well have been on fire.

"Excuse me," the voice from behind called. "Are you Sharon?"

"Yes." Sharon turned around. Long lashed eyes looked her up and down.

"So young. And pretty. My name is Abila."

"Hi. Thanks." Sharon wasn't exactly sure what to say to her boyfriend's ex-wife. "This is my friend Steph. She was friends with Sameed."

"He will be greatly missed," Steph filled in.

"Yes," Abila agreed. "How long did *you* know him?" she asked Steph, knowing perfectly well Sharon hadn't known him for long despite their intimacy.

"About four years. I live above The Likable Daisy," Steph answered. Abila addressed Sharon once again.

"This must be a *very* difficult time for you." Steph wondered if Sharon picked up on the passive aggression.

"It is," she said slowly. It seemed she hadn't. "It must be hard for you too."

"Well, I should probably help in the kitchen. It was nice to finally meet you."

"It was nice meeting you as well," Sharon replied with candor, having expected worse.

Sharon and Steph slowly made their way

back through the hall, single file. As more and more relatives had arrived, it was standing room only. Behind them Steph heard Abila say, "*…la libertine qui a volé mon mari,*" pointing at Sharon. Rusty as it was, Steph's high school French told her that was incredibly rude and probably untrue based on what Sharon and Jane had relayed.

Twenty feet turned into a mile, and claustrophobia started clawing at Steph. She didn't know any of these people, but more importantly none of them knew or wanted her. She felt unwelcome. She wondered if it were ruder to leave quickly or remain.

To distract herself, Steph focused her mind instead on the vibrancy and intricacy of Leyla's collection of Arabic calligraphy hanging on the walls. It was quite different from anything Henry or her in-laws had shown her. Some even formed images. A tigress leapt out at her, and she wondered what it said. In college, she'd learned that in some Islamic traditions, depictions of living creatures were banned to avoid idolatry, so art found a new mode of expression in calligraphy.

The lively brush strokes distracted her temporarily, but indignation continued to raise the temperature of the hall. Mourners wondered at the two strangers in their midst. They could guess at the significance of at least one of them and cast their pity on Abila. Even though Sharon didn't understand what was being said, she felt it. Fruit already delivered, she nervously clutched the fabric of her skirt in one hand instead.

Wordlessly, Ayman brushed past them to return to his mother's side and assist her with a large basket. Steph and Sharon had finally reached the doorway. Standing to the side, the two women lingered just long enough to catch Leyla alone again, but before they were able to get her attention, a gray-haired gentleman and softly wrinkled lady with henna-dyed hair approached.

"*Excusez moi, vous êtes Sharon*?"

"Yes," Sharon responded. He shook her hand.

"*Je m'appelle Farez.*" He touched his chest. "*Je vous présente ma femme Ghashmira.*" This time he gestured toward the woman next to him. Thankfully for Steph, Farez had intentionally slowed down his speech, though the meaning was still lost on Sharon.

"*Bonsoir*." To Sharon's surprise, among others, Ghashmira kissed her cheek. Sharon smiled. She knew them.

"*Bonsoir*," she tried to repeat, then turned to Steph. "Do you know French?"

"A little." Steph pinched her thumb and index finger together. Her experience with the language only included the textbook Parisian accent. "They said their names are Farez and Ghashmira and 'good evening.'"

"Oh. Thanks. Can you tell them I know them because Sameed told me about them, and I'm glad to finally meet them." Steph tried her best.

"Mon amie m'a dit qu'elle vous connaît parce-que Sameed… eh… Sameed vous a présentés. Elle est enchantée." They smiled. Steph assumed they understood.

"Nous sommes vraiment désolés pour votre perte." Their faces turned somber.

"We are so sorry for your loss," Steph translated.

"Merci," Sharon replied. She knew that much. "Can you say, 'and my condolences to you too?'"

"Et mes condoléances à vous aussi."

"Merci."

They stood a moment in silence unsure how to proceed. A small, elegant woman in an ivory hijab came forward, speaking in rapid French to the couple. They waved goodbye, stepping into a sitting room, while the petite woman turned to Sharon and Steph.

"Leyla," Sharon greeted. "Thank you for inviting me. This is my friend Steph. She was a good friend of Sameed's."

Deep brown eyes peered up at them through rimless lenses. Though barely over five feet, Leyla looked like she could manage two strong-willed boys with a single word. Her presence was formidable.

"My sincerest condolences to your family," Steph said. "Here." She handed over the check. "I didn't know where to put this, but it's a donation to the charity your family suggested."

"Thank you. My son Sameed was passionate

about this organization. It's a mentoring program for teens interested in entrepreneurship," Leyla explained.

"I'm sure he inspired many," Steph consoled.

"Thank you again for inviting me and my friend," Sharon said. "I hope you find peace and comfort. Sameed is in a better place now."

"To Allah we belong and to him we shall return."

Steph and Sharon headed back to Sharon's car. Once safely inside Sharon turned toward Steph.

"Well, that went better than I thought it would," she said. "With Abila especially. I mean, I didn't think she'd be vicious in public, but she seemed pretty nice actually." Steph remembered enough French to know Abila had not been as nice as Sharon assumed. Even her English had been laced with condescension. Steph wondered how much she should divulge. Sharon continued.

"I'm sorry for her, really. I don't think their marriage was ever happy. Their parents introduced them, and Sameed was desperate to please his family. They both were, but they were a terrible fit together. He wanted to settle down. She wanted to live it up..." She sighed. "They both knew it was a mistake. It's a shame she took so long to sign the divorce papers. We probably would have been married by now if she hadn't, but maybe she was ashamed or in denial. Who knows." Steph thought it was sweet of Sharon to give Abila the benefit of the doubt. She decided against telling her.

"Anyway, thanks for coming to this with me. You gave me the strength I needed."

"I was glad to come. I'm going to miss him too." Sharon turned the key in the ignition. The engine sputtered a bit before igniting. They remained silent for the rest of the drive to Steph's apartment. The clock on the dash read "6:47."

"Thanks for driving me," Steph said. The car's headlights shined on the golden lettering spelling out The Likable Daisy.

"Of course. Thanks again for coming with me," Sharon replied, pulling over.

"Are you going to be okay?" Steph asked. Sharon sighed.

"One day at a time. If I'm really struggling, I know I can always go see my old therapist. Have a good night."

"Goodnight, Sharon. Drive safe."

Sharon drove off, and Steph walked back up the stairs to her apartment, where Henry and Madeline were waiting.

"How did she do?" Steph inquired.

"She was great. She finished the bottle and just had a diaper change," Henry informed.

"Great. Thanks." Steph took the baby from him after removing her coat.

"How was the reception?"

"Interesting." They went into the living room.

"How so?"

"Well, Sameed's ex-wife was there."

"And?" Henry sat down readying himself for his wife's newest conclusions.

"She was really rude to Sharon, but Sharon didn't know because Abila was speaking in French. Also, I don't think their divorce was public yet, but it sounds like she did sign the papers, according to Sharon," Steph theorized.

"So they were divorced then," he repeated.

"Yes, at least, that's the impression I got from Sharon and Abila. She didn't seem to be grieving one iota."

"Well, they were separated."

"Yes, but you'd think she'd have some feeling for the man she was married to if not sympathy for his family."

"You would think that, but perhaps not. We can only guess what their relationship was like," Henry said. Steph huffed lightly.

"You're right," she conceded. Comfortably settled on the couch with Madeline, Steph then asked Henry what he'd like to do the rest of the evening.

"We both enjoyed playing a board game last night. How about we play another one?" he suggested. Steph hemmed and hawed a little. She was pretty cozy where she was on the couch. "I can make some chocolate chip cookies too," he added. Steph jumped up.

"Do we have any frozen dough?"

"I think so."

"Perfect." She started to preheat the oven.

There was nothing more comforting or enticing than a warm kitchen on a cool evening. The sun had disappeared below the horizon, and a chill had set in the air. Steph wrapped a blanket across her shoulders. Even thinking about the cold outside chilled her.

Henry started to set up the game, getting into the mindset of Neolithic hunter gatherers, while Steph tried to quickly thaw and scoop the dough onto a baking sheet. Within twenty minutes, hot, gooey cookies awaited. Steph and Henry tried to remember to eat with one hand and play with the other. It was a perfect evening, or nearly perfect. One thought niggled in the back of Steph's mind. Sameed had been gone a whole week and she didn't feel any closer to truly knowing what had happened to him.

After an hour of dice rolling, resource gambling, and avoiding starvation, Steph and Henry packed up the game and uneaten cookies. The latter would probably be gone within twenty-four hours. Steph went into the nursery to feed Madeline once last time and put her down for the night, while Henry worked on putting his lunch together for tomorrow. He finished before Steph, since Madeline protested her mother's departure the first few times. Steph was both milk cow and pacifier, as well as personal space heater, but the baby eventually settled into a deeper sleep.

Steph and Henry reconvened in the bedroom after Steph had brushed her teeth. Pajamas on, she sidled into bed.

"How are you doing?" Henry asked his wife.

"Fine, I think, and you?"

"Doing well. Have you been sleeping okay? If you pump again, I can take over one of the night feedings."

"Thanks, I don't really want to tonight, but if I sleep terribly, then I might take you up on your offer tomorrow." Steph wanted to go to bed that minute, not in another half hour after pumping, storing, and cleaning everything.

"Alright, just let me know. I love you. Goodnight."

"I love you. Goodnight," she parroted sincerely before turning out the light.

As she drifted off to sleep, Steph thought about Abila and Ayman. Abila's long awaited signature on the divorce papers seemed to indicate she had moved on. She would no longer have a financial motive, and it suggested an insufficient personal motive, Steph surmised. Or did it, she questioned. Steph had an idea.

"Honey?"

"Mmm?" he answered sleepily.

"Divorce agreements aren't official until the court signs them, right?"

"Yeah, why? Are you thinking of getting one?"

"Of course not." She kissed her husband one more time on the cheek. "Goodnight."

"Goodnight."

Steph's mind raced with possibilities. Abila could still be Sameed's legal wife. She could still benefit from his death. Moreover, what if she hadn't been lying when she said Sharon "stole" her husband, Steph wondered. Perhaps, what Sharon had told her wasn't exactly the gospel truth, and Jane's second-hand version was also slightly incorrect.

Steph determined to find out two things, one, if Sameed and Abila were still legally married, and two, the real timeline of Sharon and Sameed's relationship. If she played her cards right, she could find out without anyone being suspect. If she didn't, who knew what danger she was putting herself in?

CHAPTER 9

Steph was conscious that she was in a dream. It was one she couldn't escape and would likely never forget. She found herself once again outside her apartment building, carrying a bag of garbage. A chill emanated from the blood red brick. Her coat had disappeared, and instead of a sensible sweater and boots, she wore pajamas and bunny slippers.

The streetlights flickered, and Steph felt a presence lurk behind her. She turned around, but no one was there. She continued around the corner to the back of the building. A black cat ran across her path and into the night, hissing. She turned again. As Steph left the sidewalk, she stepped into a pothole, and water seeped through. Floppy ears matted and drooped.

The weight of the trash was starting to pull at her shoulder. A two handed carry would shorten her steps, so Steph hiked up the bag instead, curling her bicep. She wasn't far now. The back alley narrowed, and the air became stale. Though the chill was gone, she felt colder than before. She approached the defaced dumpster, darkness concentrated in the space beside it.

As she opened the shrieking metal lid, she noticed the figure of a person against the wall. "Hello?" Steph said. There was no response. It was too dark to tell if he or she was asleep.

Steph reached into her pocket for her phone, but it was gone. Setting down the trash, she walked closer to the figure. She squinted at worn shoes and dirty pants, then limp arms and slumped shoulders. Straggly hair obscured the face leaning on the brick.

"Hello?" Steph called once more before daring to get closer. The woman didn't stir. Dread pooled in her stomach, but something compelled her to draw near. Hand quivering, she brushed aside the long brown strands. Instead of the pale visage her memory expected, the olive complexion and features of her mother stared back at her.

Tripping over her sodden feet, Steph tried to retreat from the alley to no avail. She was somehow lost. While her spine pressed coldly against an opposite wall, she still felt too close to the dumpster for comfort and wrapped her arms around her knees. She closed her eyes and struggled to ignore the creaking fire escape and whispering wind.

A distant whimper entered the alley. Heart pounding, she looked around. Her eyes stopped at the dumpster, but she couldn't place the sound there. The cry grew louder and more frantic until finally the dream released her. Madeline's hungry protests flashed on the baby monitor, and Steph's eyes once again perceived reality. She jumped out of bed, rushing to the nursery.

After tending to her baby, Steph dressed for comfort that morning. A hug from Henry would have to wait until the end of the day since he had already left for work. She wondered whether she should tell him about the dream.

She checked the forecast. The weather didn't thrill her, but it was nice enough to walk across the street. It had been some time since she had sat in a coffee shop and socialized with the regulars. On her way down, she ran into Rachel, who was once again dressed casually.

"Hey, I hope you're feeling better," Steph said.

"Thanks. Yeah, the fresh air yesterday did help, but unfortunately my headache came back. At least I only have classes today."

"That's too bad. Good luck."

"Thanks. It should be fine. I made myself some tea before I left."

Steph remembered the late nights and subsequent caffeine-fueled classes. She didn't miss them, but she did miss the regularity of working in a studio. Perhaps, later today she could crack into the watercolor set Henry bought. Art was therapy for her, but first, coffee called.

Meanwhile, a tan sedan raced across Greenway Ave, accelerating well above the speed limit. Text messages occupied the only available pair of eyes inside. As Steph prepared to cross the street, she considered aloud the things she might like to paint.

"Maybe a field of sunflowers… yellow, cheery." Now twenty feet away, the phone slipped down, and the eyes sunk beneath the dash.

"I wonder what the brushes will be like. I

hope they have a nice feel to them." The car careened closer to the sidewalk as Steph's foot lifted from the pavement.

"Wooden handles really are so much nicer than plastic even if they don't clean as easi—" The sedan zoomed past, inches away from her. Steph berated herself. "I can't believe I almost… and with Madeline too." She fretted at the thought of what could have happened. She cursed under her breath. Footsteps came up behind her.

"Are you okay?" Greg emerged from the doorway of the apartment building.

"Oh! Hey, Greg. Sorry, I almost did something really stupid. I really should be more careful."

"No, that guy was driving like a maniac. Anyway, where are you headed?"

"Black Coffee Bistro."

"Same. Just picking up lunch, you?

"I thought a change of scenery would be nice. Maybe I'll stay for lunch." Steph had said "maybe," but as soon as she smelled the ready-made food, she'd struggle not to order something.

"I hope you have a nice morning."

"Thanks. You too."

Steph and Greg crossed the street in silence. He went directly to the counter to order, while Steph scouted out a good table. Once she set her things down, she tried to take a picture of her and Madeline with her phone. They had their matching headbands on today, but Steph unfortunately wasn't very good at selfies.

"Hey, Greg?" she called out. He was still waiting for his order. "Can you take a picture of us?" Steph stood up with Madeline. Black Coffee Bistro featured large glass panes on its storefront, where customers on modern metal barstools gathered to people watch or for bountiful lighting to read by. Before noon, sunshine streamed through the East-facing windows to her back.

"Sure, no problem." He grabbed the phone, snapped a shot, and handed it back to her.

"Thanks!"

"Order for Greg," the cashier called out. Greg paid in cash, snatched up his to-go bag, and left.

"I forgot to ask him if he were busy later this week," thought Steph. "Oh, well. Next time."

Unnecessary outer layers dispersed, Steph was considering what to order when her phone buzzed.

"Hello?"

"It's Jane."

"Oh, hey, Jane! What's up?"

"I traded shifts with someone later this week, so I have today off. Can you do an early lunch?"

"Yeah, I can. Actually, I'm already at Black Coffee Bistro. Do you wanna meet me here?"

"Sounds great. I'll see you in about twenty minutes."

"Great. See you then."

While Steph waited, Madeline helped herself, with some assistance from mom, to an early meal.

Steph used her scarf to be discreet, not that it mattered much. She had ventured out to the bistro in between the breakfast hour and lunch rush, so there were few others, and none of them seated nearby. Before she knew it, Jane was waving from across the floor. She pulled out a chair next to Steph.

"Hi!" Jane said.

"Hey! I'm glad you could join me!" Steph gave her a one-arm hug, cradling Madeline on the other side.

"Me too! So what's good here? It's been a while since I was last in." Steph and Jane perused the long menu in full, which inspired some indecision. Ultimately, they chose the tried and true steak sandwich and chicken parmesan.

"This one's on me." Jane offered.

"Thanks! I'll buy next time." Steph beamed up at her friend. Jane ordered up front and sat back down instead of waiting at the register.

"I have news," she emphasized. Steph was ready for some good gossip. "Sharon's pregnant."

"What!"

"I know, right?"

"No, I mean, how do you know that?"

"So, it's true," Jane surmised.

"Yes," Steph said hesitantly. "I'm supposed to be the only person she's told."

"Well, the cat's out of the bag then. Someone must have figured it out and spilled the beans, maybe her roommate."

"How long have you known?" Sharon had

planned to tell Sameed the night he died, but Steph had no idea how long she had kept the secret before then.

"Since Saturday, after I called you about Sameed's ex-wife." Word got out before Sharon even told anyone, Steph surmised. "What about you?" Jane asked.

"Only since Monday." Jane picked up on the implication.

"I hope her family didn't find out from someone else."

"Me too," thought Steph before insisting, "Jane, you have to promise not to tell anyone."

"Of course I promise" was her perfunctory answer. Steph had heard it before and gave her a look.

"It's one thing to share news that's happy or public, but this is sensitive information, Jane. You don't know how it could hurt people." It was easier for Steph to stand up for Sharon than herself. Her voice lowered. "The same goes for Sameed. You have to keep quiet about it."

"I promise," Jane said with greater emphasis.

"Thanks."

"Steak sandwich and chicken parmesan for Jane," called the cashier. Steph was grateful for the interruption. She decided to change the topic to something more palatable, men.

"You know, my neighbor Greg is cute." Steph said after Jane returned. "Tall, dark, and handsome, and I'm pretty sure he's single."

"I don't think I can date a guy who has prettier hair than me."

"Fair enough," Steph conceded.

"Know anyone else?" Jane probed, but before Steph could answer, Jane exclaimed, "Check *him* out." A man stepped into the room, tall, sculpted, bronzed, and bearded. Metal glinted in his ears, and he pulled it off with confidence. Steph's eyes widened. "Do you know him?" Jane asked.

"That's Sharon's brother," Steph informed her, recognizing him as the man who had helped Sharon with her car earlier. "David." Though knowing Jane, she probably already knew his name.

"No way. He's cute." David headed straight for the counter.

"Hey, Tony!" David called out.

"Hey, man! Long time no see!" Tony jumped out from around the counter to greet his friend. He hugged him, slapping his back. "How ya doin'?"

"Fine, I drove by this place the other day and remembered that you worked here. Do you run this place now?"

"Eh, kinda," Tony replied, bashful.

"It looks great!" He gestured toward the monochromatic prints on the wall. Steph liked them too. The classic urban subjects felt appropriate here.

"Thanks! I see you got a tan," Tony commented. Both sat down.

"Yeah, can't avoid it in the desert."

"How long you been back?"

"'Bout a week," David answered.

"Will you be staying for a while?"

"Can't say. I haven't received new orders yet." David scanned the room, and his eyes connected with Jane. He smiled, so did she. Jane turned to Steph with a twinkle in her eye.

"How's that kid sister of yours?" Tony asked. David made a face. "Not a kid anymore, huh."

"I spend bloody how long in the desert fighting these guys, then come home and find out my sister is busy playing wife number two with one of them. It's nuts. At least she's free of the lowlife now."

"That's rough man, sorry."

"This is so good," Jane whispered to Steph, intently listening.

David looked back again at their table, smiling once again in Jane's direction. She smiled back, head tilted just slightly to get her best angle. He excused himself from the table and walked over.

"Hey, so I'm gonna need you to stop smiling at me. It's too distracting, and I'm trying to catch up with my buddy Tony here."

"Oh, really? I like a nice distraction," Jane said with a megawatt smile. David pretended to shield himself from it, strategically lifting a muscular arm in front of his eyes. Jane appreciated how his shirt stretched.

"Maybe I should take you to one of those blackout restaurants. Then I might have a chance at talking to you without getting so flustered."

"Maybe. Maybe I like seeing you flustered,"

she replied, eyes practically sparkling. She knew she had him.

"In that case, how about the carnival in town this weekend? You could watch me struggle to win you a bear."

"You better win me a bear. I don't date quitters," Jane said as she wrote her name and number on a napkin.

"Yes, Ma'am," he said still grinning. Jane reached out to give him the slip of paper, and their hands touched. "Excuse me while I get back to my friend." David dragged his fingers slowly away, prolonging the contact. He stored the number in his phone and pocketed Jane's feminine script.

Once he was presumably out of earshot, Jane effused excitement. "Steph! Did you see him?" The question was rhetorical. Jane was practically fanning herself. She removed a layer of clothing.

"I can't believe you just gave him your number! You heard him. What if he was involved in–" She lowered her voice. "–you know?"

"So what? I can find out more going out on a date with him, can't I?"

"But Jane," Steph implored. "You might not be safe."

"Well, that's my choice then. He is pretty dishy, and you know I like bad boys."

"Jane, we're not talking motorcycles and leather jackets." Steph was starting to feel like Henry. "I don't think it's a good idea."

"I'll be fine." Changing topics, Jane

suggested, "Let's dig in before these sandwiches get any colder." They finished their lunch in relative silence. When they were done eating and had chatted for another good half hour, Steph invited Jane back to her apartment, but Jane declined.

"I have a mountain of laundry and no clean scrubs for tomorrow," she explained.

"I understand. Thanks so much for lunch. See you again soon! Remember, next time it's on me."

"You're welcome, and sounds great. See you again soon!"

Steph waved to her friend. Jane waved back. She was parked just outside the café. The lunch rush was starting to hit, so Steph decided to vacate her spot in the bistro and return to her apartment.

Steph spent the rest of the afternoon in serious thought, dedicating only the necessary portion of her brain to chores and a pizza dinner. Timing absolutely mattered, and she probably needed to inform Sharon ASAP. The poor woman should at least have priority in sharing the news of her pregnancy to her own family, if they didn't already know. She started dialing.

"Hi, Sharon. It's Steph."

"Hi, Steph." Steph picked up some background noise.

"I hope I'm not calling you at work."

"It's okay. I can take a quick break. What's up?" Steph wasn't sure there was a delicate way to put things.

"I had lunch today with a friend of mine, and

she told *me* that you're pregnant. I don't know how she found out, but I thought you should know. So, you could have a chance to tell your family before they hear about it."

"Oh... Thanks. I appreciate you telling me." Sharon spoke slowly over the phone, pausing between each phrase. "I told them last night, actually. My brother didn't look too surprised, and my parents weren't exactly thrilled for me either."

"I'm sorry, Sharon." And Steph was. She felt sorry for Sharon, for the situation she found herself in, sorry that she didn't have the support of her family, sorry that Sameed was gone.

"It'll be okay."

"Does Leyla know?"

"Not yet. I wanted to wait until all the funeral stuff was over, but I'll let her know soon, maybe this weekend." She paused. "I need to get back to work. I'll talk to you again some other time."

"Okay. Talk to you then." Steph didn't know what else to say.

Sharon hung up first, and Steph pitied her. Sharon had so much more on her plate to think about now than she did even five minutes prior, what with people gossiping about her. Steph continued to ponder whether Sharon's brother had known or suspected long before she told him.

Henry's arrival disrupted her pensive state.

"How was your day?"

"Good, I saw Jane. You?"

"Fine. Did you get any painting done?"

"No, I thought about it, but then I got distracted by some news from Jane."

"What is it now?" Henry wondered what macabre detail would emerge next.

"*She* told *me* that Sharon was pregnant, so the news is already out. And, she's probably going to go on a date with David, Sharon's brother, who really disliked Sameed. I overheard David trashing him at the cafe." Henry withheld his judgment. "For the record, I told her it was a bad idea," Steph added.

"I agree, but it's her life."

"That's what I'm afraid of," Steph thought.

Later in the evening Steph received a call back from Sharon.

"Hey, sorry I hung up so abruptly earlier. I was just unsettled, ya know?"

"I understand," said Steph. "How are you today?"

"Better, I guess. I'm trying to take good care of myself. I feel like I have to. It's not just about me now."'

"If there's anything you need, please let me know," Steph offered. "Actually." An idea came to her. "Do you want to have dinner with us tomorrow? It'll probably just be roasted chicken and vegetables."

"That sounds delicious. Yes. I'd love to. What

time do you want me over?"

"Dinner will be ready at 5:30, but you're welcome to come over earlier if you want. I wouldn't mind the company."

"Great. 4:30 okay?"

"Yep!"

"Okay, I'll see you around 4:30 tomorrow."

"See you then!"

Steph realized she should probably inform Henry that they would have company over for dinner.

"Hey, Henry?" she called out.

"Yeah?" He was in the bathroom.

"I invited Sharon to join us for dinner tomorrow. Is that okay?"

"I would have preferred if you had asked me first, but fine. Do you want me to pick something up?"

"You still suspect her? And no, I think I can handle making dinner if I prep everything during Madeline's naps."

"Suspect her? No, but I think you do. Did you invite her just to interrogate her?"

"No! Of course not." If Steph happened to learn something about Sharon or her family, it would be purely by accident, she told herself.

Madeline went to bed early, which afforded the young couple enough time, and free hands, to play a more complicated board game. Steph and Henry gambled fantasy life and limb in a battle of wits, pitting different creatures and special abilities against each other.

"Henry?" He was calculating his next move and didn't look up.

"Yeah?"

"I had a dream last night."

"About what?" His hand hovered over the board as he allocated troops.

"About Sunday night." Henry put the pieces down and looked up.

"Was it about the woman you found? Do you want to talk about it?"

"It was, but there's more to it. She had my mother's face."

"Deborah?"

"No, my *birth* mother. I don't think I ever told you, but I wasn't a baby when the Smits adopted me. I was three. Sometimes I think I remember things from back then, and my mother, well, she, I heard she was a recovering addict, but she relapsed after being clean for over a year. It killed her. To this day, I keep wondering why, why her, why drugs, why then. Wasn't I enough?"

"Oh, Steph, I'm so sorry." Henry moved around the table to embrace his wife.

"I just wish I had answers, but I don't think I ever will." Her voice broke.

"Shhh. It'll be okay." He stroked her hair and stayed with her until she calmed down.

"I'm sorry I ruined the game."

"No, it's okay. I think I was losing anyway." Steph wasn't so sure about that, but she appreciated his levity. "Bed?" Henry suggested.

"Sounds good."

They changed out of their day clothes, Steph shedding some but not all of her layers out of convenience. The pair brushed their teeth in tandem, trading places in front of the mirror to spit. Once in bed they kissed goodnight. Henry quickly fell asleep, while Steph lied awake for some time.

Her mother haunted her. Sameed haunted her. It seemed like every day pointed a finger at a different person, and these were people she cared about or was beginning to. Now she dissected their every word and move. If she felt up to it, she had a chance to do that again with Sharon, but Steph was emotionally exhausted. She wasn't sure she wanted to, and she still hadn't looked up Sameed's divorce.

Maybe Henry was right. She should keep her nose out of things for her own sake. However, she couldn't resist the pull of the unknown, and tomorrow it would lead her to a violent past where she least expected it.

CHAPTER 10

Madeline had been up what seemed like every hour, mewling over some undiagnosed discomfort. Hot, cold, wet, dry, hungry, full, Steph ran through the mental checklist each time, but her baby was not in the mood to be appeased.

Consequently, Steph ricocheted like a pinball between her bed, dresser, and nightstand as she struggled to put on leggings that morning. Then she banged her hip on the doorframe and toe on the threshold of the bathroom. Finally, she burnt herself while pouring hot water for her morning tea, and her mug ended up only half full. "This is your brain on no sleep," she told herself, cracking an egg.

Once she had sufficiently recovered, Steph utilized Madeline's morning nap to do something she didn't dare while Henry was at home. Pulling out her laptop, she sat down at the kitchen table, tea ready. Divorces were public record, so she assumed she wouldn't have issues. She looked up their names.

"Sameed Ishaaq Haddad," she said as she typed. She'd seen his full name under a picture of him at his mother's house. Nothing. "Sameed Haddad." No results. "Haddad." Now she had several listings. She scrolled, but none of the names resembled his. Steph tried "Abila" and "Khoury" instead, but there weren't any divorces listed with a

Sameed.

Sharon had told her that Abila had signed the papers. "Does this mean the court never signed them?" she asked herself. "Why else wouldn't there be a record?" Pulling out a pen and paper, Steph pondered aloud and wrote down, "I am a bad sleuth and don't know how to spell." She moved on. "They married and divorced in a different state/country." Next idea. "Sameed died before it was legalized. That could be why he hadn't proposed yet to Sharon." She tapped her pen on the table. She did a quick search on divorces that weren't public and added, "Sameed and Abila convinced the court to seal their record for some reason, but that implies some kind of foul play." She put the pen tip to her mouth now. "Hmmm." Her mind already twisted toward the tawdry, she wrote, "Sameed never divorced his first wife. David was telling the truth." How would that make Abila or Sharon feel, she wondered. She knew how David felt. Giving Sameed the benefit of the doubt she jotted lastly, "Some kind of delay. Divorce legal, but not published yet. Maybe super recent." Steph put down the pen and ruminated. She had theories, but no answers. She sipped her tea. Madeline woke up. Steph quickly hid her notes in her purse hanging by the door. Henry never looked in there.

Before putting the computer away, Steph wondered what else she could look up, like arrest records. Nothing came up for Sameed, Ayman, or Abila. Next she tried David. There weren't any results. That made sense since he'd probably have been discharged from the military if he had, or never enlisted. She typed in "Sharon Andrews" on a whim.

"Holy carp." Sharon *had* been arrested and not that long ago, last year, for domestic abuse. "Did I just invite an abuser, or worse, over for dinner?" she asked herself. It was too late now. Maybe Sharon was in a better place now, reformed, Steph defended. She hoped that was the case because she liked Sharon, but this little tidbit of information didn't look good.

Gathering Madeline, Steph popped her in the baby carrier and tidied up the house, while hoping her subconscious mind would figure something out. She realigned pillows and throws, and threw crumpled clothes into a hamper. Thankfully, Sharon wasn't the in-laws. Hopefully, she wasn't homicidal. There would be no scrubbing of the baseboards today. Steph didn't mind that her home actually looked lived in. After tummy time and another snack, Madeline was once again ready for a nap, so Steph inhaled a quick lunch and started on a dinner of roasted chicken and vegetables.

Some people found their Zen state in nature, others in the concrete jungle, but Steph's was in her kitchen or studio in the chaotic middle between preparation and presentation.

She brushed the pale, goose-pimpled skin with olive oil, but soon she imagined it a beautifully crisp golden brown. Next, she generously salted and peppered it. She never measured. She could feel how much was the right amount as she cradled it in one hand and poured with the other. Lastly, she looked to her spice rack for inspiration. One could never go wrong with an Italian herb blend, and she was liberal with that too. "Awesome," she congratulated. "One thing down, one to go." She checked the clock. Madeline had been asleep for half an hour. She quickly brushed two bags worth of baby carrots with butter and set a timer for 3:45.

Steph sat down for a moment to appreciate what she had accomplished. Soon she hoped to no longer rely on a weekly pizza or delivered meal. Today made that future seem possible. She didn't rest for long before Madeline awoke. It was just after 1:00 PM. She had a few hours. The apartment looked half decent, so she thought to treat herself. She could pick up some gelato and bring it home for dessert tonight.

Steph bundled up for the crisp air below, pulling on a thigh-length wool coat, four-foot scarf, and earmuffs. Hair in a bun, she couldn't accommodate a hat. For her baby, she tucked a knit cap around silky soft hair and carried a rosy fleece blanket for further insulation. Once downstairs with the stroller assembled, they squeezed past the door.

Steph strode toward the nearest business since the cold was biting. The convenience store sadly lacked anything appealing, so she continued onward. She would have to trek another couple blocks for a proper gelato shop. The stroller bounced a little between concrete slabs in the residential area, then again as it traveled over pavers in the more high-end commercial neighborhood. At last, the gilded six-letter word "GELATO" appeared. She quickly nipped inside and closed the door. The shop kept its creamy offerings cold, but its customers warmer than outside. At least, she wouldn't have to worry about her selection melting on the way home.

Ankle boots squeaked across the white tiled floor, a smart choice to advertise its cleanliness and facilitate cleanings after the inevitable drip of its finest flavors. To be safe, and not at all because she was greedy, she told herself, Steph decided to go with three different pints. It was a better deal too. Chocolate had wide appeal and paired nicely with healthy and unhealthy toppings. Vanilla was vanilla, but a welcome addition to almost any other dessert they might enjoy later. Steph vacillated on the third flavor but ultimately went with strawberry. As its name suggested, All'Otto, meaning "to eight" in Italian, featured eight different flavors every week. However, loyal customers would swear they always left with "a lot o'" gelato because it was so good. Neapolitan seemed like a safe bet to Steph. Satisfied, she braced herself for the trip back.

The cold that day was not kidding. Steph nearly expected the season's first snow to fall any second despite the blue sky above. She walked briskly, shuffling her legs together for the added heat friction might provide. She made a mental note to do more squats. Upon seeing her building, she made a short sprint to the door. To her surprise, she saw a familiar, but unexpected face in front of The Likable Daisy.

It was Dr. Khoury. Remembering how she had called Sharon a libertine, Steph wasn't sure she wanted to make eye contact, but she was too close not to.

"Hi," Steph started awkwardly. Abila didn't respond right away, lost in thought.

"Pardon?" Her face was impassive. Steph wasn't sure what to say and wondered why she had even bothered open her mouth.

"Do you need to get into the bakery? I could call the landlord Dennis," Steph offered, trying to think why Abila would be here. Key in hand, Abila finished locking up, and Steph felt silly for asking. Of course, Abila would have a key to the bakery, Steph thought. She had been married to Sameed after all.

"No, thank you. That won't be necessary." The fashionable woman turned away from the door and walked toward a svelte roadster, keys jangling. "Wait," Abila said. She looked at Steph again. "I know you. You were at the Haddad's house Tuesday night."

"Yes, I was. I'm Steph. What kind of car is that?" She pointed and admired. Abila smiled.

"It's a 1960 Mercedes 190SL." Steph didn't know what 190SL meant, but she recognized the beauty and value of an antique Mercedes-Benz.

"It's gorgeous." Steph thought the gleaming black beauty belonged in old Hollywood. Its sleek hood, plush interior, and neat dash were luxury and elegance combined.

"Thanks. It handles turns like a figure skater." Like any proud mother, Abila couldn't help but boast about her baby. It was the only kind she could afford to ignore for an eighty plus hours a week during her residency. "I restored it myself, with a little help from Ayman."

From an early age, Sameed's brother had escaped under the hood in his grandfather's garage to tinker and organize his thoughts, while his brother passed the hours in their grandmother's kitchen. As an adult, his passion had turned into a career, first as a mechanic, then later as a classic-car flipper. The only child of car aficionado, Abila, too, found it to be a great distraction from work-related stress.

"You two did a great job. Did it take you long?"

"Four years." Steph's eyes widened. That was quite the project. "I know. That's pretty quick. I was lucky Ayman found one in such good shape to begin with." Four year was "quick." That boggled Steph's mind.

"Ayman found it?"

"Yes. It was his wedding gift to... us," Abila said. Upon being reminded of her late husband, Abila was ready to end the conversation. "Take care of that little one. It's cold out," she said before climbing into her car. As she drove off, Steph heard a dynamic aria crescendo, the tenor voice trembling with some unknown emotion.

It occurred to Steph that with Abila's career as a doctor, the restoration project, and Sameed's business, they likely hadn't spent much time together. She felt sorry for her, but between the music and the machine and possible medical school debt, Steph wondered what other expensive tastes Abila had and how desperate she might be to satisfy them.

Steph unlocked the front door. Once safely and warmly ensconced inside, she picked up Madeline, collapsed the stroller, and walked the single flight up. It only took a few minutes, as she had been familiarizing herself with the process over the last few weeks.

Baby down, gelato in the freezer, and layers shed, Steph reviewed the time. It was after 2:00, but still too early to start roasting everything. She kicked off her shoes and decided to cuddle Madeline on the couch. A short rest would do them both good, and sharing body heat equally appealed. Steph grabbed a pillow to support her arm on the side the baby nursed first. "You are going to get gelato later," Steph told her. "Lucky baby." Lucky Steph.

When the time came for Madeline to sleep again, Steph tidied a little more thoroughly. She didn't just hide things away. She returned them to their usual place. She started on a load of laundry and sorted part of the basket of clean clothes. Before she knew it, her timer went off. It took her a second to remember what it was for, but once in the kitchen she knew it had to have been for the oven.

Once both dishes were in, Steph indulged in another gardening show. The world outside offered less and less green for her eyes to devour each day as autumn shifted into winter and the grass surrendered.

The doorbell rang. "That must be Sharon," Steph thought. Sure enough, Sharon waited downstairs with a dish.

"I know you said I didn't need to bring anything, but I thought it might be nice to have pie."

"That's so sweet of you! Thank you! Please come upstairs." Steph beckoned Sharon in. "What kind of pie is it?"

"Apple. I always get a ton this time of year. Apple butter, applesauce, apple pie… I love it all."

"That sounds amazing. Your apartment must smell wonderful." Steph could imagine the sweetness of the apples mingling with warm cinnamon and buttery short crust.

"It does. That's half of why I love it so much." Sharon placed her coat on the back of a kitchen chair. "Crazy cold day today. Did you go out?"

"Just briefly to pick up some gelato. I have vanilla if you like ice cream with your pie." Steph noticed a thick gold band around Sharon's wrist. "Is that Sameed's old watch?"

"Yes," Sharon confirmed stroking it. "Leyla wanted me to have it. He had told her how serious he was about me before he died. I haven't told her yet," Sharon said, answering Steph's unasked question.

"When did she give it to you?"

"Yesterday. She wanted to give it to me earlier, but she had needed to take it in for repairs first."

"Why? What was wrong with it?" Steph recalled Sameed regularly looking at his timepiece, so she assumed it would be accurate.

"There were some scratches, she said, and the glass had cracked. It must have happened after, you know..." Sharon's face fell, and the hairs on Steph's ears prickled.

"I'm sorry. Well, I'm glad they were able to fix it." Steph tried to move quickly past the thought of Sameed's death. Sharon either was an Oscar-worthy actress, or this evening presented a rare reprieve from her very real grief. Steph determined to assume her friend's innocence. She wondered if she should even tell Henry what she thought she knew.

"Me too. I don't plan to ever take it off. It's like having a part of him with me."

Steph smiled. Hostess instincts kicking in, she offered, "Do you want to sit down? Can I get you anything?"

"Actually, something hot would be nice." Sharon sat down at the table.

"Tea?" Steph walked toward the cabinet where she kept mugs and sachets.

"Yes, please." She set two cups down on the counter.

"Black or herbal?" Steph asked, rifling through her collection.

"Black, with milk and honey if you have it." Steph grabbed the honey and placed it on the table, then started filling the kettle. Once filled, she set out spoons and the milk as well.

"That chicken smells delicious," Sharon commented, smelling the nearly finished roasting meat. "I can't wait."

After setting the tea out, Steph suggested, "Would it ruin dinner to have some pie first? It sounds so good right now."

"Go ahead," Sharon invited. "And cut me a slice too." Steph served up two slices of apple pie à la mode. When it came to dessert, go big or go home was her motto. The two dug in, delighted.

Before the timer went off, the plates were clean. As Madeline had awoken and desired only her mother's touch, Steph directed Sharon to where plates and oven mitts could be found. By the time Henry came through the door, the table was set for a simple but sumptuous meal.

"Hi, Sharon. Good to see you," he greeted, then turned to Steph. "Is it ready to eat?" Henry didn't like to burn his mouth on his food, but sometimes hunger overcame his sense of self-preservation.

"I let it cool first. We can eat now," Steph responded. She put Madeline in her bouncer.

"Great." They recited a quick prayer. The Wus habitually prayed over every meal, but Steph was slightly nervous about making her guest uncomfortable. To her relief, Sharon seemed quite relaxed and eager to taste the food before her. The crisp skin had the bite, salt, and fat of even the most satisfying potato chip, but with that much more flavor, and roasting had revealed and enhanced the carrots' natural sweetness. It was almost like candy. Sharon and Henry withheld their praise only to fully appreciate what they were eating. Their silence told Steph everything she needed to know.

When it commenced, dinner conversation started with the standard "What do you do for a living?"

"I'm a receptionist," Sharon answered. "I work for a rec center where Sameed often volunteered. That's how we met. I used to go there when I was a kid."

"Aw. When did you meet?" Steph's cheeks dimpled.

"Memorial Day weekend." Sharon smiled at the memory. "He volunteered at a dunking booth, and it was a cold day." Steph remembered, but she had appreciated the relative coolness then, having been pregnant at the time.

"So, you're originally from here too, right? Is

your family still in the area?" Steph asked.

"Yep, born and raised. My parents live just East of the city," Sharon answered.

"Do you have any siblings?" Steph followed up. "I know you have the one brother."

"Just the one," Sharon confirmed.

"He's a Navy SEAL," Steph told her husband.

"Is he currently deployed?" Henry asked.

"No, he just came back a week ago. How about you two?" Sharon shifted the attention to her hosts. "What do you do? Do you have family here?"

"I just started out as an accountant recently," Henry stated. "But I used to be an EMT. My parents and one sister are local."

"Wow. I bet he came in handy when you were in labor." Sharon looked at Steph.

"You would think that," Steph said with a laugh in her throat. "But I think it was actually hard for him to sit back and just be the spouse when push came to shove." Henry seemed a little embarrassed. Being with Steph in the delivery room had seriously stressed him out since he had felt completely powerless to help by order of the staff.

"I can imagine… So, why the change?" Steph knew the answer to this question.

"Normal business hours, so I could spend more time with family." While they had been dating, Steph had pursued various hobbies during Henry's night shifts, but the thought of building a life together and the burnout he experienced inspired them to look for another option.

"How about you, Steph? Do you work?"

"I was, am, a graphic designer. And I'm originally from Pennsylvania, so my parents are a few hours away. I have four siblings, but they're all spread out."

"Five kids. Wow. That's a lot."

"My parents had four boys, but they always wanted a girl. So, they adopted me."

"Really? Wow. Four brothers then? Man, and I thought having just one was tough."

"It wasn't so bad. They babied me since I was so much younger." Sharon returned to her previous question.

"So how do you like graphic design?"

"It's pretty good preparation for motherhood, actually. Demanding clients, long hours, and lots of sitting, but I'm not sure I want to go back."

"Really? Why?" Sharon and Henry both edged forward in their seats. Henry rested his elbows on the table.

"I don't think I want to give up being a full-time mom. I don't like the idea of Madeline becoming more attached to some other woman who isn't me. Plus, advertising isn't exactly my passion, and I'm tired after the last couple years of working. I'm ready for a change." Steph took a breath.

"Good for you!" Sharon encouraged.

"Thanks." Steph relaxed her shoulders and sat back a little in her chair. She had them convinced. She thought she had herself convinced as well. "Pie?"

"Yes." Bass and soprano combined.

"We have gelato too. I picked some up today," she explained. "Chocolate, vanilla, and strawberry."

"I'll start with pie and a scoop of vanilla," said Henry, who was holding Madeline.

"Sharon?" Steph started plating Henry's portion. The pie server hovered until Henry gestured with his hand how large a slice he wanted.

"Since I had pie earlier, I'd like to try the strawberry gelato." Steph rinsed the ice cream scooper and used some elbow grease.

"It's really good. This pint won't last twenty-four hours." She handed Sharon a bowl. For herself, she had another small slice of pie and, in a separate bowl, a trifecta of gelato. This was a judgment-free dinner table.

Sharon finished her gelato first and offered to take the baby from Henry, so he could focus on his dessert. To her parents' amazement, she went to Sharon, but she was happier looking at and hearing mommy. So, when Steph finished, she opened her arms in welcome. It was probably her daughter's dinnertime. Not long after, Sharon bid them farewell. She had to be at the rec center when it opened early in the morning tomorrow, since some people liked to fit in a workout before heading to the office.

"Thank you so much for dinner. It was a

pleasure." Sharon gathered her coat and wrapped her scarf snuggly around her neck.

"Thank you for coming, and thank you for the pie. It was delicious," Steph praised. She tried to hand the dish to Sharon, but she waved it away.

"Keep the leftovers. I'll get my dish back from you some other time." Steph's heart took such generosity as a sign of Sharon's undeniable goodness. Surely, there must have been a good reason for her arrest.

"Actually, how about Saturday? We're having a little Halloween party here at 5:00. You're welcome to join if you don't have other plans."

"I'd love to. Thanks. See you again soon!"

"Bye! And thank you for the pie!" Steph closed the apartment door. The common door would lock automatically. Turning to Henry, she concluded, "That was really nice."

"It was," he agreed.

"She seems to be doing pretty well. I mean, I no expert on grief..."

"I agree, but she probably wouldn't be so happy if she knew you invited her over to pump her for information."

"What? No! I invited her because she needs a friend."

"Okay." Steph thought his tone suggested he didn't believe her.

"I swear. I like her, and *I* need a friend, a mom friend. A friend *I* can help, so I don't feel so helpless myself all the time." Steph shut her mouth and wondered if someone had slipped truth serum into her dessert. She hadn't intended to say all that. "I did find out something though," she confessed quietly.

"Yes?"

"Leyla gave Sameed's old watch to Sharon, but it needed serious repairs first. That, to me, suggests some kind of struggle." She neglected to tell him about the searches she performed earlier that morning online.

"It's possible, but he probably damaged it trying to turn off the mixer."

"I don't think so. He wore it on his left arm and was right handed, and most machines accommodate righties. I think it's more likely that he would have injured his right hand if he were still conscious."

Henry paused to consider this. Steph's pursed her lips and tilted her head forward. "What are you thinking?" Henry asked.

"I need to talk to Charlotte again. I need to know if she saw anything else, even if she doesn't realize what she saw."

"Won't she want to know why you're asking? Please don't."

"You're right. I'll probably have to explain that I think Sameed was murdered."

"I don't think that's a good idea." Steph tilted her head, inviting an explanation. "We haven't ruled her out." Having failed to convince his wife that it was an accident, Henry now sought to discourage her from investigating and exposing herself to any kind of danger.

"You haven't. I really don't think she's capable of murder. Physically, yes. Emotionally, no. I *know* Charlotte. I know how grateful she was to have this job." She grabbed both his arms and pulled him in. "I will be careful. I promise." Henry was a little stiff, still uncomfortable with the idea of his wife asking around about a possible murder.

For the rest of the evening, Steph decided to indulge Henry and play him in chess, passing the baby as needed. As an artist, she loved the look of the handmade maple and walnut chessboard purchased last Christmas for her husband. Given the beauty of the crisp lines and natural marbling, the weight and careful design of each accompanying piece, it was a pleasure to play with such a set.

Henry, on the other hand, appreciated the creativity, complexity, and even cruelty of chess strategy. He admired the gumption of more cavalier players willing to sacrifice one piece for a devastating attack, but also the keenness exhibited by those who played the long game well, slowly turning the vise on their opponent.

When both players had studied openings, the game was like a dance, with white leading and black following. The choreography could extend to the endgame with a peaceful resolution or abruptly break.

Henry led with his queen's pawn, advancing

two squares. Playing as black, Steph responded with the king's bishop pawn, also advancing two. Despite its weakened kingside, she liked the Dutch Defense not only because of the name, but also because it allowed her to play more aggressively.

After ten minutes Henry moved his knight and called out, "Check." Steph looked at the board.

"No, checkmate," she corrected. She pointed out how her king was trapped. Ironically, she had pinned him in place, rather than protected him, with her rook. It was only a matter of time until Henry mated it.

"Oh. Do you want to play another game?"

"Sure." They played three. In the second game, Steph called out "Checkmate" once again before Henry noticed he had it, but in the third match, they drew.

"Hey, I'm improving!" she exclaimed, convinced she hadn't stood a chance. A draw was a victory in her mind.

"You say that like you're no good at chess, but you'd be great if you spend as much time practicing chess strategies as you do coming up with wild theories," Henry replied.

"Thanks," she said flatly. If she had really wanted to win, she could have suggested he have a few drinks first, but she didn't mind losing. It was no loss when she considered how enjoyable the evening had been.

They put away the chess pieces and prepared for bed. Thankfully, Madeline went down quickly.

"If you want, I could teach you a new opening," Henry suggested, referring back to his favorite game.

"Sure," Steph replied, squeezing past him to grab her toothbrush.

She briefly snuggled her husband to achieve the perfect bubble of body heat before rolling away. Stay too long and she'd burn up. They kissed good night, and she drifted off to sleep, exhaustion sinking her deeper into the mattress. With a smile on her face, she recalled how she and Henry had spent Memorial Day weekend decorating the nursery after finding out they were expecting a girl. "Was that already half a year ago?" she pondered. No, it wasn't. Sharon had lied about celebrating a six-month anniversary. Now, Steph wanted to know why.

CHAPTER 11

Madeline was up for the day before Henry had left for work, so Steph helped him pack his lunch. She wished him goodbye, and he wished her a good day and good luck. In eight hours, she would have him for the whole weekend.

"Call me if you need anything," he offered.

"Thanks. I will."

First things first, Steph embraced the previous night's resolve and emailed work, explaining that she was giving her two-weeks' notice. She held her breath and hit send. "Done," she told herself, exhaling. There was no going back now.

The second thing on her mind was Charlotte. Knowing her friend, she'd already have been awake for hours. It would take more than ten days to break a habit like Charlotte's schedule. Steph searched for her contact in her phone. Not everyone was besties with their local baker, but Steph and Charlotte had hit it off from the time Steph had first moved into the building. Charlotte had recognized a kindred spirit in her artsy friend, bonding over their mutual love of thrifting. They both relished a good deal, and old things, like leather-bound books and Motown records, felt more soulful.

Steph heard the dial tone begin, and her stomach sank a little. She wondered if she should be upfront with Charlotte about her suspicion that Sameed was murdered, or if she should follow her husband's advice. Either way, she hoped encouraging her friend to revisit that night wouldn't be too upsetting. On second thought, she should probably invite her over instead of attempting this conversation on the phone.

"Hi, Charlotte. I was wondering if you'd like to come over today for a bit and catch up."

"Sure, I'd love to. I just picked up groceries, so I need to put them away first. But I can be over in about half an hour. Does that sound good?"

"Yeah, that works for me."

"Great! Say, do you want to meet me at that new tea shop by your house instead?"

"Honey Huns? I'd love to!"

"Sweet!"

Steph looked down at herself. There was room for improvement. Next time, maybe she should remember to change and brush her hair before calling. Thankfully, she had thirty minutes.

Ten minutes, she had ten minutes because Madeline had wanted ten for herself, and it was going to take another ten walking there. She briefly set Madeline down on the bedroom floor while she used a little aerosol dry shampoo in the bathroom. She worked it into her scalp, combed her hair with her fingers, and pulled it up into a less sloppy, less greasy ponytail.

Back in the bedroom Steph tried to hop quickly into a pair of jeans, but tripped. A sweater pulled at her hair, and she wobbled when it stuck. Noticing a pattern, she sat down to slowly and carefully slip her socks and shoes on. Lastly, she put Madeline in a carrier and grabbed her purse, jacket, and stroller.

Two blocks away sat Honey Huns. The newest store on the block featured honey in nearly all of its products, which ran the gamut of health and hygiene to teas and sweets.

As Steph settled herself down at one of the tables after hustling to be on time, lead-footed Charlotte strode through the door across hexagon tiles. The honeycomb pattern repeated on the walls in a soft yellow, the light fixtures above. Botanical illustrations of flowers and bee species with their Latin names decorated the wall, giving the space a slightly posh feel.

As Charlotte approached, Steph stood up to greet her. Doubled in width by her many-layered winter wear, it was like hugging a comforter.

"Hi, Charlotte! I've missed you!"

"I've missed you too, and I've got some great news," Charlotte announced.

"Really? What is it?" Steph gestured toward the small table, and Charlotte set her wooly layers down. "Is that a new coat? It's so nice!" Steph rubbed a sleeve between her fingers. "Where'd you get it?"

"It is! Thanks! At the thrift shop on Main. By the way, do they do coffee here?"

"I think so," Steph said. "I was thinking

about getting tea."

"I'll get tea too then. Also, I brought these." Charlotte pulled a container out of her messenger bag. Inside were four perfectly risen chocolate brioche buns. "I figured two for us and two for you and Henry later. Do you think we can eat them here?"

"You are a godsend. One second. I'll ask." Steph went up to order a pot of English breakfast tea with milk and honey and asked about eating the buns Charlotte brought. The owner didn't mind.

"They said it's fine, so what's your news?" Steph asked, sitting down.

"Sameed had a business partner." The Likable Daisy wasn't necessarily dissolving, or so Steph hoped.

"Do you know who it is?" Her toes nervously tapped the floor.

"Yes, his mother," Charlotte answered.

"Really? So? Have you talked to her?" Steph was now quietly pumping one leg under the table. A server brought the tea.

"Yes. She wants to keep The Likable Daisy open in his memory."

"YES!" Steph's mind screamed.

"But she doesn't want to manage it full-time," Charlotte continued. "So…"

"Oh. My. God. She invited you to be her partner? Please tell me she asked you to become partners." Charlotte's sparkling white teeth told her everything. "Yes! Oh, Charlotte. I'm so happy for you!" Steph hugged her again.

"Thank you! Leyla told me when she first asked that Sameed had already approached her about making me a partner in the past, which is how she knew she could trust me." Sameed had trusted Charlotte. His mother, Leyla, trusted Charlotte. Steph felt she could trust her too.

"I am so thrilled for you, so when do you reopen?"

"We're planning a soft opening next week, starting Wednesday. We'll have a party that night to announce our partnership. You and everyone else in the building are invited."

"That's so exciting! When does it start?"

"6:00 PM." It was such wonderful news that Steph didn't know how to segway into her own awkward topic, though it was the main reason why she had invited Charlotte over in the first place. She poured out two cups of tea.

"Charlotte?"

"Yeah?" Charlotte took a tentative sip to see how hot it was before adding a little milk. Steph looked around to see that no one was near them. Honey Huns seemed the kind of place to buzz on the weekends, but weekday mornings were quiet.

"Do you ever wonder if what happened to Sameed wasn't an accident?"

"What do you mean?" Charlotte put down her cup, but kept her hands around it for warmth.

"I mean, what if what you saw in the kitchen were staged too look like an accident." Charlotte's eyes widened, and it wasn't on account of the caffeine she had just sipped.

"Oh my God, Steph. Really? You think he might have been… murdered?" She whispered the last word.

"Yes, I'll try to be concise. The night he died, Sameed missed an important dinner. He wasn't dressed to bake, like you said, and the ovens weren't on. He had more than one strained relationship, and," she emphasized this, "his watch was broken." Charlotte would understand its significance. Steph continued, "Is there anything else you can tell me about that night that you noticed? How did he look? Did you find anything unusual or out of place?"

"Steph, I…" The thought of trying to relive the entire night was paralyzing. Charlotte didn't know where to start.

"If it helps, and I can ask you more specific questions."

"Okay."

"Can you describe how his clothes looked to me? Were they ripped, dirty, crumpled?" Charlotte swallowed another sip of tea, while Steph prepared to take one.

"Well, he was bent over, and I saw what looked like cinnamon on the back of his shirt. I remember thinking that was weird because we never get spices on our backs. Our apron fronts? Sure. And his clothes didn't seem torn or stained or anything."

"Did his hair seem out of place?"

"I can't say for sure. Maybe there was spice in his hair too."

"Were his hands on the mixer? Did you see what was in the bowl?"

"His arms were hanging down... I only saw him for a few seconds before realizing he wasn't, you know, then I screamed and ran out and called the police." Steph was at a dead end. She pursued a different avenue.

"Was there any money missing from the register?"

"No, I don't think so."

"Was anything out of place? Messy? Knocked over?"

"I think I told you before that the kitchen was pretty much clean and ready for the morning shift, but I didn't stay in there long enough to really be sure."

"So you didn't find anything."

"No, I didn't..." she paused. "Except for the earring. No one's ever claimed it." Steph had a thought and put her empty cup down.

"You sweep the floor thoroughly before closing up, right?"

"Yes, of course."

"So this earring probably fell out after."

"I guess so."

"That means someone else was probably in the kitchen after closing, since Sameed didn't wear an earring. Do you know what this means?"

"What does it mean?"

"It's evidence, Charlotte."

"Is one earring enough?" Charlotte didn't look convinced.

"On its own, probably not, but if I can convince the police and they start looking harder, then maybe they'll find more, enough to charge someone."

"Are you going to call the police then?" Something occurred to Charlotte. "Have you already talked to them?"

"I did, once, yes. I think they thought I was being overanxious on account of Madeline, but I know much more now than I did then. I'll probably call them later today after I talk to Henry."

"Good luck." Charlotte paused. "I mean it. I just don't know what to think. It's hard enough believing he's really gone. The idea that he was murdered is so..." As Steph looked ready to explain again, Charlotte continued. "If you need me to help somehow, I will, but… can we talk about something else?" Steph felt guilty for making her friend uncomfortable.

"I understand. Thank you for being willing to talk about it." Steph considered what else to say. Thankfully, Madeline's cry pierced through the awkward silence. "Aww, have we been ignoring you?"

"Can I hold her?" Charlotte put her arms out.

"You can try, but I'm not sure she'll go to you." Steph took Madeline out of the stroller and handed her over, gently supporting her head. Charlotte cradled her in her arms. She was about the same size as a fresh loaf of bread and not much heavier.

"I think she likes me," Charlotte declared. Steph was shocked. Maybe separation anxiety wasn't a thing at this stage, she thought. Then little Madeline's mouth gaped like a fish, and her head wobbled around. She was looking for something to suck on.

"I think she might be hungry. I should probably take her back," Steph said.

"Sorry, I don't have food for you." Charlotte placed her back in Steph's arms.

"Is it okay if I…" Steph started pulling up the edge of her shirt.

"Go ahead. It doesn't bother me."

"Thanks."

"So, how are you doing?" The friends moved onto a new topic and Charlotte's incredible chocolate buns.

"I think things are going pretty well. Some nights are hard, others aren't so bad."

Steph didn't quite unload the full complexity of her contradictory feelings on motherhood. Some people weren't ready to hear the range of emotion she experienced daily. They would worry too much about her. Other people didn't need to hear that it could be the most difficult thing they would ever attempt. They needed the comfort of the joys to expect, not the trials, and Steph only wanted to encourage. Henry was the one person who fully understood how she felt, and maybe other moms.

Motherhood was the most connecting and the most isolating thing to ever happen to her. It was the most difficult and rewarding job she'd ever had, but some days felt like she had accomplished nothing. It was joyous. It was tear-filled. It was heaven and hell in the same day, but she wouldn't trade it for anything.

"I'm sorry. When do you think she'll start sleeping through the night?" Charlotte asked. Steph wished she could predict when and have a fixed date to look forward to, but she knew enough from her sisters-in-law to know it was a crapshoot.

"No idea, but I'd settle hard for two solid four-hour chunks of sleep. How's Rupert? I bet he loves having you around."

"You bet. He can bother me for food all day now, not just in the morning." When she wasn't at the bakery, Charlotte was all about that cat life, spoiling her ginger tabby.

"How many followers is he up to now?" Steph asked.

"More than I have," Charlotte complained. "Yesterday, I spent five hours decorating a birthday cake and got only a few likes, spent all evening doing hair and makeup, same thing. Cat played with a toilet paper roll on his tail last week and doubles his audience."

"People have no taste these days," Steph said sympathetically, but secretly was anxious to check out the video herself.

"Well, I should probably get going soon. I have some party planning to do. Hopefully, I can get everything I need this weekend." Charlotte got up from the table and grabbed her coat off the back of the chair. "Can't believe it's so freaking cold already," she muttered, then addressed Steph again. "And thanks for the tea."

"Good luck. Let me know if I can be of any help downstairs." Steph also stood up and walked over toward the door.

"Don't worry about helping me out. Get some sleep if you can, and eat," Charlotte insisted, gesturing toward the two remaining buns. "You know, Henry will never know if you eat them both."

"True." Steph considered it. "But guilt would get to me. I know how much he loves these too. Take care, Charlotte."

"You too." Charlotte with her unreal winter proportions audibly trudged out of the shop. The extent to which she went to barricade herself from the cold made Steph wonder if she had misread the forecast. She hadn't expected it to be below freezing. She stepped outside and barked, realizing how warm it was. All that time spent by hot ovens had made her friend a wimp when it came to the cold. Steph walked quickly back to her apartment.

Now was about the time when Henry also took his lunch. She could call him and tell him about her conversation with Charlotte now, then maybe contact the police. Madeline would probably go down soon. Steph grabbed one of the remaining buns and cuddled some more with her baby. She offered the other side for Madeline to nurse on, and the baby latched. Sleep was not far off.

Once Madeline could no longer resist the pull of sleep, Steph put the snoozing baby down in her own bassinet in the nursery before heading back to the kitchen to call Henry. However, as she picked up the phone, she reconsidered. She dialed, and Jane picked up.

"Hi," a sleepy voice answered.

"Hey, is now a good time? Did you just get off work?" Steph asked.

"No, I got off this morning. And now is as good as any. What's up?" Jane could tell Steph had something newsworthy.

"I talked to Charlotte today." Steph thought she heard something pouring in the background.

"Mhmm?" It was probably coffee. Jane did sometimes drink a whole pot. How she managed to keep her teeth so white was a mystery to Steph.

"She noticed reddish brown dust on the back of Sameed's shirt and maybe his hair. She couldn't be sure on that. Charlotte also said that the cleaners found an earring, a large diamond one, in the kitchen, which didn't belong to anyone on the staff."

"Really? Did she think maybe a customer lost it?" Jane went back to sipping the hot brew.

"Here's the thing. They sweep up thoroughly

every day before closing, especially in the kitchen. I think they would have found something like that if it had been there at closing time. No, I think the killer left it behind on accident."

"Who do you know wears earrings?" Jane asked.

Jewelry did suggest a woman, though strangulation did not, Steph thought. She didn't suspect Charlotte, who was the only woman she considered physically capable of such a thing. Did she know any men who wore an earring? Henry didn't.

"A lot of women. Men, I'm not so sure except Sharon's brother, but I guess I could keep my eyes a little more open."

"I'm not so sure it's important," Jane dismissed in David's defense. "I don't think diamonds are his style. What other points did you mention?"

"Well, I think the dust suggests a struggle, being pushed up against a wall, which would explain the watch too. Someone wants us to believe it was an accident."

"This is getting interesting." Jane sounded more awake.

"I was going to call back the police and tell them what I've learned. What do you think?"

"If you think it'll help, yes, call the police, but it is possible they already know those things."

"Okay." Her expectations lowered. She didn't have a smoking gun, yet. Sipping continued over the line. "I'm going to go refuel too while Madeline's still asleep. Thanks for picking up. I hope the rest of your Friday is relaxing."

"Thanks. You too."

Steph didn't think she'd have enough time to finish a call with the police before Madeline reawakened, so she decided to fix herself something to eat quickly instead. Leftover chicken meant she could make a chicken salad sandwich. The relative dryness of breast meat, she felt, was only redeemed in soup or mayonnaise. She could eat the leftover carrots as is.

As she chewed, she considered Jane's counterpoints. It's very likely the police noticed the same things she was just discovering now, specifically, the dust and broken watch. If so, they still came to the conclusion that it was an accident. She tried to see the circumstantial evidence from their perspective. Sameed could have brushed up against a wall to make way for someone or while heaving a large bag of garbage. Sameed could have broken his watch earlier that day or during the accident, but Steph had a hard time imaging how. Steph wondered if it were foolish to call again only with what she had gathered thus far, but then she remembered Detective Harris' encouragement to do so and decided to call anyway.

Madeline started to stir. Steph quickly finished the remainder of her sandwich and went to collect her daughter, who was easily mollified. The new mom wondered how someone so small could have such a profound impact on everything and everyone around her. Here Steph was completely and irreversibly imbued with a new sense of purpose. She hadn't felt her life unfulfilling before, but in her present state she couldn't imagine reverting to the past. It was unlivable, and yet at the same time she wondered how she had ever thought eight hours wasn't enough sleep. It was one of life's mysteries, she supposed.

Steph used a portion of the remaining afternoon to make leftover chicken and vegetable soup for dinner, then washed, dried, and folded a load of laundry. After indulging in one show while her baby snoozed again, she decided now was a good time to pick up their mail. She hadn't remembered in a while. Henry probably had, but she could go check for today.

On her way down, she ran into Rachel, who having abandoned her collegiate wear, looked resplendent in a shimmering black ball gown, silky hair artfully pulled back and stud earrings twinkling. Her heels clicked on the floor.

"Wow. Rachel, you look amazing," Steph complimented.

"Thanks. I have a concert tonight," she explained. "It's at 7:00. We're still selling tickets if you're interested, but I understand it may be too difficult with the little one."

"It won't work for us tonight, but I'd love to catch another one of your concerts sometime. I always enjoy hearing you practice."

"You can hear me? I hope I'm not too loud."

"Not at all. Don't worry. Are you taking the bus in that?" Steph asked. It hardly made sense, but she knew Rachel didn't have a car.

"No, thankfully a friend is picking me up. I didn't want to risk the bus being slow."

"Oh, that's good. Good luck tonight!"

"Thanks! Have a good evening!"

Steph opened the door for Rachel, heavy laden with her instrument, music, and possibly a change of clothes. Letting the door close, Steph took out the key for their mailbox. It was all junk mail. She walked back upstairs and dropped everything in the trash once inside. She sat on the couch, and Henry came in a few minutes later.

"Happy Friday," he said.

"Happy Friday," she repeated, moving toward the kitchen.

"How was your day?" Henry put down his coat on the back of a chair, ladled himself some soup, and sat down at the table, while Steph did the same.

"Good. I had a nice afternoon." Hearing a noise in the nursery, Steph walked away to collect to Madeline, then returned. She set the baby down in a bouncer and sat opposite her husband.

"Did you go anywhere or meet up with anyone today?" Henry asked. Steph looked down slightly guilty.

"Yes, I met up with Charlotte." She focused on her soup, waiting for Henry to respond.

"Did you interrogate her?" Henry said half joking. Steph thought it was more like an eyewitness interview.

"No, I asked her a few questions. That's all, and I found out The Likable Daisy is reopening. Sameed's mother was the other partner, and she asked Charlotte to join her."

"That's great news then. What else did you learn?" Henry suspected Steph was withholding information. She wasn't a good liar.

"Sameed had dust on his clothes and possibly hair. Also, the cleaners found an earring not belonging to any of the staff."

"You should call the police."

"That's what Jane said." It occurred to Steph after speaking that maybe she should have called Henry first.

"Were you even going to tell me if I hadn't asked?"

"Yes, I was. I just did, and I'm going to call the police, promise."

"So you haven't yet," Henry more stated than asked.

"No, I'm just afraid it won't be enough for them to take me, it, seriously, but I talked to the first person on the scene. Charlotte was the only person who saw him dead." Steph tried to convince herself it wasn't a fool's errand to call again, then paused to consider the truth of her statement. Someone else *had* seen Sameed and ruled his death an accident. Henry watched Steph's face as the gears in her brain clicked into place. "Henry?"

"Yes?"

"The coroner would have examined him, right? And that's public record." Though eager to dissuade his wife from investigating, he knew she'd double check anyway, so he responded once again with a slow "yes." She reached across the table to grab his hands, spilling soup.

"I can't say for sure what you'll learn," Henry added. "The coroner did rule it an accident." He refrained from reclaiming the spoon he dropped for the moment.

"But maybe I could see the autopsy notes and suggest there be a second opinion. If a different doctor disagrees, then, presto, that would persuade the police to open an investigation." Eyes gleaming, Steph regained some of her forgotten vigor. "Do you think we can go tonight?"

"If they're open, but they probably aren't," he said, hoping this was true. Steph looked it up.

"Closed! And they don't reopen until Monday morning." She'd have to wait an entire weekend. That felt like a lifetime.

Steph got up to grab a napkin for her earlier spill and sat down to eat the rest of her soup.

After Madeline had tummy time, dinner, and a diaper change, Steph got to work on putting her down for the night, while Henry tidied up the kitchen. After the baby went down, Steph eased into the couch next to him and prepared a few notes to have on hand during her call with the police. She dialed, and a receptionist took the call.

"Hi, I'd like to speak with Detective Harris? Is he available?" Steph thought it might help to at least speak with the same person. She looked to Henry for reassurance and waiting for some time on the phone before her call could be transferred.

"Detective Harris speaking."

"Good evening, Detective. It's Stephanie Wu. I called about a week ago about my neighbor Sameed Haddad."

"Yes, I remember."

"You said to call if I heard anything else? Well, I have learned a few things."

"What have you heard?"

"That Sameed had reddish brown dust, like the brick on our building, on the back of his shirt. That his watch face had been broken and needed serious repairs." She looked at her bullets. "And there was an earring found in the kitchen not belonging to any staff, and they clean thoroughly at the end of every day. It must have been dropped the night he died."

"Mrs. Wu." Steph imagined her father was about to explain something to her five-year old self. "Thank you for calling. We noted the condition of his watch and clothes, but we weren't aware of the earring. It's just as possible that a customer lost it. Is there anything else?"

"No, officer." Steph hated admitting that. She knew she had lost, and he wasn't convinced.

"Thanks again for calling," he dismissed

politely. "Have a good evening, ma'am."

"You too." She hung up and rested her head on Henry's chest. She curled her feet beneath her. They sidled closer together, sliding into a more comfortable arrangement. Something was playing on the TV, but Steph didn't look up, just rested. She nearly fell asleep. When she realized what was happening, she pulled herself and Henry to standing and walked toward their bedroom. She considered skipping tooth brushing, but she would probably dream about her teeth falling out. She did the minimum required to ease her conscience before spitting and slipping into bed. Her day clothes were comfortable enough to function as pajamas.

Henry and Steph wished each other, "Good night. I love you," and turned out the lights. Steph felt a little sick to her stomach. She hoped the feeling would pass.

Half an hour later, her phone flashed. It was Jane. "On a date with David. Tell you all about it tomorrow."

CHAPTER 12

A day in the life of Jane

Friday morning, while others were starting their day, Jane was clocking out at work, thoroughly exhausted after a twelve-hour shift.

"7:05. Awesome," she said, checking her fitness tracker. "Finally leaving on time for once."

"Hey, Jane!" Deanna called out. "Can you come over here for a minute? I've got a Chocolate Hostage and need help administering an enema."

"Never mind," she thought to herself.

Around 8:05 Jane finally left the hospital. She resisted the urge to caffeinate before driving home. Falling asleep while the sun shined was hard enough without coffee.

At the door, she kicked off sneakers normally meant for geriatric patients, but even these didn't completely spare her feet. In the hallway between her bedroom and bathroom, her head turned from left to right, considering which sounded better first, sleep or a shower. Ultimately, she looked down at her soiled scrubs and decided to strip right then and there, cranking up the hot water.

She was quick and efficient. Once she felt sufficiently disinfected, Jane wrapped a robe around herself and headed toward her room. Her feet still throbbed, and they would continue protesting until she was horizontal. Hair drying would have to wait.

The minutes ticked by. "Why is everything so

loud?" she questioned. From the humming of a dishwasher above to steps in the common hallway, every noise was magnified by her intense desire to sleep. She told herself, "When this lease is up, I swear I am moving into a house." Just a few more nights shifts, and it was a financial possibility, she hoped.

Try as she might, Jane couldn't get the eight full hours of sleep research dictated she needed. Sometime around two, she rolled out of bed and brewed a pot of medium roast Guatemalan beans. While she waited, mesmerized by the *drip, drip, drip* of her coffee pot, her phone rang. It was Steph. Normally, her friend waited until a little later to call just in case Jane had worked a night shift. This meant Steph probably had good gossip, so Jane picked up and poured herself a cup of joe, adding a splash of creamer to cool it just enough. From the sound of things, Steph was on the right track with her investigation, and maybe Jane could help. She put her phone down.

An unknown number flashed across the screen. She almost ignored it, except the sneak peak of the text showed her, "Hey, Jane. It's Da–"

She picked up her phone, swiping eagerly to unlock it. Of course, it misunderstood her passcode twice and nearly locked her out. "Stupid phone, get it right," she ordered. She pulled up the text. It *was* David. He was asking her out on a date. Tonight. She felt more awake just thinking about it.

Jane tried to sort through her like-to-dos and

her must-dos. The more time she had to prepare for tonight, the better, especially when her hair stuck out like wet hay.

She really only needed to feed herself and – a yowl interrupted her thinking. "Not again," she groaned. Her neighbor's cat was probably in heat. She could have sworn it was the second time this month and wondered why her neighbor didn't just get the randy feline fixed.

Jane picked something to wear for the afternoon. She needed more time to decide what to wear for tonight and wouldn't want to dirty it anyway. After straightening her hair and throwing on some foundation, she exchanged the cacophony of sounds from adjacent apartments for the hum of an engine.

The grocery store was quiet, blissfully so. Jane lingered in the aisles, trying not to make too many impulse purchases. She was saving for a down payment after all, and her discretionary spending typically only covered her dancing habit, not cave-ripened cheese, organic wine, and Alaskan king crab. A sliver of triple crème, however, cost less than $3.00. "Mine," she claimed quietly, dropping it into her cart.

Back home, Jane spread the smooth indulgence over toast with two eggs over easy, sopping up the runny middle with extra bread. It was cheap and filling, and she had eaten out with Steph earlier this week. Thankfully, tonight's meal would likely be covered. Free was in her budget. If

David wanted to go Dutch, she could always call a ride and hope the driver was cute, but she still needed to investigate. Perhaps the reward for solving a murder would cover dinner.

Jane spent the afternoon laser-focused on clothes. Once again, she had enough dirty laundry for a load. She almost always did after work, and some stains required pre-treatment. She used her remaining time to perfect her bob, beautify, and select a sufficiently warm but also flattering outfit. Skinny jeans and ankle boots would show off the results of years of dancing, while some green around her neck would tempt him to get lost in her eyes, or so she imagined.

David called back to confirm a time and place to meet up. Though it was safer to bring her own car, Jane liked being picked up. She could tell a lot about a person by just sitting in their vehicle, and it felt more like a date. If it went sour, it was easy enough to order a car. If it went well, she'd save herself the gas money too.

He was five minutes early, texting her that he was there. Ready, Jane locked up and walked down, and David came out of his truck to greet her.

"I like a lady who's ready to go."

"And I love a man who's on time." David opened her door and helped her in before closing it after her slowly. She had chosen her jeans well. Jane looked around while David circled the truck. The inside was neat, no spare change or crumpled wrappers lying around.

As they drove off and David started to tell her about the carnival they were going to, Jane noted the smooth, quiet ride. The hum of the engine became white noise as she focused on the sound of his voice. The way he spoke wasn't slow, but deliberate and clear.

When they arrived, the crunch of leaves beneath their feet testified it was autumn. Sweetness filled the air as kettle corn, cotton candy, and caramel apples lent their sugary filigree. Any colder that night, and it might have crystallized, but Jane didn't notice. Wearing flannel, David looked like he'd jumped off the cover of a camping magazine. The sight of him was enough to keep her plenty warm. David too couldn't take his eyes off of Jane in a fitted leather jacket and scarf that brought out her emerald irises.

Entering the carnival, Jane noticed right away a booth with prizes. "Hey, there's that bear you promised me," she said. "You better win it, or I'll find someone else who will," she joked.

"Target acquired. I'm moving in," he said with feigned gravity. The price to pay was $5.00 in exchange for a chance to knock over three milk bottles with a softball. From his first throw, Jane could see that David had a strong arm and one heck of a big hand as it wrapped around the diminutive looking softball. Despite all this, the bottles barely moved. The guy behind the booth smirked.

David slapped down another fiver. He squeezed the ball and tossed it lightly in the air to feel its weight coming down. He frowned. The ball felt a little light to him, but he thought maybe if he aimed more strategically, then they'd fall. He aimed lower. The softball flew right where he wanted it, but only the top bottle wobbled and fell.

"Better luck next time," the attendant told him. Angrily, David pulled out another ten dollars. The attendant handed him back five and another softball. David tested this one too.

"Do you have any others?" he asked.

"No, they're all the same," the attendant fibbed. For demonstrations, he had a heavier ball. David threw one last time. He stepped back to put his whole body behind the throw. The booth attendant moved a few steps away. Bullseye, the softball slammed into the two supporting bottles, and no prize. The top bottle fell easily – *clink* – but one of the two below it made a leaded thud.

David leapt over the counter to pick up the last bottle standing, while the booth attendant sputtered protests. It was no wonder that sad excuse of a softball couldn't knock a tower of three bottles down. Two of them easily weighed ten pounds a piece.

"What kind of racket are you running here? Do you like cheating people for a living?" David towered over him. Jane tried to pull him back by his sleeve.

"Hey, man. I just run the booth," he defended nervously. Regardless, David felt the man must have known how impossible it was to win. He loomed over.

"David, it's fine. It's just a bear," Jane protested, hoping to deescalate the situation and wondering if his fuse was just a little too short.

"You want a bear? Here. Take one." While the other man could stand up to lesser patrons, David didn't seem the sort to cross. He also knew that the stuffed animal wasn't even worth the $15.00 already spent, so it wasn't much of a loss.

David walked out of the booth and handed the bear to Jane, who was red from embarrassment.

"Here," he said, then apologized when they were further away. "Sorry. I hope I didn't scare you, but did you see the look on his face?" He laughed. "Guy probably thought I was gonna kill him, and over a stuffed bear too."

"Did you jump over the counter just to mess with him? Sadist," she teased, smiling.

"All's fair in love and war," he replied.

"It is a nice bear," she said. "Thanks." She gave it a hug.

"I can carry it for you if you like. Or, how about we drop it off in my truck, then go get something to eat?"

"I'm starving. That sounds great." The pair walked back to a grassy area where they had parked, carnival lights singing in the background.

As they turned around and headed toward the food trucks they'd seen earlier, David said, "I don't know much about you, except that you're gorgeous and quick as a whip. I don't even know your last name, or should I just call you Jane Doe?"

"Not while my heart's still pumping." She laughed. "It's Moynihan."

"We'll see about getting it to skip a beat," he teased, making her blush. "Jane Moynihan," he repeated. "Sounds Irish."

"It is."

"Well, that explains your incredible green eyes then." Jane blushed. "Tell me more about yourself."

"I'm a nurse," she said proudly. "Been doing it for five years now. I love to go salsa dancing and sing karaoke, and I'm a bit of a film nerd. You?"

"Enlisted in the Navy in college, became a SEAL two years ago. Give me enough alcohol and I'll dance and sing. What kind of movies do you like?"

"Sometimes I watch Korean horror movies if I really want to be scared, but what I really love is French cinema and Spaghetti Westerns."

"Can't say I care for ghosts, and I don't know French," he admitted. "But I like Westerns. So, do you prefer cowboys or Indians?"

"Neither," she replied. "I always had a thing for the sheriff. I like a good law man," she hinted.

The smell of smoke and frying oil broke through the wall of sugar, alerting them of their proximity to food. "Are you feeling *Nacho Daddy's Tacos, The 'Que Stick,* or *Roll Up And Fry*?" he asked, pointing at the trucks nearest to them. "Or something else? Whatever you want."

"I like the sound of gourmet mac 'n' cheese," Jane replied, pointing out a truck with the slogan "Sweet Dreams Are Made Of Cheese" further away. She wanted to avoid messy condiments and fish breath, and macaroni was easily shared.

"Mac 'n' cheese it is," he said, ordering their most decadent. "Don't forget to save room for dessert," he added.

"Well, in that case, we better share this." Rather than waste a second fork, Jane and David handed the one back and forth, electricity passing from fingertip to fingertip, as they strolled through the fairgrounds. Once the tray was empty, they dumped it in the nearest bin and finally let their hands meet. David's large hand folded over Jane's easily, flooding it with warmth. They looked at each other.

Seeing her breath, he asked, "Are you cold?"

"No, I'm used to it from working in hospitals."

"You sure? It looks like I could buy you some hot cider over there."

"I'd rather have a hot toddy, actually, or whiskey neat." David grinned broadly, and Jane found her strategy for getting him to talk, sing even.

"Well, in that case, I know a place. Were there any rides you really wanted to go on before we leave? And I promised dessert."

"Maybe one ride on the Ferris wheel to get a good look of this whole place," she suggested. "I'll save my stomach for something stronger."

"Alright."

Up in the sky, Jane marveled at the stars and the contrast of the cool air with David's warm body. Thighs and shoulders touching, she thought, "This is nice." When the ride experienced some turbulence, David's arm shot out across her chest to make sure she didn't slip out, firmly staying in place until their gondola stabilized. They were up quite high, she noted, and David seemed a little tense.

Once no longer aloft, Jane was happy to have her feet on the ground and her hand again in David's. They walked back to his truck.

"My heart is feeling kind of weird," David said seriously. Jane the nurse reported for duty.

"Really? Is there any tightness in your chest right now? Can you see clearly? Describe what you're feeling." Jane pushed up his sleeve to take his pulse. It was elevated.

"Feeling a little lightheaded to be honest." Jane's mind raced through possibilities. Heart attack. PTSD. Stroke. Drugs. Two of those were unlikely for a man of David's fitness, but he had just returned from a combat zone.

"Okay. Anything else? Your pupils are a little dilated, and your heart rate is fast. Any shortness of breath?" Jane edged closer. She put her hands on his shoulders to help her look more clearly at his eyes.

"There is now." David's arms snaked up behind Jane and brought her mouth the rest of the way to his. She briefly gasped in surprise before melting into the warm embrace.

Once they separated she said, "You know, you're lucky you didn't try something like this at the hospital. Both of us could get in trouble." She smiled.

"Is that so, Nurse Jane? Well, how are you going to punish me?" His grin was wicked. Jane for once didn't have anything to say. She felt as though she'd just downed a shot of corn-fed bourbon, and she wanted more. "Looks like I might be contagious," he assessed, noticing her racing heartbeat and wild eyes. She blushed. Reading her sustained nearness and silence as good signs, he added, "Still wanting to have a whiskey with me?"

"If you're buying."

David and Jane drove off together. David rested a hand on Jane's thigh. She didn't move it. Her phone buzzed. It was a message from her manager confirming a shift Monday.

"Friend making sure you're still alive?" David asked, seeing the bright light in his peripheral vision. Jane jumped in her skin a little.

"Work. It's nothing," she replied, putting the phone away. They continued driving, heading back into the downtown area.

David pulled up his truck to a scotch bar. "You mentioned you liked whiskey," he said. "Have you tried this place before?"

"No, I've been meaning to, but my friends

aren't big whiskey fans."

"Their loss." He got out and opened the door for her, helping her down. Looking at his face, she appreciated once again the strong jaw, neat beard, and thick hair. She wanted to run her fingers through it. Her eyes were drawn to a metal glint in his ear, and in the back of her mind she puzzled out the pieces of his personality, wondering if he fit the profile of a murderer. She could find out more inside the bar.

David started with an order of two whiskeys served neat, treating them both to a pricier 12-year-old malt to start. As the night progressed, they switched to less expensive bottles, and Jane offered to buy a round or two.

"Maybe on the next date," David refused confidently. Once they both had a little liquor in them, Jane and David started to ask more personal questions. "So, am I competing against any other guys right now?" he asked.

"Not at the moment," she replied. "A couple months back I was seeing someone, but it fizzled out. No chemistry. I moved on. What about you?"

"Well, it's slim pickings when you're deployed. The last woman I dated seriously decided life married to someone in the military wasn't for her."

"I'm sorry."

"Don't be. It's better she figured it out sooner than later." He paused. "As a nurse you could find a job anywhere."

"That went serious real fast," Jane thought. Anyone else, and she'd have been seeing red flags, but something about David's cut-to-the-chase attitude struck a chord instead.

"That's true," she said, weighing her response. "I wouldn't mind seeing the world, with the right person, of course." David smiled.

"You wouldn't miss your family?" It was a valid concern.

"I could still travel to see them, and they're not close right now anyway. My parents live downstate, and my brother's still in school. What's your family like? Are they local?"

"They are. Dad's a cop. Mom's a teacher. Good, solid people."

"Any siblings?" Jane played dumb.

"I have a sister."

"What's she like?"

"She's real sweet, but I worry about her." He ran a hand through his shaggy hair.

"Really? Why?" Jane probed. She hope that he'd had enough whiskey for the truth to slip out if he weren't already inclined to disclose it.

"She doesn't always have the best judgment…" Jane gave a knowing, sympathetic look. "…with guys, especially. It's been that way for a long time, and I can't keep bailing her out of bad situations." Jane wondered just how far he was willing to go to protect Sharon.

"That's too bad. I've got friends like that. They trust anyone and everyone, but not everybody deserves the benefit of the doubt." While some might disapprove of her methods, Jane found gossip was a great tool for filtering out sub-par men.

"Exactly," he agreed. "You don't seem like that though," he complimented.

"You calling me picky?" She acted slightly offended.

"No, smart." Good answer. "So, do I meet your high standards so far, miss?"

"We'll see. A few more whiskeys, and my standards might be lower." David laughed. Seeing him so relaxed made Jane want to let go of her suspicions and simply enjoy the evening. "One second," she excused. She texted Steph briefly and put her phone away for the rest of the night. "Another round?"

Conversation bounced from army life to nurse rounds, religion – "bad Catholics" – to kids. Jane felt she was in her semi-buzzed happy zone at this point.

"D'you think you'll ever go back to being a 'good' Catholic?" David asked.

"Someday," Jane replied. "When I'm married, have kids. My work schedule makes it difficult to attend."

"So, you want kids?"

"Eventually, I'm not in a hurry. The only clock ticking is my fitness tracker here." She tapped her wrist. "What about you? A whole platoon of Navy brats?"

"No," he laughed. "I think I'd be hard-pressed to find a woman who'd want to have sixteen or more kids with me." Jane hadn't realized how big platoons were. "And who knows. I might not even be in the Navy by the time I start having any."

"Why's that?"

"From what I've seen, it's hard being away from a wife and kids for months at a time." That made sense.

"Well, one woman looking after sixteen is asking for a lot, but with a little persuasion, maybe some lucky lady will meet you halfway."

Another round and Jane felt she was losing more than her edge, and she felt high on something else too. David was quite possibly too good-looking.

"Maybe I should take you home," David suggested.

"Okay." She sidled out of her chair, almost missing her footing. "Whoops." David came beside her, and she gave him another megawatt, albeit slightly goofy smile. She leaned into him and sniffed. "Mmm, you even smell nice." She hadn't meant to say that aloud.

David drove her back to her place, helping her up the stairs and with her keys.

"Are you going to be okay?" He asked, concerned.

"It's so cute when you care," she said. "Definitely not a killer." David looked at her confused, and Jane gave him a scorching kiss. It was definitely getting hot in the apartment. When the kiss ended, David tried to ignore her bewitching, bedroom eyes. Her legs betrayed her, so he carried her to her room, got her a glass of water, and left her there.

"I can stay a while if you want."

"No, I'll be fine," she promised. "Thanks for taking me out tonight."

"You're welcome. Goodnight, Jane."

"Goodnight, David."

After he left, Jane reconsidered some of the things she'd inadvertently blurted. Her accidental overindulgence in whiskey and verbal diarrhea trembled in her stomach, and she rushed to the porcelain bowl. Thank God her hair was short and David wasn't here to see this. "At least I don't have work tomorrow," she told herself, "But what am I going to tell Steph?"

CHAPTER 13

As Saturday morning rolled in, Steph groggily rolled out of bed herself. She slipped on a robe for warmth and walked into the living area. Madeline was doing just fine with Daddy, so Steph brewed some coffee for the two of them. If Henry didn't want his, she'd drink it.

After mellowing out and trading places, Steph stayed home with Madeline to observe regular nap times and clean, while Henry left to do some shopping. After he had gone, Steph heard their buzzer ring.

"Hello?" No one responded. It must be a delivery of some sort. She grabbed Madeline and went downstairs to investigate. Sure enough, just outside the building was a cake box. Steph popped open the lid, and a human skull grinned up at here. However, this one smelled of chocolate, not decay, and there was a frosting message piped inside too.

"RIP Steph," it read, listing her birth year to present underneath.

Steph eyes widened to the size of dinner plates as she tried to think who would leave such a thing for her and why. She quickly poked her head outside the door, checking both directions. No one. Maybe someone had realized she'd been snooping around, asking questions. She hadn't recognized any passersby yesterday when she was at Honey

Huns with Charlotte, but maybe she had missed someone. "How could I be so stupid," she berated.

"Okay," she told herself, pacing the floor, "What am I going to do next? Is there any chance this thing is poisoned?" She looked around again, realizing she had said that aloud, then went back upstairs to call Henry, but he wasn't answering. She put the phone down, and her fingers tapped on the counter. The police department was within walking distance of her apartment, maybe a little far, but doable. Steph frantically dressed to go outside, gathered Madeline and the stroller, and gingerly placed the cake in the stroller basket once unfolded, treating it like a live bomb.

Nervous, her determined pace kept her warm. Her mind raced. "I can't believe someone is actually trying to kill me. I should have listened to Henry. What was I thinking playing detective? Are we gonna have to move now?" After a rushed twenty-minute walk, Steph huffed her way inside the police department.

"I have something I need to show Detective Harris," she stated with purpose. A receptionist pointed to a desk where a middle-aged man sat. He was not young like Steph had assumed and looked as though he'd played football, but not for two or three decades. She wondered if he wouldn't be a little gray at the temples if it weren't for the fact that he had a flat top.

"Excuse me, sir. I'm Stephanie Wu. I've called before. Look, this morning I received this."

She pulled out the box and opened it to reveal the deathly dark chocolate treat. "I think someone is trying to send me a message. Is there any chance it's poisoned?"

"Ma'am, do you have a reason to suspect someone would poison you?" Harris looked around his desk at the stroller parked beside it, lowering the volume of his voice.

Luckily for Steph, the hustle and bustle of the station provided sufficient white noise for Madeline, who slumbered peacefully.

"Because I've been investigating my neighbor's death," she explained. Harris put two and two together. So, this was the woman who had been calling in tips.

"Are you sure this isn't a prank? Have you asked if one of your friends sent it?" Steph hadn't.

"Not yet," she admitted, embarrassed, wondering, "Why didn't I think of that?" She pulled out her phone, texting Jane and Charlotte first, then Sharon and Rachel, among others. She waited in the chair feeling awkward. "Can you test it?" she asked.

"Ma'am there are so many different types of poisons we would have to test for. If you think it's poisoned, it's best to just throw it away. Don't even take a chance." Steph gazed longingly at the chocolate cake. Her phone buzzed. Charlotte claimed the cake.

"A friend sent it," she confirmed, cheeks reddening.

"Do you suspect her?" he asked.

"Do I?" she asked herself internally. She had told Charlotte her theory yesterday, and Charlotte had in fact benefitted from Sameed's death.

While she was silent, Harris added, "You know, I've seen a lot of weird things in my career and met a lot of dumb criminals. It's unlikely she'd poison the cake and claim it, but you'd better not risk it, for that one's sake." Harris thought it couldn't hurt to encourage someone trying to investigate to lay low and play it safe for a while. He dropped the cake in the trash.

Steph felt a simultaneous *thud* in the pit of her stomach, regret already creeping up and gripping her. She had thrown away what was probably a perfectly safe and incredible tasting cake from Charlotte. She wanted to dive into the trash and rescue it. Her distress evident, Harris felt sympathy for the young mother.

"You're in luck," he said. "Someone in the department had a birthday today, and we have some cake left over if you'd like a slice."

"Thanks. I would." Harris got up from his chair to get two servings of sheet cake from the rec room. While he was gone, Steph tried to subtly review the papers on his desk, seeing if there was anything related to Sameed. Nothing. Harris came back, giving her a slice with a red frosting balloon. Having more frosting usually cheered up most people.

They enjoyed their cake together, exchanging tidbits about their respective families.

"I have four kids," Harris informed Steph.

"Four! Wow."

"Yep, in four years."

"That must have been tough when they were little."

"They still are," he said. Steph wished she could have eaten her words, feeling guilty for overestimating his age. "Just kidding," he said to relieve her tension. "They're actually teenagers now, but I long for the days when their worst tantrums were over a toy."

"I believe it," Steph said. "I was a terror in high school. Thankfully, I straightened out before graduation."

"That's what we're praying for." Harris was only half joking.

After finishing her slice, Steph told him, "Thanks for letting me have a piece." She left not a crumb or smear on her plate. It was completely clean, and as for Harris, it was his second slice already that morning.

"You're welcome. And Ma'am? Don't be afraid to come back if you hear something new, but please leave the investigating to us."

"But you're not investigating," Steph thought before saying aloud, "I won't. Thanks."

"You won't stop investigating?" he asked, a little incredulous.

"No, I mean, yes, I meant I'll come back if I hear something."

"Good." Harris waved goodbye as she left.

As soon as Steph exited the police station, Harris pulled the cake box back out of the trash and stuck his fork in. After trying a bite, he said, "O'Brian?"

"Yes, sir?"

"If I die, look into this case, and if I don't, find out who made this. It's amazing."

"Yes, sir." He paused. "Can I have a slice of that cake, sir?"

"No," Harris replied. "You'd best protect yourself. Stick to the sheet cake."

Outside, Steph felt a little disappointed in herself. "They must think I'm crazy." She checked the time. Henry would likely be done running errands soon. Lucky for Steph, Madeline snoozed blissfully unaware of her mother's mood.

Back home, Steph figured she'd burned off the cake and needed to refuel. She had carefully carried Madeline and the stroller back up the stairs. Greg's husky Alaska had made a sudden, short bark, likely excited by her footfalls, and almost woke the baby, who now snoozed happily in her own bed.

As Steph grilled a cheese sandwich, Henry came through the door laden with groceries.

"Do anything this morning?" he asked. Steph debated whether or not to tell Henry she freaked out over a cake. She decided not to mention it.

"I went on a long walk with Maddie," she answered. "It was a little cool, but sunny out."

"That's nice." Henry started putting some of

the groceries away in the refrigerator and cabinet. "Can you make me one too? I'm pretty hungry."

"Sure. Here, you can have this one." She slid the first grilled cheese sandwich onto a plate for him.

"Thanks." Soon enough, Steph sat down herself, but Henry had already finished his by then. "I got the drinks and snacks. What's left to get done before tonight?"

"What do you mean?" Steph asked.

"The Halloween party we're hosting," he reminded. "Did you forget?"

"The Halloween party, of course. How could I forget?" That was why Charlotte had dropped off a cake. Now, she felt like an imbecile. This was her worst case of mommy brain to date for sure.

"Are you alright? Do you want to cancel?" he asked, disappointment written on her face.

"I'm fine. It's just... silly of me to forget. I'm looking forward to the party, really."

"Okay. Well, I have something fun for you to do once Maddie's asleep."

"Ooh, what?" Steph perked up.

"I bought a pumpkin for you to carve." Oooh, she thought. That *did* sound like fun.

"Will you put some kind of a playlist together?"

"I can do that."

Henry and Steph cleaned and decorated together, alternating keeping Madeline entertained while she was awake, before going to their respective tasks.

Thirty minutes before the party was to start, they heard a knock at the door.

"Hi." It was Dennis dressed in a hockey jersey. "I brought some chips."

"Thanks," Steph said, slightly forcing a smile. She didn't feel ready to receive any guests. She took the bag and poured some out in a party bowl.

"What are you two dressed as?" he asked, pointing to Steph's purple outfit and Henry's blond wig and orange ascot.

"Fred and Daphne. From Scooby Doo." The show was a childhood favorite of Steph's.

"Oh. Does the baby have a costume too?"

"Yes, you'll see." Madeline was at that moment sleeping in an orange long-sleeved onesie with a red tutu and orange thigh highs. Her fake glasses wouldn't likely stay on for more than one picture, if even. "Please sit down. Can I get you anything?" Steph offered.

"I'm fine," Dennis assured, sitting on the couch and waiting for others to arrive, while Henry and Steph worked around him. Eventually, Henry left the last minute details to Steph and engaged Dennis in a game of chess, letting his guest play as white first.

Next to arrive on time was Greg. As she opened the door, Steph could hear Alaska complaining about being left behind in the background.

Greg broke from tradition, donning a white t-shirt that showed off his collection of classic American beauties. To this he added dark shades, a few bracelets, and a top hat.

"Ozzy Osborne?" Steph guessed. She didn't know her rock stars very well.

"Slash," he corrected. "From Gun N' Roses. He is my guitar, and overall, hero."

"Ooh. I should have known. Do you want anything to drink? We have soda, water, coffee, beer, and some other things Henry picked up. There's punch too. It's spiked," she warned.

"Thanks. I'll grab something myself." Greg left to peruse Henry's liquor selection.

Rachel arrived next, apologizing.

"I'm sorry. I didn't have much time to plan a costume. I was so focused on being ready for last night's performance."

"No, no. That's fine. You look great," Steph encouraged. "Karate Kid, I presume?" she said based on the headband with a neatly rendered sharpie flower.

"Yeah, this is my taekwondo dobok. Are you Daphne?"

"Yep." She paused. "Are you really a black belt?" Steph pointed at Rachel's waist.

"Yes," Rachel said proudly. It occurred to Steph that Rachel's limbs now counted as lethal weapons. She had dismissed her size before. Interested, Steph probed deeper.

"Do you still practice these days? I know you're busy with school."

"I do," Rachel answered. "I go every Monday if I can. You're welcome to join me next time if you're interested."

"I think that'd be a lot of fun actually, but we'll see if it works out with Madeline. What's the name of the studio?"

"Of course. Master Kwon's Taekwondo."

"Well, thanks so much for coming. Can I get you anything? Punch is out on the counter. Other drinks are in the fridge. Feel free to help yourself to snacks on the table."

"Thanks. That punch looks pretty good, and that pumpkin next to it. Did you carve it yourself?" She pointed at the howling wolf and dimpled full moon with realistic craters.

"I did. It's always been one of my favorite things about Halloween."

"Wow," Rachel admired. "You're really talented."

"Thank you!"

"I'm going to try some of that punch," Rachel said, smiling. She walked off to pour herself a cup and struck up a conversation with Henry about the music playing.

"Did you do the playlist?" Rachel asked.

"Yes," he replied.

"Is this what you normally listen to?" There was a mix of pop, rock, and other Halloween themed music.

"Not exactly. I like jazz, some new grass, and math rock," Henry admitted. "Steph listens more to the radio."

"Really? Well, if you like math and music, you'd probably appreciate Beethoven," Steph heard Rachel suggest.

Steph poured herself half a cup of soda. She'd like to try the punch later, but she was waiting until after Madeline fed to imbibe any alcohol. In the meantime, she awaited the next guest and wondered who else was busy on Monday nights, the night Sameed had died.

Instead of a knock, this time the buzzer sounded. It was Sharon dressed like a hippy flower child in a loose floral dress beneath her coat, gogo boots, large peace sign earrings, and beach blond waves. Steph wondered if the shape of the dress were strategic, but it would probably be too early for her to show, she concluded.

"Sharon! Welcome! I'm glad you could make it on such short notice."

"Me too! Thanks for inviting me. So, who else will be here?" She shrugged off her coat, but held on, unsure where to put it.

"Here, let me take that into our room," Steph said, grabbing it from Sharon. "Just other people from the building and my friend Jane. You know Henry. Next to him is Rachel. She's a grad student. She lives upstairs and plays violin." Rachel was already swaying to the music. Steph thought Henry had chosen well. "Over by the couch dressed like Slash is Greg. He's a photographer. He's upstairs too, and next to him is Dennis, our landlord."

"Great! Thanks!" Sharon drifted over toward Henry and Rachel in the kitchen, while Steph put Sharon's coat in their bedroom. Out of sight, she checked her phone. She was still waiting on Jane and Charlotte. Charlotte. Steph asked herself what she was going to tell her friend about the incredibly realistic skull cake the officer had suggested she toss out. Her phone vibrated with a text. Jane said she was running late and bringing a guest, if that were okay. Steph texted back, "That's fine," thinking one more person in their apartment was no big deal.

As she walked back toward the front of the apartment, she heard the buzzer go off again. Dreading Charlotte, she let Henry, who was closer, answer, while Steph nipped into the nursery to get Madeline up.

Coming out of the nursery, Madeline snuggled against her chest, Steph invented possible excuses to give Charlotte. Henry opened the door. She winced at the thought of the awkward conversation to come, but it was Jane and… David.

Steph looked at Sharon to catch her reaction. She didn't seem pleased. Sharon walked up to Steph.

"You didn't say my brother was invited. How do you know him?"

"I don't. I mean. I met him at a café earlier this week, but I didn't invite him. My friend brought him." Sharon believed her, but was slightly peeved. Steph figured she still must not be on very good terms with her family after everything.

"Jane! Hi! And, David, right?"

"Yes, nice to see you and the little lady again," David answered. Underneath a black coat, he wore a long sleeve Punisher tee pushed up to his elbows, denim jeans, and combat boots. He liked the vigilante, anti-hero type, Steph surmised, but was he one, she wondered. Despite being covered up, it was obvious to anyone in the room that David could out lift and out press them all.

Next to David slinked Jane dressed as Catwoman, striking quite the figure in an all-black ensemble, pointy ears, and mask.

"Hi, Steph! Thanks for letting me bring David. I was going to call you earlier, but I ran out of time." Jane looked up at David. Steph figured she must have really hit it off with him and likely spent the day together as well.

"That's okay. You look amazing, by the way."

"Thanks," she purred, giving a "mrow." Steph knew very well how attractive her friend was and hoped David saw that there was so much more to Jane than her pretty exterior. More importantly, for Sharon and Jane's sake, she hoped David wasn't a murderer.

"Help yourself to anything in the kitchen." Steph gestured broadly behind her. "Can I take your coats?"

"You've got your hands full. Where can I put them?"

"Thanks. Go down the hallway. The open

door leads to our bedroom." David walked off. "So, how'd it go last night?" she pried.

"I had a little bit too much," Jane admitted, holding back her "killer" comment for the moment. "But overall I had a great time." She smiled. "He seems like a genuinely nice guy, a little protective, maybe, but for good reasons. I'll tell you more later," she promised.

"Alright," Steph thought. "I can wait 'til later." Steph milled around the open kitchen and living room, talking to various people. She had Sharon take a photo of her, Henry, and Madeline altogether. Greg was still talking to Dennis, discussing something in depth. It seemed the guys in the building got along well enough, maybe she could propose a poker night. That way, she could figure out if anyone else were busy and had an alibi for Monday evenings, which was when Sameed had died.

Steph's phone buzzed again. It had to be Charlotte. "Hey, so sorry." It read. "Had to feed Rupert again. Be there any minute."

"Any minute." The words rang in Steph's head as she mentally prepared herself. Charlotte was certain to ask about the cake. Over the music and the conversation, Steph still thought she could hear each and every one of Charlotte's heavy steps, and when she opened the door, Rosie the Riveter greeted her.

"Hi!" Steph enthused.

"Hey, Steph! Good to see you again so soon.

Nice decorations," Charlotte said, appreciating Henry's fake spider webs. Steph had been too short to help much with those.

"Thanks! Do you want me to take your coat?"

"Not yet," Charlotte replied. "By the way, is there any of my cake left?"

"Cake?" Steph's mind momentarily forgot the morning's fiasco.

"Hello, the one I dropped off this morning? The skull cake that said 'RIP Steph' because your social life is over and you clearly haven't been sleeping?" The joke finally reached her.

"Right. That cake," Steph said. "Umm, I'm really sorry, but I accidentally dropped it on the floor. I had to throw it away." It was partially true.

"Throw it away? Are you crazy? Steph, do you know how long I spent on that cake?"

"I know. I know. It was really stupid of me. I saw the skull and freaked out." Steph wasn't quite ready to admit she took it to the police station.

Charlotte just laughed hysterically, silencing the rest of the room.

"Scared of a skull? How old are you again? Girl, you *really* need to get some sleep. Make Henry wake up with the baby."

"That's probably a good idea," Steph said, thinking it might actually work on the weekends.

"Just do it," Charlotte insisted. Finally warmed up, she took off her coat and flexed her Rosie-worthy guns. "Mmm, I think I'm gonna try some of that punch."

As Charlotte walked away to serve herself, Steph returned to her previous idea, scoping out people's schedules. She walked over to her husband.

"Hey, Henry?"

"Yeah? What was that all about?"

"I'll explain later." He gave her a look. "Do you like the idea of a poker night? We could host. That way, you could have some guy time and not feel like you're abandoning me."

"Sure, okay."

"I was thinking we could invite Dennis and Greg, maybe even David, and some other friends of yours."

Henry nodded. He was a little confused by the addition of Sharon's brother, but he thought maybe his wife saw longevity in David's relationship with Jane and thought getting to know him worth pursuing.

"Great. I'll ask which days might work best." While in the kitchen, Steph noticed Rachel pouring herself another cup of punch, now singing along with the playlist.

"Heey, Steph," Rachel greeted.

"Hey."

"This playlist is soo goood." Rachel took her phone out and pointed in at the stereo, pressing a button several times. It caught Steph slightly off guard.

"Thanks. Henry made it. Do you like the

punch?" Steph asked. "I'm waiting to have some myself."

"It's de*li*cious," Rachel confirmed. "This is my fourth cup, but why are you waiting?"

"There's alcohol in it, didn't I tell you?"

"No."

"Sorry. I hope Henry didn't make it too strong." To be polite, Rachel finished what she had, then started drinking water.

"It explains why I tried to adjust the stereo with my phone."

"Oh, it is too loud? I can turn it down," Steph offered.

"Not at all," Rachel said. "I was trying to turn up the volume."

Steph was glad the building's resident musician approved of the playlist. She thought the party was going quite well, though Rachel seemed a little tipsy. Steph went up to Dennis and Greg, who were discussing their costumes.

"You must be Cameron from Ferris Beuller's Day Off," Greg guessed, pointing at the Red Wings jersey.

"No, I'm a hockey player," Dennis corrected.

"Right. People only want to pretend to be someone they're not on Halloween," Greg subtly jabbed, but the joke was either lost on Dennis or he didn't care.

"Hey," Steph interrupted. "Thanks again for coming tonight."

"Thank you for hosting," Greg replied.

"I was wondering, we're thinking of starting a poker night. We would host. What do you think?"

"I'd be down," said Greg. He wasn't about to say no to free food and drinks.

"Sure," Dennis added. "When were you thinking?"

"Monday night? Would that work for you?"

"I'm free."

"Me too."

"Great! This Monday then?"

"Sure."

"Can we bring anything?" Dennis asked.

"Umm, let me ask Henry. I'll get back to you." Steph looked down at Madeline's gaping mouth and decided it was a good time to feed her.

She passed by David and Jane and stopped quickly to ask him too.

"Hey. Henry is having a poker night Monday. You'll welcome to join," she said.

"Cool. I'll think about it," David replied. Jane nudged David to tell him she thought it was a great idea, while Steph went to the nursery for privacy.

The room was dim and quiet, though she could hear the hum of music playing. After a few minutes, she also started to make out some other loud noises and possibly the buzzer again. She rested Madeline high on her chest and left the nursery to investigate. Pandemonium.

"Stop treating me like a kid!" Sharon yelled at her brother, looking ready to pick a fight.

"Then stop acting like one," David bellowed

back. "Are you off your meds again?"

"I can't believe you'd say that!"

Unlike most disasters, Steph couldn't help but look away. Instead, her eyes were drawn to Rachel darting toward the kitchen sink. It looked like she was going to– the sound of retching reached Steph's ear.

Being closer, Henry hurried to help their neighbor.

"Sorry," Rachel said weakly.

"You don't need to apologize," he told her. Next, Steph heard the door open, and Greg, still dressed like a rock star, was slipping out while Charlotte held it open to Steph's in-laws.

"Thanks for the party, Steph!" Greg shouted. "Gotta catch another. See ya again Monday!" Her in-laws stepped aside to make room, looking disturbed. A red cup rolled to her feet, and she picked it up, walking toward the door.

Li Ming held what was obviously a meal for them, probably the closest attempt at an apology to date. Steph burned with embarrassment. They saw a party out of control, Steph's dress askew, her baby crying, guests going crazy… what a terrible, horrible spectacle, Steph thought.

She walked up to them, red solo cup in one hand, Madeline cradled in the other. She tried to thank them graciously for dropping off the meal. Charlotte, seeing her friend in distress, grabbed the containers of food, walked over to Henry, and replaced him as Rachel's nurse, while Henry came to Steph's rescue. He gently led his parents outside their apartment and closed the door to explain.

"It's done. I am never going to recover from this," Steph lamented internally. "I could use a drink." However, she crushed the cup and abandoned any plans of trying the punch. She needed her wits about her. Instead, she filled a glass of water and checked on Rachel.

"Rachel? Are you okay? Can I get you some Tylenol? Do you need a new shirt?" Thankfully, Rachel's hair had already been tied back, and she had managed to dash to the sink in time. Her clothes were clean.

"I'm fine. I… I just need to sit down."

"Okay, if you want someplace quiet, you can go in our room, then someone will help you upstairs when you're ready. Promise." Charlotte led Rachel into the bedroom and helped her sit down, showing her where the entrance to the bathroom was in case she needed the toilet. Rachel was petite and had spent her college weekends studying and practicing violin, not drinking and partying.

When Jane came out of the bathroom, Steph quickly told her, "I need you to intervene. Thank you for coming, but please take David somewhere else."

"Done." Jane walked over to her date, pulling him away from his sister. From the look on her face, she tried to keep it light, lure him away from this party to something more enjoyable, perhaps for both of them.

Steph wished her friend a silent "thank you" and walked over to pacify Sharon, rubbing Madeline's back.

"I'm really sorry," she told Sharon. "I had no idea Jane would bring David."

"It's not your fault, and I'm sorry. You invited me here. I should have just ignored him." Steph wondered what they had argued about. Jane will likely know. At least, she'll know David's side of the story. Steph noticed Sharon looked a little off.

"Can I get you something?"

"Do you have ginger ale? My stomach's upset."

"Yes, we do. It's right in the door of the fridge. And we have Tums too, if you want."

"I'll try the ginger ale first. I can get it. Thanks." Sharon walked off to the kitchen, while Henry came back in through the door. His face told her that his conversation with his parents hadn't been a pleasant one. Steph mouthed "Sorry," dreading the play-by-play to come.

Steph looked over in the corner. There was Dennis, poor Dennis, looking lost and out of place.

"I'm so sorry," she apologized to her guest. "This wasn't how I imagined this party would go."

"I'm sure it wasn't," he replied.

"So, do you think you'll still come Monday night for poker?"

"Uh." He thought about it. "I think so."

"Do you want anything?" Steph offered before leaving her guest in peace.

"No, no thanks."

Steph walked back toward her bedroom, knocking first.

"Rachel, do you need any help upstairs? You don't have to go now, only if you want to."

Charlotte came back out supporting what looked like a female drunken master after a tough fight.

"I'm so sorry," Steph apologized again for forgetting to mention the punch was alcoholic.

"It's okay. I feel better now," Rachel reassured sleepily. Charlotte and Rachel left for her apartment. Stairs seemed beyond her capabilities at that moment. It occurred to Steph that she could help Rachel to her apartment and check her jewelry box for a solitary diamond stud, but she abandoned the thought. Taking advantage of her neighbor's current state to root through her things was unconscionable.

Sharon came up to Steph next.

"Thanks for the ginger ale and the party," she said. "I should probably get going since I have work tomorrow."

"Of course. I hope you feel better," Steph wished, bidding her friend goodbye.

That left only Dennis, who was sitting by himself on the couch. Steph was relieved when Henry approached him.

"Another game of chess?" Henry offered. Dennis accepted. This time Dennis was black. After Henry moved his king's pawn up two squares,

Dennis responded by moving his queen's pawn up one square.

"Going for the French defense? Giving up already?"

"No, the French is solid."

"It's just a military joke," Henry explained. "The French *is* a great opening."

Steph left the room to finish nursing Madeline in peace and put her down to bed. What a night. By the time she had finished, Dennis had left, and Henry had started cleaning up, beginning with the rancid kitchen sink.

"Thanks," Steph said, opting to sweep up chips and various other crumbs. "I'm sorry about tonight," she said.

"Why are you sorry?" he asked.

"Well, I should have suggested Jane not bring David, for one."

"Did you know she was bringing him?"

"No, I–"

"Well, then that's not your fault. They chose to argue."

"I guess, but Rachel too. I must have forgotten to mention the punch was alcoholic." She sighed. "This whole mess probably made things much worse with your parents, didn't it?" Henry was quiet for a moment. Steph took that as a bad sign.

"Rachel could have guessed the punch was alcoholic, and I neglected to tell her too. As for my parents, they were here to apologize for last week."

"I was right," Steph thought. "And now I've gone and blown it." Henry continued.

"Yes," he said, answering her previous question. "It was shocking to them, but it can't be all blamed on you." Steph wasn't sure "can't" was the best choice, more like "shouldn't," which didn't negate the possibility of it still being blamed on her.

"I know, it's just one more thing going against me. I don't feel like I'll ever measure up," she confessed.

"You're more than enough for me," he said. "And for Madeline. That's all that matters." Steph wished she felt as sure of her maternal ability as her husband did, but she feared the things she might have inherited from her birth mother. Not to mention, she knew nothing of her father. "Come here," he ordered gently, bringing her in. Steph didn't mind that his hands were probably dirty. She was going to change out of her costume anyway.

Looking up at Henry and seeing the platinum wig still perched on his head brought a smile to her lips.

"You know, I kind of like you as a blonde," she commented.

"Don't get your hopes up," he replied, smiling back. "You, however, look stunning as a redhead."

"Thanks, but I don't think I'll be dying my hair any time soon. *Maybe* when I'm done breastfeeding." Steph inched closer to her husband and tilted her head back, asking for a kiss. He obliged. They soaked in the moment before going back to cleaning. A good night's rest appealed to both.

Preparing for bed, Steph realized she now had to plan for a poker night in two days. She could remind Henry tomorrow, she told herself. She also needed to check up on Rachel's taekwondo alibi though it was unlikely that she was the killer. Steph couldn't imagine what would possibly motivate her diminutive, sweet neighbor, but if she could cross even one name off her growing list of suspects, it would bring her one step closer to figuring out who killed Sameed.

In a residential neighborhood not far away, Inspector Bertrand Harris, better known as Bert by his family, indulged in another bite of Charlotte's irresistible skull cake. He had managed to sneak it past his wife, who would give him the eye if he so much as thought about sugar. Alone, in his home office, surrounded by stacks of paper and dusty mementos, he devoured the last bite, telling himself it was a rather small cake, and it had been quite a long day.

He pulled the salad his wife had packed for his lunch out of his bag and wondered how best to dispose of the evidence. He could try to dump it in the trash while his wife rounded up the kids for a late dinner if that hadn't already eaten without him. He hoped college scholarships awaited them in the near future. It seemed half his paycheck went to feeding them.

Slipping into the kitchen, Bert decided he'd better not risk Florence finding his salad in the garbage. She hated food waste. He'd pretend someone brought in lunch. Perfect. He placed the salad back in the fridge.

"Hey, honey. How was work?" Florence came into the kitchen when she heard her husband's footsteps.

"Not bad. The woman who's been calling in tips came in with her baby today. Pretty cute."

"You better be talking about the baby. You're not thinking of having more are you?" she teased.

"No. Four is definitely enough. I'll be in diapers by the time a new kid's out of them." Florence laughed.

"We aren't that old," she replied. "Are you hungry?"

"I'm good. They had some food at the station today, so I ate already." Florence looked at him suspicious. She came up closer. She gave him a kiss.

"*Why* do you smell like chocolate?" she accused, quite the detective herself.

"Baby, I–"

"And *why* are there crumbs on your shirt? Have you been eating in your office again? You know you're not supposed to be eating that stuff. What did your doctor say?"

"He said I need to cut back," he recited joylessly.

"And you should listen to him." Bert started to tune out his wife. He felt a strange pain in his abdomen. "Are you listening to me? You need to listen when I'm talking to you." Bert grabbed at his shirt and leaned on the refrigerator with one arm.

"Flo."

"What? Don't try and cover your sneakin' around. I bet your salad is in the fridge too for the second day in a row."

"Flo," he tried again. "Take me to the hospital."

CHAPTER 14

Florence hit the gas pedal like never before. Bert gripped the door of the passenger seat, sweat dripping down his temple. The other arm clutched his side, his hand in a fist.

20, 30, 40, 50… Through clenched eyes, he watched the speedometer climb, concerned. His wife had never received a ticket before, and not because her husband was an officer. This was the closest he'd ever been to thinking he was dying.

"How are you doing?" Florence asked. Bert groaned, doubled over, and vomited on his feet.

He thought of his four, beautiful children. He thought of his wife, her fingers and their vise-grip on the steering wheel at nine and three o'clock. Through the corner of his eye, he witnessed the intense look of terror and concentration on her face. How could he do this to them, he asked himself, and for what, cake?

Cityscape blurred by. He couldn't be sure if they had been in the car for five minutes or fifty. The pain was incredible and inescapable. The car suddenly stopped, and for a moment Bert wondered if they had been pulled over. Moments later, he heard the door open on the passenger side, and his wife helped pull him to his feet.

As Flo struggled toward the entryway, ER staff rushed to assist her and find out what was the matter with the detective.

"Thank you, Jesus," Bert heard his wife say quickly as they hurried him into a room. The pain was so intense he could hardly focus on his surroundings. A medical professional came in to ask questions. Florence helped fill in some details. In between bouts of pain, Bert told them it was possible he'd been poisoned, and all the color left his wife's face.

Within minutes a nurse was there to take blood for testing. Bert looked away from the needle. At some point, another nurse gave him water to stay hydrated. After two cups, he asked to use the restroom. Florence got up from her chair beside the bed to assist him. She helped him to the door.

"Do you want me to come in with you?"

"No," he replied. "I can do it." His wife looked unsure, but she respected his request for a moment's space.

He was even more relieved to have gone in alone when the bowl starting turning red. He washed his hands and hobbled out of the restroom, back to his hospital bed without saying anything to Florence. When she left for a minute to update the kids, he called the nurse and told him what he'd scene.

"Still in pain?" the nurse asked.

"Yes," Bert admitted. The nurse left and returned with two white pills.

"For the pain," he said. "And keep drinking water."

Florence rejoined him a few minutes later.

"The kids are fine," she said. "Patricia said she'd make sure the other girls went to bed on time. Clarence was already in his room. I think he's worried about you. *I'm* worried about you. How much longer are we gonna have to wait? And why do you think you've been poisoned? How is that even possible?"

Bert relayed the afternoon's events and informed O'Brian he was at the hospital.

"You ate a poisoned cake? I can't believe you."

"I didn't think it was really poisoned," he defended. "Her friend claimed the cake. What kind of criminal is dumb enough to do that?"

"What kind of detective is dumb enough to test it?" Florence put her face in her hands. Bert had no response. In the middle of the awkward silence, a doctor in a long white coat entered.

"Mr. Harris?"

"Yes, Ma'am."

"Hi, I'm Dr. Horowitz from the Urology Department. We want to have an ultrasound done on your kidneys to see how serious your condition is."

"Do you have the results of the blood test yet?" Florence asked.

"No, I'm sorry, but we'll let you know as soon as we do."

Uncertainty and fear festered in the air. Florence always knew one day she might be called to the ER or worse, but since her husband had become a detective, that nightmare had faded to the back of her mind. Now it was at the forefront.

The nurse returned. "Sir, if you please, come with me. Ma'am, I'm going to ask you to wait here." Florence kissed her husband, then sat back down, hands folded in prayer.

"Sir, let me know if you need any assistance," the nurse offered in the hallway.

Once in the room and on the table, Bert was prepped for an ultrasound.

"The pain is on your right side, correct?" the technician asked. Bert nodded to confirm. The gel was cool on his skin. The transducer probe pressed into his side, moving around to get a clear picture of his kidney.

"Am I going to be okay?" Bert grit his teeth, since he couldn't hold his side. The medication the nurse had given him earlier had only touched the surface.

"Sir, I'm just a technician, but we'll have a doctor review your results shortly. We're all done taking pictures." The tech put the equipment away and helped Bert remove the gel before he pulled his shirt down.

His nurse returned to help him back to his room, where his tired wife waited. Anxiety eating the both of them, Bert and Florence held one another's hand, and after a number of minutes, Dr. Horowitz reentered the room.

"Mr. Harris, you have a large kidney stone

on your right side. Because of its size, we recommend ESWL, that is extracorporeal shock wave lithotripsy, to try breaking it up into smaller, more passable stones. If that doesn't work, then you may require surgery."

"What? What about the blood tests?"

"Your blood work came back normal. To be honest, after looking at the results, I'm surprised you're not in here for a heart attack, Mr. Harris. Your cholesterol is sky high. So is your blood pressure, and you need to lose weight. You're lucky to be alive." The doctor paused briefly. "I'll be back in a half hour or so for your ESWL."

Bert was gobsmacked. A kidney stone, that's all it was, and he thought he had been dying. No longer fearful of her husband's life, Florence was on him in seconds.

"You heard the doctor. You need to take better care of yourself. You could have died today. You could die tomorrow. Please. Eat healthy. Exercise. Take some time off work. Do it for me. Do it for our children. And you!" Florence pointed at Detective O'Brian, who had just entered the room. O'Brian pointed to himself, looking stupid. "You better keep all that garbage at work away from my husband, or I will tell your wife that you're still smoking."

"Didn't you quit months ago?" Bert asked.

"I tried," O'Brian admitted. "But it's been hard giving it up. I swear I'm down to less than a pack a day, but how did you know?"

"Shoes, hand, smell," she said pointing at each clue on his person. Sure enough, once he got closer, Bert could faintly make out some ash on O'Brian's shoes, easily mistaken for dirt, and the fingers clenched reflexively, but no characteristic odor.

"I don't smell smoke," Bert said.

"It's air freshener, and a bit too much of it," Florence explained.

"Please don't tell Michelle. I only smoke outside the station, but I'll try quitting again, I swear."

"Promise me you won't let Bert eat any more junk food. I don't care if he's your senior."

"Yes, Ma'am." O'Brian turned to Bert. "So were you poisoned? You look terrible."

"No." He groaned. "Kidney stone." O'Brian winced just thinking about it. "Thanks for coming though. You can hold off on finding out who made that cake. I think it'll be a long time before I have another," he said, looking at Florence.

After receiving the prescribed therapy and having a second ultrasound to check what was left, the hospital staff sent Bert and his wife home with painkillers and muscle relaxers.

"Drink lots of water," Dr. Horowitz advised. "Come back if you feel severe pain again, nausea, bloody urine, or high fever and chills. I would take it easy the next 48 hours."

Under the influence of more than one medication and still in some pain, Bert was happy to let Florence drive back home. He looked at her, her weary eyes focused on the road. "She must be exhausted. Hopefully, the kids are asleep," he thought. "What a phenomenal woman." If he wanted to stay by her side for another twenty years, he needed to do better.

As they pulled into the garage, fourteen year-old Clarence ran up to meet them.

"Dad!" he exclaimed, pulling him in for a hug. Bert tried to hold back a wince, but he didn't shy from the embrace. Clarence wrapped his arms around him, already nearly as tall, but about half the size, of his father.

"It's gonna be okay, son. Now, go back to bed." Happily, Clarence bounded up the stairs back to his room, knowing his father was fine.

In the living room, Bert's eldest daughter Patricia was asleep on the couch. The television was still on. He figured she must had tried to stay up. Bert turned off the TV and put a blanket on her. She went by Tricia, or Trisha – he couldn't remember which – at school, but she'd always be his sweet little Patty Cakes.

Upstairs, the twins, Tiffany and Monique, slept quietly in their room. He couldn't resist checking in on them too. Normally, the room was an explosion of creative thought, but in the dark, new ideas developed silently in the back of their minds. If they ever became famous, he wouldn't be surprised.

Bert shut the door quietly behind him. The

lights in Clarence's room were out, and he assumed its sole occupant was already asleep. He walked on and stepped into his bedroom.

After tidying up downstairs, Florence joined her husband on the second floor of their Victorian home, water bottle in hand. She passed it to her husband before making her way into the en suite bathroom. She came out in a robe and facemask, looking even more tired.

"I love you," Bert told his wife. "And I'm so sorry. I'll start taking my health more seriously, I promise."

"I love you too," she replied. "You know I'll help you any way I can."

"I know. Goodnight."

"Goodnight."

As Bert fell asleep with the dawn, he wondered about his recent encounter with death. He had been lucky it was just kidney stones that put him in the hospital, not poison or heart failure. However, this wasn't the first time his life had been in danger, and as a detective, he was sure it wouldn't be his last.

CHAPTER 15

Sunday morning, the sun slowly emerged hazy and warm. Steph took her time as well and was happy to see Henry still asleep beside her. It was one of the things she loved most about the weekends. She chose to lie in bed and soak up the rich, cozy atmosphere. Turning back into her indentation, she carefully clutched the blankets as she shifted so as not to let in a draft.

Thankfully, Madeline waited until a decent hour by baby standards to rouse, then was up for the day. Steph slipped on a robe and carrier to hold Madeline, and then walked toward the kitchen. There, a few dishes remained from the previous night, but she decided to make her tea first. She could deal with those while the water boiled. As steam from the kettle slowly accumulated, Steph placed the dirty plates in the sink and started on the clean ones in the dishwasher. A *click* alerted her when her water was ready, and she grabbed a sachet of Earl Grey.

Atop her steaming mug, Steph placed a stroopwafel. The waffle sandwich cookie sat perfectly on the rim, trapping the steam, which softened the underside and the caramel in between. Waiting for a molten, gooey center was ideal, but Steph usually lost her patience a minute or two in and was happy enough to bite a little harder into the disk. It was still delicious.

Sugar-satiated and caffeinated, Steph set Madeline down in her bouncer and finished putting away the dishes, making the occasional *clang*. A yawn interrupted her and betrayed Henry's position a few feet behind. "I must have been a little too loud," Steph reckoned, looking back guiltily at her sleepy husband.

"Hey, how'd you sleep?" she asked.

"Fine," he answered. "You?"

"Alright." Henry started putting dishes away as well.

"Do you want to go to church this morning?"

"I think so," Steph replied. She moved onto loading the dirty dishes in the sink, keeping her mug out in case she wanted more tea later. "We should have enough time to get ready and not be too late." Eggs scrambled, bread toasted, and coffee brewed, they ate quickly and packed the dishes away as soon as they finished. Picking up Madeline, they headed back toward the bedroom to change.

Unlike old order Mennonites, who sported brims and bonnets, Steph and Henry dressed casually, as did the rest of their peace-loving congregation. For Madeline, Steph settled for a cute headband that screamed, "Girl." It showed some effort, while also being a time saver.

The family of three bundled in layers for the expected cold. Henry and Steph shivered in their compact car until it warmed up, while Madeline was nice and cozy under her fleece car seat cover.

The drive was brief, and they hustled through the opening door as a greeter welcomed them.

"Wow, you guys made it! I thought you'd still be desperate to catch up on some sleep. We use our kids to get out of going places all the time. Not that I would ever not want to be at church," Richard, the greeter, said smiling.

"We are. Well, Steph is. I sleep fine. Steph gets up with the baby. We were here last week actually," Henry replied. "What's your excuse? Did your daughters want to watch the Bills game?"

Richard laughed. "Speaking of it, it was a great game. They actually have a team this year. I'm already thinking of all the ways they're going to break my heart. Missed field goal. Fumble at the one-yard line. Botched handoff. Oh, the possibilities."

"By the way," Henry added. "I know it's last minute, but I'm having a poker night tomorrow. Do you think you can make it?"

"Sure. I don't know the rules, but sounds like fun. Should I bring anything?"

"It's easy to learn. Just bring $5.00."

After stepping through the entrance, a few others in the lobby greeted and smiled at them as well, happy to welcome new life into the building. Once again, the Wus sat near the back in case Steph needed to retreat for privacy and sound proofing, but Madeline allowed her to sit through an entire service on Cain and Abel.

There was no escaping it.

Suspects lived in Steph's building, and seemingly every time she left her house she ran into another. Now even at church, murder was being discussed from the pulpit. While sitting upright in the pew, Steph tried to wrap her head around the original murder mystery.

"Why did Cain kill Abel? Why did God prefer Abel's offering? What does any of it represent or mean?" There were theories but no definitive motive provided. Was it a precautionary tale about man's pursuit of advancement over reliance on God, she wondered, or a simple account of human nature.

In Steph's mind, perhaps the easiest and truest explanation was jealousy. Cain, bitter over the favor shown to Abel and not himself, had killed his brother. As a child whose biological father had rejected her, knowingly or not, Steph could relate to the intense desire for approval.

Ultimately, the speaker argued playing the comparison game was a dangerous thing, no matter what age or era. It distracted from the blessings of the present and led to resentment. Moreover, Jesus warned against anger, as murder began in the heart.

As the sermon ended and members milled around for coffee hour, Steph considered jealousy as a potential motive in Sameed's death. A jealous brother, a jealous wife, a jealous girlfriend… any of those were possible. Thankfully, someone brought in donuts to distract her from her musings. Steph helped herself to one, while friends and acquaintances drifted past eager to get another glimpse of the baby. Henry asked if he could get Steph some tea or coffee, but she declined. For the sake of Madeline's nap, they should head out soon, and chugging a blisteringly hot drink didn't appeal to her.

They hurried to the car once again to minimize exposure to the cold. Soon, they were back on their cozy, shop-lined avenue. They pulled into an open spot on the side street and walked around to the front door.

Once inside, Henry started rifling through the cabinets.

"What are you doing?"

"Looking for something to eat. I didn't grab a donut." He closed the cupboard and looked in the fridge a few times.

"Umm," Steph thought back to last night. "There's the food your parents brought." Steph wasn't sure she could stomach it herself, feeling ashamed again just thinking about it. Henry grabbed a container of homemade Chinese food and ate it cold. Steph much preferred her food warm, but everyone made choices in life. Henry eating, however, made her peckish too. She fixed herself a sandwich. They sat down at the table, although Henry quickly finished.

After she put her plate away, he asked, "Do you want to play a game?" Steph looked at the clock.

"Something quick. I don't think Madeline will give us much time."

"Blitz chess then?"

"Sure." Henry went to get his chess set and placed it in the middle of the table. Steph helped set up, but he corrected the placement of her queen, as her focus strayed from the game to other subjects. When she saw things weren't going well, she tried a few desperate trades and eventually knocked over her king to signal surrender.

Madeline still wasn't up yet, so Steph went to check on her. Every now and then her maternal instincts went into hyper drive, and she suspected the worst might have happened. However, Madeline was still sleeping soundly, and the angelic face inspired Steph to get her camera. Sensing the dark room, the flash went off, and Madeline stirred. Steph could have kicked herself. At least it was time for her to wake up, and their chess game was already over. Steph checked the photo. The quality could be better, but how could she delete any picture of her child, she thought, keeping it.

"I should go see Greg. He could do better… Hey, Henry?" she said, coming out of the nursery with Madeline.

"Yeah?" Henry's voice came from the bedroom. Steph stepped into the doorway.

"I want to talk to Greg for a second and see if maybe we can schedule a photo session with him."

"Okay. Do you want me to hold her?"

"No, I'm fine." Steph walked toward the

front door.

Up the single flight of stairs she went to the third floor. She knocked at the door. An eager tail thudded against the adjacent wall, ready for the door to open. Greg answered, asking who was there.

"It's Steph." He opened the door. Alaska pushed it further ajar with her snout and slipped out. Greg's hair was pulled back for once.

"Sorry if I disturbed you. Are you sick?" She pointed to a facemask around his neck and took a step back, but couldn't resist giving the dog a few scratches around the ears.

"It's nothing, just developing film," he said. Even so, Steph backed up another step and turned her body away from him in case of residual fumes, since she was holding Madeline.

"Anyway, I was wondering if your schedule was open sometime soon to do pictures. I can see that today is no good."

"Yeah, sorry."

"Let me know some other time that works," she said, starting to complete her turnaround.

"Sure." Greg whistled to Alaska to come, then closed the door. Steph walked back to her apartment. Henry was reclining with a book upon her return.

"So?"

"He's busy."

"That's too bad."

"Yeah." Before she could think of another

subject, the incessant *beep beep beep* of a truck backing up interrupted her train of thought. Steph looked out the window and saw Charlotte directing a white vehicle toward the rear end of the bakery for what must be a delivery. For a moment, Steph thought she also noticed a familiar pickup truck parked across the street, but it sped off before she could confirm.

Once out back, the delivery guy pulled out a dolly for sacks of heavy, dry ingredients and crates of fresh ones. Steph watched him zip in and out of the door. Charlotte must have propped it open for him. For a moment she wondered if her friend might need help unloading, until she noticed another employee – it looked like the newest one, John, she thought – helping her out. Steph was stronger than she looked, but she wasn't that strong. She recalled Charlotte telling her a little about him. He started at The Likable Daisy not knowing much about baking, but he had arm strength and could work a register. With some training, he could help out more in the kitchen.

From her perch, Steph watched the traffic downstairs and wondered what the party would be like. If it were anything like the events they'd hosted before, there would be plenty of food and, likely, things she had never tried before. There would also be people she suspected of foul play and the frustration of not having figured it out.

Sensing his wife's dour mood, Henry suggested, "How about we go to the park?"

Successfully diverted, Steph located her coat, hat, and scarf, while Henry did the same.

The intrepid family headed out despite the temperature to take advantage of the sun while it still shined, something they'd miss in a few short months. They waved to Charlotte, who was inside the bakery getting ready for the soft opening. Charlotte waved back, but was evidently too busy for a quick chat. Steph would catch up with her later.

Instead of walking to the nearest park, they ran back into the car for a short drive and forest views. The glen was beautifully still. Rain overnight had saturated the landscape and deepened every hue. Steph inhaled the clean, damp air and drank in the burbling stream. She wished she had at least packed a sketchbook, itching to etch the feeling the scene gave her. Hopefully, a couple poor pictures would do to keep her inspired later.

"Thinking about painting this?" Henry asked, standing beside the stroller.

"Mhmm." Her eyes remained on nature, snapping another photo with her phone.

"What do you think you'd use? Acrylic? Watercolor?" Steph considered which she'd prefer. Though used to oil-based paints, they weren't the best choice in a small apartment with a baby.

"I'd have better luck getting richer colors with acrylic paints, but the watercolors you bought would blend more nicely, help give it a dreamy feel." Henry smiled.

The couple stayed out as long as they dared, periodically touching Madeline's darling face to check its warmth. Everything else was bundled up and out of sight. After an hour of meandering through sodden leaves and soft, earthen paths, the family of three harkened to hunger and returned home.

The baby fussed during the drive. Steph sat in back in an attempt to soothe her, but Madeline wouldn't go down until she was fed and stationary. After their return, the remainder of the afternoon was quiet with Madeline's intermittent naps. Steph started to sketch the brook that had captured her attention earlier, but her thoughts were divided. She remembered about Rachel's taekwondo class and figured now was a good time to call. She could pick up her sketch again later.

"Hey, Henry?" He looked up from his book. The thickness suggested Tolstoy or Dostoyevsky.

"Yeah?"

"I think I'm going to call and ask about the taekwondo class Rachel mentioned."

"Really? Isn't it a little early for you to start exercising again?"

"Maybe, but it can't hurt to learn a little more about it in advance."

"Okay," Henry said. "I would have thought you'd get back into running."

"Oh, I will, but I think it might be fun to try something new too. And it's never a bad idea to learn self-defense." Henry agreed and went back to reading.

Steph looked up the number for Master Kwon's Taekwondo, then dialed as she walked toward the bedroom. This way, she wouldn't disturb Henry's reading, and Henry wouldn't ask her about the questions she was about to pose.

"Master Kwon's Taekwondo. How can we help you?" A male voice answered. Steph wondered if she were speaking to Master Kwon.

"Hi, I heard you have an adult class on Mondays? Is that correct?"

"Yes, we have a class from 5:30 to 7:00." It sounded as though a class were going on at that moment, but one full of children with their high-pitched shouts.

"Oh, wow, it's an hour and a half long?"

"Yes. Does that time work for you? If not, I can suggest another adult class."

"No, it does. Are there any other women who could spare with me?"

"There are, though you probably wouldn't spar if this is your first time."

"Oh, okay. So, how many women attend the Monday class, and how regularly do they attend? I don't want to spare with men if possible."

"There's Rachel. She's here every Monday night, and she's a black belt. You could learn a lot from her. And, there's Minju. She started earlier this year and comes every Monday and Wednesday. Actually, the Wednesday night class usually has at least three or more women in it, if that works better."

"Great! Thanks! Should I buy my own uniform before I start classes, or can I get one there?"

"You can wear regular workout clothes at your first lesson. We can help you order the right size dobok at the studio."

"Oh, good. Thanks so much for your help."

"Of course. We look forward to seeing you."

Steph hung up the phone and walked back out to the living room. Hopefully, the man who answered the phone didn't expect her tomorrow or any time soon. That said, Steph's conscience would likely hold her to her unspoken promise of attending at a later date.

"So, are you signed up for classes?" Henry asked.

"No, I'm going to wait, but they have a class Monday from 5:30 to 7:00."

"How's that going to work with a poker night?"

"Oh, you're right," Steph said. "Well, we'll wait and see. If I end up really liking taekwondo, then we can move poker night to another evening. They have a Wednesday night class too, but Rachel doesn't go to that one."

Having had little for lunch, Steph and Henry ate their dinner early, then packed the leftovers for Henry's lunch the next day. In the evening, they decided on a hand-drawn animated feature from Studio Ghibli. With a soothing soundtrack and gorgeous images, it thoroughly charmed and put their busy minds at ease. By the end of the night, Steph required less mental effort to let her suspicions rest, and anticipation of Wednesday's events took over. Visions of chocolate croissants and foamy cappuccinos danced in her head as she eagerly awaited the return of her favorite indulgences.

Madeline fell asleep during the movie. Laid in her bed, she seemed so small and so perfect. Life was certainly fuller having her out than still in, and as Steph walked toward her own room, she remained in awe of the tiny person she and Henry had created together. She came up behind her husband and held him close. They slid around each other to be face-to-face and kissed before splitting and both heading to the bathroom. They brushed their teeth, snuggled their customary snuggle, kissed again, said goodnight, and went to sleep.

As Steph's mind drifted, she reflected on the day's sleuthing. It suggested Rachel was innocent, not that Steph had ever strongly suspected her, and she was glad to rule out her friend. However, Sameed's killer remained unknown. Tomorrow, the coroner's office was open, and what she discovered would shock her.

CHAPTER 16

First thing Monday morning, Steph couldn't wait to call the coroner's office. She eagerly helped Henry get ready for work rather than laze in bed. The early start to the day would be worth it.

"Goodbye! Love you!" she called out after kissing him.

"Love you too," he echoed. "See you later, princess," he added, addressing Madeline, who looked pretty in pink.

Tummy full, Madeline wriggled happily in her bouncer, while Steph looked up the coroner's office at the kitchen table, coffee brewing.

"Record information requests... Monday through Friday ten to three," Steph read aloud. "Dang it." She would have to wait a few hours.

In the meantime, she could help get the apartment ready for poker night. Tidy up, check their supply of snacks and drinks, and locate a deck or two of cards... that was it. "Shouldn't be too difficult, right?" she told herself.

Thankfully, the party left them fairly well stocked, but the cards were nowhere to be found. She tried to think of the last time they had used them and drew up a blank.

"Where are poker cards?" she texted Henry.

"No idea." Dead end. Oh, well, she could always go out and buy more. Cards were cheap.

Steph indulged in a quick episode with the volume off while Madeline nursed and settled down. Seeing gardens reminded her of the walk in the park yesterday, and her desire to get creative reemerged. But, it would have to wait.

Once Madeline was down in her room, Steph dialed the coroner's office.

"Office of the Medical Examiner."

"Hi, I'd like to request a copy of a recent autopsy report, it should be under the name Sameed Ishaaq Haddad." Steph recited the letters of each name to the receptionist.

"I'm sorry. We have no autopsy reports available under that name. Do you want me to connect you to another office? It's possible someone else performed it."

"No. No, thank you. Perhaps, I was mistaken. Thank you for your help."

"You're welcome. Have a nice day."

"You too. Bye."

Steph hung up the phone wondering why there would be no results. Sameed had died here. The local police had briefly investigated his death before determining it was an accident, so it was unlikely his case would have been moved to another county.

"What if there never was an autopsy?" Steph considered, reviewing the timeline of events, her neighbor's death, an almost immediate burial with family only, and the flower-less reception. Sharon had told her the reason for the rush and other funeral arrangements was religious. Maybe the lack of autopsy was for religious reasons too.

Steph's fingers typed in a flurry of activity, searching for more information. The quick burials were for purity, and same sex relatives were responsible for cleansing the body. She kept reading. Sure enough, most Muslims avoided autopsies unless absolutely necessary to avoid "breaking the bones" of the dead, which Muhammad compared to breaking those of the living. Since Sameed's death had been ruled an accident, his family would have had little reason to desire an undesirable procedure. If Steph wanted the police to reconsider, she'd need to convince Sameed's family of its necessity. Her stomach lurched, and she wondered if there was any way around it.

There were noninvasive autopsies. She hoped that would be enough to be decisive. "But what if his family is guilty?" she asked herself. It would be a waste of time or worse to try to bring it up. At the very least, she should try to establish an alibi before approaching Ayman, who likely had prepared his brother for burial.

"Think. Think. Think," she commanded. "What were Ayman and Sameed arguing about in the bakery?"

There had been a woman, most likely Sharon, and a missed evening prayer. She kicked herself for not remembering earlier. Perhaps, just like Rachel, Ayman regularly attended on Monday nights. Steph called up Sharon. She would know which mosque the family went to and might even have Ayman's number, but Steph also didn't want to suggest murder at this time either. She'd have to come up with an excuse for asking.

"Hi, Sharon?"

"Hi, Steph. What's up?"

"My church is planning an interfaith event, and I was wondering if you knew the name of the mosque the Haddad family attends."

"Sure, it's called the Islamic Center. It's right off of Exit 15."

"Thanks."

"Of course. Let me know once you've picked a date. I'd love to attend," Sharon said. Steph thought, "Now I need to plan an interfaith event too, not that that's a bad thing." One of these days, she'd get to it.

"I will. Do you also happen to have Ayman's number? I thought I might reach out to him with the idea first."

"I do. Hold on just a sec. He gave me his card recently." Sharon dug through her purse. "I should probably put it in my phone," she said more to herself. After finding it, she recited the number to Steph, who heard other voices in the background.

"Thanks again. Am I calling you at work? I should probably let you go, right?" she asked, hoping to move onto the next step of her investigation.

"Yeah, I can't talk for long, but maybe we can

meet up again later this week."

"Speaking of later this week, before I forget, The Likeable Daisy is reopening. Leyla and Charlotte are throwing a party Wednesday night to celebrate. I'm sure you're welcome to come."

"Leyla already invited me, but thanks for letting me know. I guess I'll see you Wednesday night then."

"Great. I'll see you then."

Two calls down, at least one or more to go. Steph looked up the mosque's number, but before she could dial, Madeline started to fuss in the nursery, the monitor in the kitchen broadcasting her complaint.

Steph picked up the sweet, little burrito, unwrapping her to check if she were wet. Swiftly, she unsnapped buttons, changed the diaper, and re-snapped the pajamas closed, covering up the tiny toes. Maybe, there was a safe art project she could do with those adorable feet, something to research later.

It was noon. Steph took a quick lunch and played with Madeline before setting her down again to call Ayman.

"Haddad Auto Renovation & Repair." Steph scribbled down the name quickly to look up the address later.

"Hi, my name is Jen-ny," Steph introduced, trying to countrify her voice. "And I'm callin' with the National Center for Abrahamic Faiths. Do you mind if I ask a few questions for a survey on religious practice? It won't take more 'n five minutes."

"Sure."

"Do you practice one of the three Abrahamic religions, Islam, Judaism, or Christianity?

"Yes, Islam."

"You're quick. That was my next question. And, how often do you attend a religious service, prayer, or other practice outside of your home?"

"Several times a week."

"Do you mean one to two, three to five, six to seven, or more than seven?"

"Three to five."

"On which days do you attend services typically?"

"I try to go every two days, Monday, Wednesday, and Friday, but sometimes I attend other prayers."

"At what time are these prayers scheduled?"

"I attend evening prayer most days, which takes place after sunset, and *Jumu'ah* on Friday, which is just after noon." Steph realized she'd need to look that up to get more specific times.

"How long do those services last?"

"Prayer is a few minutes long, but on Friday, there is also a lecture."

"And how long is that?"

"About the same length."

"Thank you. So, each service would be fewer than fifteen minutes, between a quarter and half an hour, between half and a full hour, or more than one hour?"

"No more than thirty minutes," he answered. Steph thought that wasn't very long at all. She tried to think of another question. She knew in other religions, it was necessary to wash before entering a holy place, and it seemed Islam also valued cleanliness from her knowledge of Sameed's funeral.

"Sir, do you prepare before you attend prayer?"

"Yes, I practice ablution." That was a new word for Steph. She quickly looked it up.

"And how long do you spend on... ritual purification?"

"A few minutes to a half hour, longer for *Jumu'ah*."

"You've answered all my questions, sir. Thank you so much for participating in our survey to increase awareness of national religious practice."

"You're welcome."

Steph quickly looked online. Two weeks ago, Ayman would have been at the mosque around 6:15. It wasn't impossible for Ayman to have been at the bakery after closing and killed his brother, but it was looking highly unlikely for him to race back to clean up himself, collect his sons, and be on time for evening prayer. Moreover, Steph's only chance of getting the police involved was convincing his family that an autopsy was necessary. She looked at the piece of paper in her hands. It was time for more detective work.

After Madeline went down for another nap, Steph called Jane with the latest.

"Jane!"

"What?" Jane was grateful her shift hadn't started because she was sure Steph had something.

"There was no autopsy."

"What? How's that possible?"

"Ruled an accident, family didn't want one…"

"I'm surprised, but some things don't show up right away."

"What do you mean?" Steph asked.

"Bruising, for one. Haven't you ever knocked into a table, then were surprised by a big purple splotch a few days later? Like that."

"Jane, you genius! The medical examiner saw the tie in the mixer, cause of death, and made a quick determination. There was no time for fingers to leave a discernable mark and suggest otherwise."

"Maybe," Jane said. "What are you going to do next?"

"I, well, I need to convince his family to request an autopsy."

"You what? Don't you suspect his brother?"

"I did, but…"

"But what, did you learn something new?"

"He was at evening prayer that night. I find it really unlikely."

"Okay." Jane didn't want to think about who

was still suspect. "So, are you going to talk to him?" Steph thought it over. She made up her mind.

"Yes, but I want to do it in person. Can you help me?"

"What do you want?"

"Drive me to his garage, today, now even, if you can. Watch Madeline for me."

"You're crazy. I'll be there in ten."

True to her word, Jane was there within ten minutes, a bag of hospital clothes packed in the back in case she ran out of time.

"Do you have to go to work soon?"

"I've got time. Don't worry about it. Where are we going?"

Steph pulled up the address of the business associated with the number Sharon had provided.

"Here. It's a car repair shop." It was in a manner of speaking. As they pulled up, Jane and Steph "oohed" and "aahed" over the vintage and classic models parked to the side and being worked on in the garage. There was a familiar 1969 Mercedes sitting outside, ready to be driven off. Bidding goodbye to the aged but still handsome Ayman was Abila herself. Steph peeked over the car door, not wanting to be recognized.

They seemed to be standing pretty close to each other, Steph noted. She need not have worried about being seen, for their eyes only looked at each other. Ayman handed Abila her keys back, and she smiled, thanking him. Judging by his clothes, he must have worked it on himself. Abila drove off none the wiser of Steph's proximity.

"So, what's your plan?" Jane asked.

"His shop seems like a good, visible place to meet him, just in case I'm wrong about the alibi. He'll probably have an office for privacy. I'll have my phone on me. Text if Maddie starts to get upset. I'll try to be quick."

"And if you're right?" Steph's stomach dropped.

"Then I'm about to drop an emotional bomb on the poor man at work."

Steph left the car, heart pumping. She walked toward where she'd last seen Ayman. Another mechanic approached her.

"Can I help you?"

"I'm looking for Ayman."

"He just got under a car. One second. I'll get him." The mechanic walked over to a cherry red Austin-Healey. "Ayman! Lady here wants to talk to you." Ayman rolled out from beneath. All of a sudden Steph was parched.

"Hi," he said, cleaning himself up briefly. "I know you, don't I? One of Sameed's friends, is that right?"

"Yes," Steph said, clutching her purse in one hand. "Actually, I wanted to talk about him if you have a minute." Ayman wasn't sure what to expect. He gestured toward his office. Steph took note of the dark windows and the noise of the work around her. Perhaps, this wasn't as safe as she had thought.

Knowing his crew was watching, Ayman

made sure all the blinds were raised to maintain a sense of propriety. Steph relaxed. She sat down in one of the two chairs she assumed were for clients, noticing a prayer rug in the corner.

"What did you want to discuss?" Ayman sat behind his desk. Two photographs showed two different families of four. In one, there was Ayman, Sameed, their late father, and mother, and in the other, Ayman, his two sons, and a woman who must have been his late wife. Steph pitied him for all that he had lost in a few short years.

"I'm sorry," Steph apologized in advance. "But I have reason to suspect your brother was murdered." Ayman didn't move.

"How is that possible? The police said it was an accident."

"I believe the accident was staged. I've talked to the head baker, who described the scene to me, and my friend, who's a nurse, says bruising doesn't appear immediately. So, it's possible the medical examiner didn't have enough information."

"How can you be so sure? What business is it of yours?" Ayman hadn't lost his composure, but he seemed affronted.

"I don't know what the police know," she started. "But I do know that your brother had dinner plans. I know that he wasn't dressed for baking, nor was the kitchen prepped. I know that there was dust on the back of his shirt and that his watch was broken." Ayman was quiet for a moment.

"What do you want from me?"

"I think if someone reexamined the body now, they would come to a different conclusion, and the police would investigate."

"I buried my brother, and you want me to disturb his body? Do you know how important it is not to do that? I want the police's opinion. Have you told them these things?"

"Forgive me. I understand the religious significance. I know there are specific rules related to timing and ceremony. You were there for the ritual cleansing, correct?"

"Yes, I was there," he said, his voice lowering as he recalled the washing and wrapping.

"Did you notice any bruising on the body?" Ayman weighed his options. He could cut this interrogation and all the personal questions short, or he could entertain the idea that his brother was murdered. As different as they were, as much as he disagreed with his brother's choices in life, Ayman loved his brother, and a part of him believed Steph.

"Yes."

"Can you describe it?" Steph asked. His face was like granite. "I know this is difficult," she added.

"Do you? Can you imagine what it's like lowering your lifeless little brother into the ground, never to see him again? Wondering, how could this have happened? We were boys together. We became men together. You hardly knew him." Though she knew he was speaking out of hurt, her guilty feelings returned. A moment later, he added, "There were bruises on his back… and his neck, of course."

"The bruises on his neck, were they in a straight line? Were they even?"

"Yes." Steph's shoulders dropped, thinking her theory was toast. "And no. There was a line across his neck, but it was also mottled in places." She sat up straight again.

"Didn't you find that suspicious?" After the words left her mouth, Steph could have kicked herself for saying something so rude to the brokenhearted man.

"My brother was dead. The police ruled it an accident. Wouldn't you want to grieve and move on?"

"I'm sorry. Of course, but it suggests your brother was strangled by humans hands, not a machine. Anyway, I think you should tell the police, if you want to, that is. But you should know if they consider your brother's death a homicide, then they're going to order an autopsy." Ayman was silent.

"I should go. I'm so sorry, Ayman. Truly." Steph started to rise. As she did, Ayman imitated her and moved toward the door.

After she walked out, Ayman closed the door and all the blinds. Steph could only imagine his pain.

Back at the car, Steph found one of the mechanics chatting up Jane. Typical.

"I can hear your timing is off. I can fix it for you right now for free if you agree to go on a date with me," he offered.

"No, thanks," Jane said, decisively. "I have a boyfriend. He's a Navy SEAL."

"Sure, he is. Well, it sounds like the timing's not right with me too, but if you change your mind, you know where to find me." Jane thanked God that he walked off after that.

"Phew, close call. Glad you're okay."

"How's Madeline?" Steph inquired.

"Oh, she's fine. How'd it go?"

"Well enough. I'm alive, right?"

"But did you convince him?" Jane cut to the chase.

"I don't know. I hope so."

Jane drove back, stopping once at a gas station on the way. Seeing the ads for the lotto reminded Steph of the upcoming poker night. After Jane filled up, Steph entered the station to purchase two packs of cards, paying quickly.

Back in the car, the baby informed her mother that she was about to reach her limit.

"By the way, is David coming tonight?" Steph asked.

"I told him he had to," Jane said.

"I'll count that as a yes then."

Jane returned them to their abode, wishing her friend a good evening.

Emotionally exhausted, Steph collapsed on the couch. She didn't have the energy to even think who might have killed Sameed, let alone consider whether she would tell Henry. She lounged on the couch with Madeline, not even watching anything, just letting her mind wander.

In the middle of her blank state, she received a message from Henry.

"Can you pick up a bottle of something for tonight?"

Steph thought about it. There was a small liquor store not that far away, and she could always make herself some caffeine if necessary. Once Madeline awoke from her catnap, Steph loaded her up in the carrier and started walking.

A few blocks away sat Fischer's Liquor & Wines. Steph and Henry had been going to the shop for years, and while other stores boasted larger selections, they always found something they liked at Fischer's.

Normally, Steph gravitated toward wine or champagne, for special occasions, so she felt a little lost looking at stronger offerings without Henry. She stared for some time at the wall of spirits, trying to discern the merits of one over the other.

"This one has a buffalo on it, that's seems manly, but that sounds like a Scottish name. And Scots are known for their scotch, right?" Her eyes read one description after another, each bottle claiming epic founding or rarity. As a graphic designer for an ad agency, Steph knew the labels reflected less fact than fiction, but it didn't help her pick one.

The owner, a third generation Fischer, sensed her indecision and came over to offer his expertise.

"What are you looking for?" he asked, a simple question.

"Umm, I don't know," Steph confessed, then realizing she was wearing a newborn quickly explained, "It's for my husband's poker night, not me."

"I wouldn't judge you if it were. What does your husband like?"

"Whiskey?" She wondered if she should go aged eight or twelve years, oak barrels or bourbon. There were a few too many options for Steph even at this shop.

"These two are popular," the salesman offered, pulling down two different bottles. "One is single-malt and the other is blended, but I'd recommend something else if you're planning on making mixed drinks."

"No, I'll take those," Steph said, checking the price. Surely, getting two was a better bet than risking one, only to find out later that Henry didn't like it.

"Have a nice day!" Mr. Fischer said after wrapping up her purchases.

"Thanks, you too."

Steph walked back quickly, eager to pick up the pace before any passersby realized she was carrying not one, but two bottles of whiskey in a paper bag. She made it home in record time.

Now physically tired, Steph plopped back down on the coach with Madeline. After a few minutes, she decided coffee wasn't such a bad idea, even this late in the afternoon, so she place the baby in the bouncer, while she brewed. This was how Henry found them when he returned home.

"Hey, how was your day? Making coffee this late?"

"Yeah, I came back from Fischer's not that long ago. I hope I found something you'll like. I bought two different kinds of whiskey just in case. One is scotch."

"I'm sure they'll be fine," Henry reassured. "Thanks for picking it up. What else did you do today?"

The truth came spilling out.

"I called the coroner. They said there was no autopsy, so I went to go see Ayman to ask what he saw."

"You went to go see Ayman? In person?" Henry looked incredulous.

"Yes, but I was pretty sure he was at the mosque when it happened because when I called and asked–"

"You what? I can't believe…" Henry abruptly turned about face and walked to their bedroom without another word.

Steph winced as the door clicked to a close, considering what her husband must have felt or was feeling.

Betrayed. Livid. Scared that his wife went to meet with a potential murderer. As urgently as she wanted Henry to come back into the room, so she could say she was sorry, she also dreaded his return. Under hear breath she wondered aloud, "Should I go in there now, or should I leave him alone? If I don't go, he might fume even longer, but if I go in too soon…" She didn't think she could stomach another second of that injured look in his eyes plus the silent treatment.

Guilt ate at her. Minutes ticked away. Fretfully, Steph looked for something to tidy up to burn the nervous energy. She made two sandwiches instead. She also razed the cabinets to see what they had in terms of ingredients, hoping she could fabricate a worthy apology out of carbs and sugar. She haphazardly threw wet and dry together. As the first tray of cookies clanged on the oven rack to bake, the bedroom door opened, and heavy steps creaked on the old hardwood floors.

Surprised, Steph bumped the inside of her forearm on the hot metal, letting out a four-letter word as her skin sizzled. It wasn't her first second-degree burn, nor would it be her last, but it would smart for the rest of the night and probably scar. Feeling stupid about her rookie mistake, she couldn't help but look angrily when she turned around.

Steph closed the oven door and set the timer, waiting for Henry to say something. Neither could make eye contact. Two minutes on the digital display passed, and Steph couldn't bear the silence any longer. She stated the obvious in forced cheeriness, her face directed at the oven, maintaining the pretense of needing to keep vigil over her baked goods. "I made cookies. The first batch should be done soon." The insufficient admission of guilt glued Henry's tongue, and it grated on her.

Whether intentional or not, Steph hated when he concealed himself, his thoughts and his feelings, from her. She felt it was wrong to hide from each other, chastising herself as well. Steph turned and beheld his totem pole-like stance. Finally, he spoke, keeping his distance. She strained to hear.

"What if something had happened to you?"

"I'm sorry. It was irresponsible and dangerous of me," she admitted. "I should have talked to you first. Ayman, he, I saw his face at the reception and today at the garage. That man was broken. I don't think he could have laid a finger on his brother, no matter how mad he was."

"You think, but you don't know, Steph. It boggles my mind how someone so smart can be so reckless." Arrows pierced her. Henry concluded his case succinctly. "I can't afford to lose you. Madeline can't afford to lose you. Please don't *ever* do something like that again."

"I promise," she choked. In silence, she grieved how stupid she felt, how thoughtless she had been putting herself in danger. She mourned her frustration and fatigue, the weeks of not sleeping, her residual pain, and the isolation. She leaned back against the oven for warmth and support, wrapping her arms around herself. She would have preferred a hug from her husband, but she feared being rebuffed, though he never had before.

"I'm sorry." Henry walked over and put a hand on her shoulder. "I just… you're home and you're safe now, and that's what matters." Steph sniffled and leaned into the touch. "Why do you need this so much," he asked after a moment. "Why can't you let it rest, leave it to the police?"

"I… I don't know."

The timer went off, and he grabbed the oven mitts.

"We can bake the rest some other time," he said, turning off the oven. "Is this for me?" He pointed to the sandwich. Steph nodded yes. "Thanks."

She changed topics. "I picked up some cards earlier."

Realization dawned on Henry's face. The thought of poker night had been a million miles away. "I invited my coworker Jason earlier. He said he could make it, and Richard from church texted me back too, saying he's free tonight. Who else is coming?"

"Dennis, Greg, and David. Is that enough people? Too many?" Steph knew very little about poker.

"No, that should be good. You said you picked up some cards?"

"Yes. Are two packs enough?"

"Yes, thanks."

"Wait, what about poker chips? Don't you need something to bet with? Do we have any? Drinks? Do we have enough? Besides the two bottles of whiskey." The last thing Steph wanted was for tonight to be another failure. She felt she owed it to Henry to provide an enjoyable evening.

"We have poker chips," Henry assured her. "And we should have plenty enough drinks even if they all turn out to be hard drinkers. Jason will probably bring something. Maybe others will too."

"Oh, okay. Good." They were all set then. Steph could relax, leisurely prepare the kitchen for hosting, then maybe get back to her sketch in another room while they played.

Once again Dennis was the earliest to arrive and came with a snack offering. Thankfully, it was only a few minutes before the hour. Next were David, Jason, Richard, and Greg. It didn't surprise Henry. It seemed people who lived the closest always showed up last to events, parties and church services, overestimating how much time they had. A less gracious host would assume impoliteness.

Before he sat down, David pulled out a bottle of bourbon, setting it on the counter by the glasses Henry had pulled out.

"Sorry about Saturday," he said, referring to his argument with Sharon.

"I know what it's like to have a sister," Henry replied sympathetically, though he hadn't caught the topic of dispute. "Thanks for bringing the bourbon."

Jason too pulled out a bottle but of wine.

"This is a 1998 Château Mouton-Rothschild, and I brought some Camembert and Roquefort to accompany it." He pulled out two cheeses. Greg looked at him like "are you for real?" wondering what kind of person brought expensive wine to a poker night. One glass probably cost more than the entire pot.

"Thanks, Jason!" Henry put the proffered bottle and appetizers on the counter, then grabbed a couple wine glasses and a corkscrew. These joined six small plates, a bowl of salted nuts, sliced salami, cheddar, and a tray of crackers, as well as a bottle opener. "There's also beer in the fridge and hard liquor in this cabinet here, for those who are interested. Help yourself."

Richard cracked open a pale ale and stabbed a few cubes of cheddar and salami. David grabbed a few slices of salami and chips, and poured himself a dram of scotch, trying one of Henry's. Greg started with the single-malt Henry's father had brought the week before, while Jason poured himself a glass of wine and held out the bottle, offering it to the others. Dennis accepted, as did Henry, who also poured a finger of David's offering.

"What do you think?" Jason asked. "Are you getting the berry liqueur and floral notes?" Dennis looked like a kid surprised by a pop quiz.

"It's good, fruity," he answered honestly. Jason wondered if this perhaps weren't the right crowd to appreciate the wine.

"That's intense," Henry said, guessing, "hints of chocolate?" He hoped to make his friend feel a little more comfortable.

"Yes." Jason smiled.

"I bet Steph would like this too." Henry poured a half glass for his wife and brought it to her, happy to see her scribbling away. "Jason brought this. It's good. There's cheese to go with it too if you want."

"Yes, please. And thank you." Steph looked up and beamed at him. Henry had told her about Jason, but she hadn't met him too many times. From what she knew, the wine and cheese wouldn't disappoint. Henry left for a minute, returning with a plate of Camembert and salami. "You didn't have to bring me so much. You have guests," she protested weakly. It *did* look good.

"We have plenty. Don't worry."

"Good. Can I help with anything?"

"No, we're fine."

"Okay, have fun!"

"Thanks."

Back in the kitchen, Greg had already starting cutting one of the new decks, snapping the cards as he shuffled them. David picked up the other deck and followed suit, so they'd be ready to play a second hand right after the first.

"I can deal," Richard offered, enjoying what felt like a second dinner. "I know nothing about poker, so it's for the best."

"No, you should play," Henry insisted. "I can help explain." He got up to grab a sheet of paper. "Here, I printed out a ranking of hands. Anyone else want a copy?"

"No thanks," a few said. The rest were comfortable with their poker knowledge.

"I guess I should introduce everybody," Henry said, starting with his neighbors to his left. "This is Greg."

"Hey," Greg said before taking another sip of whiskey.

"He lives upstairs. And this is Dennis, our landlord."

"Hi."

"On my right…" Henry continued, gesturing toward Richard, who lowered the poker rankings and a handful of nuts. "…is Richard, a buddy from church. Next to him is Jason, from work, and across from me is David, a new friend, just back from Afghanistan, right?"

"Sir, yes, sir!" David saluted in mock seriousness.

"I didn't know people in the military could have beards," Greg said. "What were you doing over there, selling rugs?"

"It is their largest export," David informed

him. "But no. Special forces are allowed beards in certain areas."

Henry set the example, being the first to deal. He flipped a card to Greg, then moving clockwise to Dennis, David, Jason, Richard, and finally himself before repeating the circle. David, Greg, and Henry peeled up the ends of their two cards, while Richard picked his up.

"Keep your cards lower," Henry advised. "Otherwise, everyone else can see them." Richard lowered his cards. Dennis and Jason pulled their cards up high and tight, quickly taking a look, then setting them back facedown on the table.

It was David's bet. The stakes were low, a $5 buy-in, but that didn't mean tensions didn't run high.

"Gotta spend money to make money," he said, pushing a short stack of chips into the middle of the table. He bet double the big blind.

Jason picked up his cards again as if they might have changed in the last few seconds. He frowned, folded, and pushed his cards toward Henry.

"What am I supposed to do?" Richard asked.

"You can either match David's bet or fold."

Richard cautiously added his chips. Henry did as well.

Greg raised it to fifty, double check bet size. Dennis fiddled with his glasses and folded. Jason followed. David threw in the required twenty to match Greg. Once again, Richard looked to Henry.

"If you want to stay in the game, you need to add twenty."

"Or I fold?"

"Or you fold. Remember, I am going to lay down three more cards, which will count toward your hand and everyone else's."

"Okay, I'm out," Richard said, tossing a pair of eights, which resulted in a few raised eyebrows.

"Don't flip over your cards after you fold," Henry advised before he too folded, cards facedown. He then turned over the flop, revealing an ace, nine, and three. Greg bet one hundred.

"You can have this one," David said.

"I'll take them all eventually," Greg replied confidently.

"I'm going to take all this cheese if you guys aren't going to eat any," Richard threatened.

"Hand some over here," Dennis called out.

"And here," David added after disposing of his cards.

"So, how huge is your wife now?" Henry asked Richard, while Greg dealt.

"Pretty big, ready to burst any minute. The last kid was way past the due date too, so we ate tons of Indian takeout. Spicy food is supposed to encourage labor. I guess it kind of worked, but I felt sorry for my wife. Spicy in, spicy out, not a pleasant experience when you've got stitches down there." Greg looked thoroughly disgusted.

"I didn't think I wanted kids before, and now I never will," he swore. "A dog is good enough for me."

"Dogs are great," Richard agreed. "I had to put mine down last week." Greg got up and left the table to pour himself some of Jason's wine after he finished dealing.

"Sorry, man," David said.

"That's too bad. How'd the girls take it?" Henry asked.

"Better than I did. The vet handed me a pamphlet on grief. The girls asked me when we were getting a new puppy."

"That's enough of that," Greg said. "No more dead dog or diarrhea talk." He returned to the table to sit and look at his cards. As Jason did the same, David noticed his wrist.

"Nice watch," he commented.

"Thanks. It was a gift from a client." Jason unstrapped the watch and turned it over. "It has a transparent case back, so you can see all the mechanisms, and a moon phase sub-dial."

"Are you a werewolf or something?" Richard asked. A few chuckled at the obvious dad joke.

"No," Jason replied.

"That watch is dope," Greg said. "Mind if I take a look?"

"Sure, no problem." Jason handed it over.

"I wish I had a client like that," David said. "Must be nice."

"Don't you work for the U.S. government?" Dennis asked.

"As a Navy SEAL, not a defense contractor."

"Time to make your bets," Greg reminded. People added their chips and refilled their glasses in turn.

Dennis paid the small blind. David paid the big, as did Jason and Richard. Henry raised it before Greg overbid once again. Everyone folded except David.

"You're not getting away with that again," David warned.

"Hey, I've gotta pay off my student loans somehow," Greg defended.

Henry stopped the bidding after three raises and flipped over a seven, a queen, and a ten.

David raised the bid again, and Greg didn't back down. It was time for the final reveal.

Henry flipped a jack and a four.

The last to raise the stakes, David turned over a queen and a four. Greg too revealed a queen. A king in the same suit followed.

"Ooh!" Someone exclaimed.

"Yeah!" David shouted, slamming the table with one hand. "That's how I like it!" He pulled the pile of chips over to his side of the table. Greg relaxed back in his chair as if he hadn't just lost the majority of his stash.

Henry, Dennis, and Richard switched to beer. Jason continued to casually sip wine, as Greg and David consciously or unconsciously committed to a drinking contest. They seemed equally tall, though David was broader.

As the night progressed, a dozen bottles of

beer dwindled to two, the ice ran out, and the whiskey was more than half drunk. The snacks had depleted a mouthful at a time, as players crunched in concentration. After his big win, David had held onto his lead with more conservative bets. Coming hadn't been so bad after all for him.

"Same time next week?" Henry suggested.

"If you're hosting," David said.

"Sure," the rest agreed. It had been fun, and five dollars was nothing.

"Does anyone need a ride home?" Henry asked.

"I'm good to drive," David said.

"Same," Richard and Jason added. Henry knew Greg and Dennis could easily walk to their respective apartments. "Thanks for the invite."

After she heard the other men leave, Steph popped her head out to help Henry clean up.

"So, how'd it go?" she inquired. Henry looked a little tipsy, and he was normally talkative when he was.

"It was fun! Greg played loose and aggressive, like a snake, over-betting often. Dennis and Richard, pretty mousy, prey for the ballsier players, but every now and then, when Dennis was backed into a corner, he would come out with a great bluff to stay alive. And Jason had no discernable strategy."

"What about David? Did he have a good time?" Steph hoped Henry got along with David, since Jane was so keen on him. She swept the floor for crumbs, while Henry put away glasses.

"He better have. The guy won!"

"Really?" Steph looked up from the dustpan.

"Yeah. He was goaded a few times into big bets, but overall came out on top. Most of the game he went after small and medium-sized pots, but he knew when to retreat and not waste chips. More conservative than Greg," Henry assessed. "But always pushing forward."

"Sounds like a great night. So, are you going to have another one?"

"I hope so, especially if Jason keeps bringing $800 wine."

As Steph and Henry settled for the night, Steph was grateful for a fun-filled evening to replace the memory of her misadventure. Tomorrow was a new day. The case was in someone else's hands, and she prayed for the best. Now, if only her conscience would leave her alone and let her sleep.

CHAPTER 17

Tuesday morning, a fist rapped on the glass door marked The Likable Daisy.

"We're closed until tomorrow," Charlotte shouted.

The rapping continued. Who could it be, she wondered, dusting her hands on her apron, but instead of a customer like she expected, there stood Detective O'Brian.

"Oh, sorry," she apologized, unlocking the door. "How can I help you?"

"Are you Charlotte Jeffords?" O'Brian asked.

"Yes."

"Is it alright if I ask you a few questions?"

"Of course." Charlotte sat down at the nearest table. O'Brian joined her.

"Where were you Monday evening two weeks ago?" Charlotte tried to think back.

"Probably at home with my cat."

"Were you alone?"

"Yes."

"Did you work in the bakery earlier that day?"

"Yes, I did. I started at 5:00."

"And how late did you work?"

"'Til about 2:00. After that, I left the register to John, the new guy, and..."

"And?" O'Brian probed.

"And Sameed. He stays, stayed, until closing, then locked up."

"Did he always stay until the bakery closed?"

"Yes." O'Brian scribbled some notes down.

"Did anything unusual happen that day?"

"Nothing too out of the ordinary, except Sameed argued with someone, I think maybe his brother."

"Do you recall what they argued about?"

"It wasn't clear. I was in the kitchen, and I think they were speaking Arabic."

"Who else was in the bakery at that time?"

"John and some customers."

"I see. What are his hours?"

"9:00 to 5:00."

"After closing, are there any employees around after hours?"

"No, not unless Sameed had some business to do in his office."

"Did he usually stay late?"

"Not that I'm aware of."

"Are you the first employee here in the morning?"

"Yes."

"How do you get in?"

"I have a set of keys." Charlotte patted the pocket where she kept them.

"Does anyone else have keys to the building?"

"Yes, Leyla, his mother, his ex-wife Abila, and Dennis, our landlord."

"Who has Mr. Haddad's set of keys now?" O'Brian asked.

"His mother," she answered.

"They never went missing?"

"No, they didn't."

"How long did you know Mr. Haddad?"

"Seven years. We met working at a restaurant together, then he invited me to join him when he opened up The Likable Daisy," she explained.

"Can you think of anyone who would have reason to kill him?"

"No."

"Is there anyone you know who benefits from his death?" O'Brian held his pen suspended over the paper, waiting for any lead.

"Maybe his ex-wife, but I'm not sure she would."

"Who owns The Likable Daisy now?"

"Leyla and I are partners," Charlotte said, wondering how many more questions O'Brian would ask.

"That's all for now. Thank you very much, Miss Jeffords. I'll be in touch."

"You're welcome."

Charlotte followed the detective to the front door, locking up. She slumped into a chair, thinking Steph was right. Sameed was murdered.

Not long after, a knock on the door

interrupted the flow of the morning before Henry left for work.

"Who could that be?" Steph asked. Henry shrugged his shoulders and went to answer.

"Who is it?" Henry said.

"Detective O'Brian," a voice replied. Henry cracked open the door. "I'd like to ask a few questions if that's alright."

Henry saw the badge and opened it wider. O'Brian walked in with a pad and pen. "Please sit down anywhere." Henry gestured toward the kitchen table and living room.

"Thank you. I'll only be a few minutes," the detective promised. All three adults sat down, O'Brian in the armchair, the Wus on the couch. "Mr. and Mrs. Wu, correct?"

"Yes."

"Where were you Monday night, two weeks ago?" Steph and Henry looked at each other, surmising that the police were, in fact, investigating Sameed's death.

"Here," they both replied.

"All night," Steph emphasized.

"Did you notice anything unusual earlier that day?"

"No." Steph replied first. "I stopped by The Likable Daisy that morning for a cappuccino and talked to Sameed. It seemed like a normal day except that Sameed argued with his brother." She felt a little guilty mentioning it after having spoken to Ayman personally.

"About what?"

"I think Sameed's girlfriend, and Ayman wanted him to go to evening prayer that night."

"Anything else?"

"That was all I heard," Steph answered.

"And you?" O'Brian directed his head and question at Henry.

"I only walked into the bakery for a minute. Charlotte, one of the bakers, wanted me to give Steph a few cinnamon rolls in case she wasn't feeling up to making an in-person visit later." O'Brian's pen scratched across the paper every now and then, but it didn't seem like they were helping him much.

"And did you notice anything unusual or out of the ordinary while you were there?"

"No, I was in and out. Sorry."

"Later that evening, did you hear anything downstairs, after the bakery closed?"

"No, it's pretty quiet after they close. It's one of the reasons why we like living here," Henry explained.

"Actually," Steph said, thinking back to that night. "I recall hearing the backdoor slam."

"And that was unusual?" O'Brian followed up.

"Yes. I didn't think it at the time, but Sameed never let the door slam as a courtesy to his neighbors. I remember because I was so surprised – it's quite a loud door – I dropped a bowl and broke it."

"Around what time was that?"

"Um," Steph tried to recall. "Maybe a little after six, we were cleaning up dishes after dinner, and Henry's usually home by 5:30."

"I see." The officer scribbled down some notes. "Do you have any reason to suspect your neighbor's death wasn't accidental?" Steph wondered what he already knew.

"Yes, we found the circumstances to be suspicious. He was a talented baker. It seemed unlikely for him to be killed by his own mixer."

"Were there other reasons?"

"Yes," Steph answered curtly. Madeline looked annoyed, probably hungry. "I've already explained them to the police, but I can list them again if you need."

"Right! You're *the* Mrs. Wu, the one with the cake!" Steph reddened with embarrassment, having hope he hadn't noticed her at the police station. Harris must have told him. At least Henry wouldn't have time to ask before he needed to go to work. "Got it," he continued. "Thank you. Do you suspect anyone at this point in time?" Truthfully, she did, but Steph knew she didn't have enough to indict any one person. And she didn't want to cause anyone any additional grief without being sure. She held her tongue.

"I don't know, sir. His death surprised all of us." O'Brian looked to Henry.

"I don't have a clue," he answered. Madeline started fussing audibly.

"Thank you for your time," O'Brian said, standing up abruptly. "If you think of anything else, please call."

"Of course. We will," Henry assured. He followed O'Brian to the door and bid him a good day, while Steph hustled to the nursery before Madeline started wailing.

When Steph walked back quietly into the living room with a satisfied baby, Henry was still standing in the kitchen, ready for work.

"I thought you would have gone to work already," she said, heading toward him. "Did he say anything to you after I left?"

"No, nothing important. Just apologized for the inconvenience. I think he felt bad about Madeline."

"So, what do you make of the police coming over here?" Henry started, wanting to know how his wife felt.

"I think Ayman must have called, or someone else came forward with more information," she concluded. "I hope the police find something." Henry was happy to hear her leave it to the authorities and promptly left for work.

Upstairs O'Brian continued onto Rachel's and Greg's apartment. He started with the former.

"Detective O'Brian. May I come in and ask a few questions?" Rachel opened the door, dressed for class.

"Yes, sir." O'Brian noticed the pink accents, music stand, and studio layout, guessing she was a student of some kind.

"Can you tell me where you were Monday night two weeks ago between the hours of 5:00 and 7:00?" The pair sat down at a small table with two chairs by the kitchenette.

"I was probably still here at 5:00, but I left soon after to go to taekwondo class."

"And when did you return to your apartment?"

"Maybe 7:20, depends on the bus. The class runs from 5:30 to 7:00."

"What's the name of the studio where you practice?"

"Master Kwon's Taekwondo."

"Is there someone who can corroborate your story?"

"My story? Any of the other students, the instructor, the receptionist... can I ask why you're asking so many questions?"

"The police are investigating the death of Sameed Haddad." Rachel sunk into a chair. "Do you have an idea of who might have wanted to kill him?"

"No," she replied meekly.

After a few more minutes of questioning, O'Brian left Rachel practically in shock. He offered to make her tea before he left, but she declined. As he closed her door, he could hear what sounded like an older woman on the phone. He deduced the poor girl must have been calling her mother. He knocked on the final apartment door.

"Hello?"

"Detective O'Brian. I'd like to ask some questions." Alaska lunged forward as the door opened. O'Brian jumped back, expecting the worst, but the dog wagged her tail and tried to lick him.

"Nice dog."

"She's a sweetheart," Greg said.

"Do you mind if I come in?"

"No, not at all. Sorry, there's not much for seating."

"Don't worry. I remember my first apartment."

"So, why are you here?" Greg sat down on his futon, which Alaska must have taken a few bites out of, while O'Brian pulled up a chair. Alaska laid in her bed, alert.

"I wanted to ask you a few questions about the night your neighbor, Sameed Haddad died. Where were you?"

"I was here all evening, working," Greg answered.

"Did you hear anything unusual after 5:00 PM?"

"No."

"Did you go to the bakery or see Mr. Haddad elsewhere that day?"

"No, I didn't."

"How long did you know Mr. Haddad?"

"Not very long." Alaska whined, and Greg

scratched her ears.

"How long have you lived in this building?"

"A little more than a year."

"Did Mr. Haddad have any enemies that you knew of?"

"No, but I didn't know him all that well," Greg admitted.

"If you had to guess, who would you suspect?"

"Maybe our landlord Dennis. I've heard them use some choice words with each other."

O'Brian asked a few more questions and was on his way.

Meanwhile, Steph's mind raced. If the police were investigating, Steph figured that meant someone had to be guilty. Someone's fingers left deep purple blotches on Sameed's neck, and he or she had twisted Sameed's tie in a mixer to cover it up. Unfortunately, the cleaners or the dump likely already erased any possible clues. And, if she understood correctly, family had washed the body prior to burial.

"I hope Jane's right about the bruising," she said aloud. She hoped too that an autopsy would uncover more evidence, but she doubted how much would be left. Charlotte had the one earring, but that might not have any traces of DNA left at this point either. What the police really needed was someone living, a witness or a confessor.

Steph first considered the former. Security footage from surrounding properties might suggest a few characters, but it was unlikely. Regardless, the staged accident happened inside the bakery, and there would be no footage there to mine.

Assuming there had been a witness, Steph considered why one wouldn't come forward. She named, "Fear, loyalty, guilt…" She imagined two or more people lurking behind the building and considered whether Sameed himself had witnessed something. Steph had assumed his death was personal given his strained relationships with his brother, ex-wife, and Sharon's family, but she could be wrong. In any case, the police were better equipped to find a witness, she told herself. She moved on.

A confessor. People generally didn't confess to murder out of guilt. She'd read that something like almost half of murders go unsolved, especially those in a city. Steph looked down. Madeline pawed at her for another nibble.

She might be sleepy this time, Steph thought.

She sat on the couch and offered the baby what she desired, then continued her line of thinking. A murderer might gloat, but that was more the Hollywood serial killer type. The guilty party might confess to some degree for a lighter sentence, but there would have to be pretty convincing evidence. Or, the murderer would have to believe there were. Before she got her hopes up, Steph reminded herself she hadn't narrowed down her suspects yet, let alone accumulated enough reason to suspect any particular one. She slouched, feeling frustrated. She told herself that at least the police were investigating now, which meant she hadn't been imagining things all along. Itching to get away from the building where the murder took place, Steph decided Madeline could sleep in the stroller.

Once out the door, Steph realized it was cold. However, Madeline slept soundly, and Steph had dressed in layers just in case. She continued toward the promise of a change of scenery and maybe even adult conversation, something her darling child couldn't produce yet.

Dennis too was outside, scrubbing away at something on the glass storefront with what looked like a metal sponge.

"What's that," Steph inquired.

"This?" He pointed to the sponge. "It's bronze wool."

"And what's—" Steph's mouth gaped. "Bye, sand n—" was written on the glass, the remainder already removed. Steph could guess the rest. "I can't believe someone would do that."

"We've had some graffiti before," Dennis informed her, "but nothing like this." He stretched high above his head to reach the top of a red letter, then slowly bent down for the drips.

"Has this happened many times?" She hoped not. The "d" of "sand" disappeared.

"No, maybe once a year at most, and usually

out back." Once a year seemed like a lot to Steph. She tapped her foot in annoyance.

"I wonder who would do such a thing. It's so…" she struggled to find a word strong enough to convey her disgust. "Hateful!"

"Who knows?" Dennis shrugged his shoulders.

"Have you reported it to the police?" This was a new angle she hadn't considered, a possible connection between a racist vandal and Sameed. Her fingers itched to start pushing the stroller while her brain walked in a new direction.

"I did the first time, but there wasn't much they could do. It's too expensive to put cameras around the whole building." The first and final "n" faded away. Steph thought a few cameras weren't such a bad idea after recent events.

"That's too bad."

"Are you out on a walk with Madeline?" Dennis changed the topic, asking the obvious.

"Just gonna drop by Black Coffee Bistro, see if anyone is there."

"Well, enjoy." Dennis turned back to his small bucket of water and scrubbing. Steph turned her mind to the perp. Calling this mystery person a graffiti artist was inappropriate. There was no art. She puckered her lips.

Taking another good look at the heinous writing, she noticed the height and execution. Not that she had any respect for someone who'd write that, but it was pretty bold of him to use spray paint during daylight hours. If some snot-nosed kid did this, then it must have been his first time, since he didn't know how to avoid drips. He probably even had paint on his shoes. "Or her shoes," Steph supposed, but considered it less likely.

Inside Black Coffee Bistro, Steph easily found an empty table, coming in between the pre-office and lunch rush. Caleb, the retiree, was there.

"Hey, Steph! How are you?" When he noticed the slumbering baby, he lowered his voice to a whisper. "Sorry. Didn't realize she was asleep."

"You're fine," Steph said softly. "Things have been pretty crazy since I last saw you."

"Busy with the baby?"

"No, I mean with everything that's happened at The Likable Daisy." She got an idea. "Hey, have you been here all morning? You didn't happen to notice someone spraying graffiti across the street today, did you?"

"No, sorry. I've been here for maybe twenty minutes, just reading the paper. That's a shame about the graffiti." Deflated, Steph moved on to other topics.

"What's the real estate market like these days?"

"Depends where. Are you looking?"

"Maybe," Steph said. She wasn't so sure her family belonged above the urban bakery when there were safer, greener options.

"City or suburbs? The suburbs have the best schools, but there are some good ones in the city too."

"I'm not sure at this point. Probably suburbs. I'd like a yard, but we haven't thought about it in depth. Thanks though. How've you been? Still retired, or getting back into real estate?"

"Still retired," he said. "I just keep an eye on the market for fun. Let me know if you ever want any help looking. Free of charge, of course."

"Thanks, Caleb. I'll take you up on that when we're ready."

Back at the police station, Detective Harris called in Ayman Haddad, Abila Khoury, and Dennis Kaplan.

"Thank you for coming," Harris said. "I'm so sorry for the loss of your brother."

"Thank you, Detective."

"I would like to ask you some questions about the day he died."

"Of course. What do you want to know?"

"I heard you argued with your brother the morning of. What did you argue about?" Ayman sighed, regretting that was their last conversation.

"A woman he was seeing."

"Anything else?"

"His lapse in attendance at the mosque."

"What about this woman?"

"My brother was in the middle of a divorce, and our family did not approve of the new girlfriend."

"And how did his ex-wife feel about it?"

"My brother did not deserve Abila, and we are ashamed of his treatment of her."

"What you do mean treatment? Did he abuse his wife?" Ayman squirmed almost imperceptibly in his chair.

"No, but he was not the kind of husband she deserved," he said, weighing his words.

"Can you elaborate, please?" Harris didn't enjoy squeezing information like this out of people who were already in pain, but it was necessary. Ayman sighed.

"Abila made sacrifices to finish medical school and become a doctor. It's a taxing career. My brother should have left the bakery in the hands of someone else every now and then to spend more time with her." Harris knew Ayman had been married and widowed and got the impression that he had been a devoted husband to his late wife.

"Thank you. And where were you the evening your brother died?"

"At the mosque, in prayer."

"When does that take place?"

"After sunset."

"Was anyone with you?"

"Yes, my sons and many others."

"Thank you, Mr. Haddad. Now is there anyone you suspect?"

"No, I think most people liked my brother."

"We only need one person who didn't," Harris reminded. Ayman sighed again.

"I honestly don't know."

"Thank you. That's all for now, Mr. Haddad. I'll let you know if I have any other questions."

"Of course. I will do anything I can to help."

The next person to come in was Dr. Abila Khoury, still in a white medical coat.

"Excuse me, what's this about?"

"Ma'am, the police are looking into the death of your husband Sameed Haddad."

"Why? I thought it was ruled an accident." Harris noticed she didn't seem startled by the suggestion of murder.

"New information has come forward, and we are treating it as a potential homicide. Now, I'd like to ask you–"

"Am I being detained?" Abila interrupted, eyes narrowed. Harris imagined she was the kind of doctor to make an accurate diagnosis in a heartbeat, but he doubted her bedside manner.

"No," Harris answered.

"In that case, I'm leaving. If you have any further questions, you can call my lawyer."

Harris released her and moved onto the landlord.

"Dennis Kaplan?"

"Yes?" Dennis turned his head toward Detective Harris as he entered the private room and sat down.

"Where were you the night your tenant Sameed Haddad died?"

"At home."

"Did you go out at all that night?"

"No, I ordered delivery, watched TV, that's it."

"Do you live with anyone?"

"No, I have the place to myself."

"How far are you from the building you manage?"

"Just a few minutes away."

"Do you manage any other buildings?"

"One other, a duplex."

"Did Mr. Haddad pay his rent on time?"

"Yes."

"Did you have any issues with Mr. Haddad or the bakery?"

"They had a bit of a trash problem, but generally no."

"Were you otherwise on good terms with Mr. Haddad?"

"Yes."

"I have reports that you may have used a racial slur while speaking with him, is this true?"

"What? No, I mean, not seriously, as a joke." Dennis looked down, pinched the bridge of his nose where his glasses sat, and then tried to meet Harris' eyes again. "We joked with each other. He was my friend."

"Is there anyone you suspect who might have wanted to kill Mr. Haddad?"

"I wish I knew, but I swear it wasn't me."

After a few more inquiries, Harris took a break from questioning. He only had one more scheduled for the day. He looked over his notes. This could be interesting.

"You are Sharon Andrews, correct?"

"Yes."

"You were the late Sameed Haddad's girlfriend?"

"Yes," she responded, her tone lowered.

"How long had you been dating Mr. Haddad?"

"Since Memorial Day weekend," she replied honestly.

"So, for a few months?"

"That is correct."

"Were you aware Mr. Haddad was still married to his wife at that time?"

"They were legally separated," she argued. "He had filed for divorce, but she was dragging her feet."

"So, yes?"

"Yes," she said resignedly.

"I'm not judging you, Ms. Andrews. Just establishing a timeline." Harris made a note. "Did you see Mr. Haddad earlier that day?"

"No, I was working and had a doctor's appointment, but we had dinner plans."

"When were you supposed to meet him?"

"5:30, at the restaurant. We had reservations."

"Were you there on time?"

"Yes."

"How long did you wait for Mr. Haddad?"

"Half an hour."

"I have a report that says you went to The Likable Daisy to look for him, is that correct?"

"Yes. He wasn't answering his phone, and the bakery wasn't that far away."

"Were you angry with him?"

"Kind of, yeah."

"Did you lose your temper with him?"

"No. I didn't even see him." Underneath the table, Sharon's fingers began to clench the fabric of her pants, sensing where the questions were going. They itched to play with her hair instead, an old school habit.

"Ms. Andrews, I have a record here stating charges were pressed against you by a previous boyfriend for domestic abuse less than two years ago."

"No… I mean, yes, but you've got it all wrong. He was abusing me, and I fought back one time. One time! Sameed was different. Kind. I would never…" Blond locks cascaded, covering her face, as Sharon rested it in her hands.

That evening, when Henry returned, Steph still felt a little on edge over the graffiti and the ongoing investigation, but she was relieved that the police were finally involved.

"How was your day?" Henry asked once in the door.

"Good. I saw Caleb at Black Coffee Bistro."

"How's he doing?"

"Enjoying retirement. He offered to help us look for a home if we wanted."

"Do you want to?" Henry asked. "I thought you loved living here, especially now that the bakery is reopening."

"I do, but... maybe it's not the right long-term choice for us."

"Maybe not, but our rental agreement is only for one year."

"So, you don't feel... unsafe?"

"No, do you?" he asked, concerned.

"No, if you feel safe, I feel safe," she said, smiling. Henry raised an eyebrow.

"Are you sure? I thought you'd feel better now that the police are investigating."

"I was, but there was some sick graffiti on the building today, and the dead woman a week ago..." her voice trailed off.

"We can look," he assured her. "And if we can't afford to buy, then we can rent somewhere else for a while." Steph's shoulders relaxed. "By the way, what's this about a cake? First Charlotte, and now the police officer."

"So," she started out awkwardly. "I might have taken a cake Charlotte made to the police, then thrown it away thinking it might be poisoned. It wasn't. Charlotte was just bringing it for the Halloween party. I think the detective ate it after I left." Henry laughed hard. "It was scary looking!" she defended.

"Well, at least you're finally developing a sense of self-preservation, but all this talk of cake is making me hungry. What's for dinner?"

After a simple, but satisfying meal, the couple returned to their normal hobbies, reading and drawing, but Steph found her mind struggling to focus on the autumn landscape. She decided to play with Madeline instead, remembering to schedule in tummy time despite her baby's protests.

"Are you really okay?" Henry asked. Normally, Steph liked to chat a bit more in the evening, since she spent most of the day with their currently nonverbal offspring. "I know the last few weeks have been a lot."

"I know. I feel like it's been ages since things felt normal, and I don't mean because we're parents now. That's different, but a good different." Steph took a breath. "I just hope that some sense of normalcy returns after the bakery reopens tomorrow."

However, rather than return to normal, Steph would return to the scene of the crime, her mind astir, as she rubbed elbows with Sameed's killer.

CHAPTER 18

The day of the soft reopening arrived. Steph was thrilled that the beloved bakery wouldn't be shutting its doors, but her mind was still troubled, feeling that Sameed's killer remained unknown.

To support Charlotte and Leyla, Steph, having received a 6:00 AM wake-up call from Madeline, went downstairs when The Likable Daisy opened. She was their first customer. After downing a delightful cappuccino and sweet turmeric roll, she stayed behind to help finish setting up red, white, and green streamers and balloons for the evening celebration, leaving briefly for Madeline's nap. While she decorated, she witnessed the happy trickle of regular and new customers through the polished front doors. For the moment, the layout of tables and chairs reflected their usual positioning, and guests seated themselves. A suitable arrangement for tonight's party could wait until later.

The smell of baking flour filled the air with a pleasant roasted aroma that accompanied bitter coffee beans. The westward-facing window front and soft recess lighting contributed a gentle glow, perfect for reading a morning paper or slowly coming to consciousness.

Some of the guests stopped over to where Steph was working, eager to hear what was new with the baby and why she was putting up decorations. Were they for Christmas, they wondered. Steph explained that those were the colors of the Lebanese flag. Since Charlotte and Leyla had limited the list of invitees to the party, Steph refrained from mentioning it to those who asked about the decor, so they assumed it was just for the reopening.

The party was going to be a celebration not only of the culture Sameed and Leyla wished to share with the world, but also what this space represented to the people who loved it most. Steph looked around, appreciating the sparkling clean glass, marble, and stainless steel. Almost everything reflected the beauty the shop had always possessed, but there was something she hadn't noticed before.

"Has that always been there?" Steph pointed above the front door. Charlotte, who had been behind the counter, turned toward her.

"No, it's new," Charlotte confirmed, then returned to her yeasted dough that she was punching down. Leyla too was stationed in the kitchen, making phyllo for baklava, her apron spotted with flour, while John managed the register.

"Hey, John," Charlotte called. "Can you take out the trash? And don't forget to prop the door, or else you'll be locked out," she reminded.

"Sure." John left, while Charlotte temporarily took his place.

To Steph's surprise, her friend leaned over the counter and whispered, "By the way, I forgot to tell the other tenants. I was so busy preparing, it slipped my mind, but I don't want Leyla to know. Can you go and invite them for me?"

"Of course," Steph replied quietly, then more loudly. "Hey, Charlotte. I'm gonna go upstairs to change Maddie. Can I take anything on my way out," Steph asked.

"We're good thanks."

Steph grabbed her purse, then through the front doors and up the stairs she went, stopping at the third floor with Madeline safely ensconced in the wrap carrier. She knocked on Rachel's door. Once unlocked, Rachel shuffled into the open doorway in house slippers, her lustrous hair disheveled for once. Steph felt a little guilty and wondered at the time. Maybe she should have waited until later.

"Hi, Steph," said Rachel. "What's going on?" Behind her all the lights were out and her blackout curtains were drawn.

"Oh, I'm sorry if I woke you. I didn't realize it was so early." It was 10:27 AM actually.

"No, no. It's just that I was playing at an event last night and didn't get back 'til late."

"Ah, I see. Sorry. Was just stopping by to let you know The Likable Daisy is reopening today, and the new owners, Leyla and Charlotte, have asked me to invite all the neighbors to join them at 6:00 to celebrate."

"Really? That sounds great," Rachel said, yawning. "Should I bring anything?"

"No, just yourself."

"Okay, thanks for telling me."

"No problem. Sorry again for waking you," Steph apologized.

"It's fine." Rachel yawned again. "Wait, does this mean they're open now?" she inquired, excited.

"Yep! And the turmeric rolls are as delicious as ever. See you later this evening, or maybe earlier," Steph said, reading Rachel's obvious desire for sweets. Her neighbor smiled.

Rachel gently closed the door, and Steph moved on to Greg's apartment. She knocked on Greg's door, hoping that he would be more awake.

Greg called out, "Who is it?"

"It's Steph."

"Just a minute," he called back. Steph wondered if he weren't fully dressed. "First Rachel, and now Greg," she muttered. Wow, her timing was bad. Greg opened the door. Behind him Steph noticed the eggshell white walls of yesteryear and in one corner a large cellaret. Bottles of amber liquid in more than a dozen different shades gleamed inside the cherry cabinet where crystal snifters also hung in display. The place screamed "Bachelor pad." A woman's touch was clearly lacking, not a decorative pillow or otherwise to be seen.

"Nice bar setup!" Steph praised. "Remind me to let you host the next poker night."

"Thanks," Greg said, sliding in front of the door. "I don't think I have enough chairs, but anyways, what's up?"

"Well, I wanted you to know that there's going to be a party downstairs to celebrate the reopening of The Likable Daisy. Leyla and Charlotte are hosting. All of us are invited, and it starts at 6:00." Remembering Rachel's question, she added, "You don't need to bring anything."

"Great."

"By the way, where's Alaska?"

"She's at the vet. She hasn't been feeling well."

"Sorry. Poor thing. See you tonight."

"See you tonight," Greg echoed, turning back into his apartment.

In retrospect, maybe Steph should have asked Dennis to tell them. Speaking of Dennis, she whipped out her phone and quickly called to let him know as well.

"Hello?" a male voice answered.

"Dennis?"

"Yes."

"Hi, it's Steph."

"Yeah?"

"Leyla and Charlotte are throwing a party downstairs tonight to celebrate the grand reopening. You're invited. It's starts at 6:00."

"Okay. Thanks for letting me know."

"You're welcome. See you later."

Steph looked down at Madeline. The baby gazed back up at her with heavy lidded eyes. It was probably time for her to take another nap, so Steph went back to her apartment instead of the bakery.

She called to let Charlotte know that she could return to help more in an hour or two.

"Don't worry about it," Charlotte said. "We're pretty much done. The rest is all baking and cooking. We'll see you at 6:00."

"Great!" Steph replied. She went back inside her own apartment and got comfortable in the armchair in the nursery. She carefully withdrew the sleepy infant from the carrier and rewrapped her in a swaddle. A short snack later and Madeline was out for the count. Steph too tried to take advantage of the quiet hour by sleeping, but something kept nagging her in the back of her mind. She paced the apartment instead. Maybe a hot shower would dislodge whatever thought or idea was stuck there, she thought. At the very least, it wouldn't hurt to be clean for the party tonight.

Water pouring down her back, Steph reviewed everything she had done this morning and tried to pair it with a similar conversation or circumstance she had come across in the last two weeks. A hazy picture was coming together in her mind, but it still remained out of focus as she stepped out of the steamy fog. She turned on the bathroom fan.

Steph had a few more hours before Henry would be home and the party would start. Whatever it was needed to simmer in the back of her mind for a while longer. Now seemed like a perfect time to take out her watercolors.

When Henry walked through the door after work he found his wife and child surrounded by a sea of impressionist images. When he looked closer, he recognized the scene from the glen, the storefront of their building, and a face he didn't know but found familiar.

"Who's that?" he pointed to the third image.

"My mother," Steph replied.

"You mean your biological mom?"

"Yes."

"I don't think I've ever seen a picture of her before. Do you have one?"

"No," Steph replied, a little morose. "This was from memory."

"She's beautiful, and you look so much like her."

"Thanks." A part of Steph had been worried inheriting her mother's looks also meant inheriting her mother's vices, but that voice was much quieter now.

Henry held Madeline while Steph washed out her brushes. Thankfully, watercolor brushes were easy to keep nice.

Thirty minutes later, Steph and Henry went downstairs with Madeline ready for a sumptuous feast and an interesting evening. All the neighbors were there, as well as Sharon and her family, Ayman and his family, even Abila, and– *Bang*! The back door slammed shut, and Dennis walked in. He must have parked closer to the rear entrance, Steph thought.

Ayman said a word over the meal, then welcomed people to dive in. Before them a glorious wall of food appeared. Still sizzling beef, chicken, and lamb saturated the surrounding air with the scent of black pepper, cinnamon, and fenugreek, among other spices, while sharp, fresh flavors lent by tabbouleh, fattoush, and baba ghanoush cut through the mouth-watering fattiness. Finally, pita, pilaf, falafel, and other carb-heavy sides soaked it all up into one harmonious blend. Another table featured mountains of sweet breads, anise and turmeric buns, sticky baklava fragranced with orange blossom water, an aromatic rice pudding, and a number of desserts Steph didn't recognize, but was dying to try. Her sweet tooth ached just at the sight.

Steph loaded up her plate, and she wasn't the only one to do so. Henry loved Mediterranean cuisine and was already acquainted with a majority of the offerings. Sharon seemed close to embracing the idea of "eating for two." Rachel, being a grad student, didn't shy from free food, and neither did Greg, though his plate was mostly meat, which was in contrast to her vegetarian one. Dennis seemed less familiar and a little more hesitant, but well-seasoned beef and fresh pita easily appealed to him, as well as Sharon's family. Ayman's kids tried to go straight for the sweets, but their father intercepted them, while Abila helped dish out healthy portions of vegetables.

Steph, Henry, and Madeline sat at a table near Sharon, her parents, and her brother David. Steph's wondered whose idea it was to extend the invitation to them, Leyla's or Sharon's.

"Hi, I'm Steph," she introduced.

"I'm Henry." Henry reached across the table in greeting.

"I'm Pam," said a mature woman with a graying bob and runner's physique.

"And I'm Nelson." A firm hand jutted out to shake theirs. Like his wife, Sharon's father had the lean, wiry musculature that implied a preference for long distances.

"Do you know our son, David?" Pam asked.

"Yes." Steph put her hand out toward him.

"Good to see you again," David said. Up close, Steph noticed a scar on his hand, wondering if it were from shrapnel or something else.

"Good to see you too."

The golden silence following the brief introductions signaled the food was delightful. Some small talk and chitchat filled the gaps in between chewing, but more often the not the only sound heard was that of a utensil scraping a plate. In between bites, Steph asked Sharon's family about their careers.

"So what do you two do?" Steph directed her question at her friend's parents.

"I'm a middle school math teacher," Pam answered, as her husband's mouth was full.

"And I'm a police officer," Nelson supplied.

"Retired. How about yourselves?"

"I'm an accountant," Henry responded.

"And I'm a stay-at-home-mom," Steph said. "For now. We'll see."

"Good for you," Pam told her. "I took a few years off when my kids were little and never regretted it."

"Thanks." Steph appreciated the validation.

Plate empty, she got up to fill it with just dessert, and since Madeline had nursed just before dinner, she felt at liberty to indulge in some champagne too. By the time the baby would want to eat again, the alcohol should be out of her system.

The bubbly hit her throat, cool, refreshing, and titillating. Steph helped herself to one more effervescent glass before walking back to her table.

As she sipped, she paused a moment to consider the people who were here and the one person who wasn't. Just like The Likable Daisy, Sameed had been sweet, neat, and welcoming. Though not everyone was exactly whom they seemed, and there was one person whose motivations seemed obscured or incongruous of late. While she was deep in thought, a little bit of champagne slid down the wrong pipe, and Steph wheezed.

"Are you okay?" Henry made a sideways glance at the flute she grasped.

"I'm fine. I'm fine," she protested, flushing from embarrassment and possibly alcohol.

"How many have you had?" Before she

could answer, Leyla and Charlotte began their prepared speeches.

"Please grab a glass." Leyla gestured to the already filled flutes on the tables. Those who had been seated with their backs to the register turned their chairs around.

"Thank you, everyone, for coming tonight. It means so much to us to have the support of such wonderful family and friends. In case you didn't know, I have asked Charlotte to be my new business partner," announced Leyla, her brown eyes smiling. Everyone cheered.

"A toast to a new partnership and a new beginning." Leyla held up a glass of sparkling cider, and everyone took a sip from his or her own flute. Charlotte took a step forward.

"Since I will be helping run the business," Charlotte said, "We'd also like to announce that Sharon will be joining our team. She will be the new face of The Likable Daisy, greeting and serving our customers up at the front." Sharon waved and smiled.

"A toast," Charlotte called, "to excellent pastry and even more excellent people." After another sip and a cheer, attendees returned to small talk. As she turned her chair back around, Steph remembered the new installment above the entrance. She handed Madeline to Henry and walked outside to make a phone call.

"Excuse me," she said, slightly scraping her chair. "I need to make a quick call."

In Steph's absence, Henry restarted the small talk with Sharon's parents.

"You live in the suburbs, right? East of here? How are the schools?"

"Excellent," Pam answered.

"Do you teach there as well?"

"No, I actually teach on the West side, but I know other teachers who do. Are you thinking about moving for this little one?" Pam smiled at Madeline.

"Eventually." Henry turned to Nelson. "Crime's low too, I'm guessing."

"That's correct, certainly lower than in the city," Nelson replied.

"Of course."

Steph returned from outside.

"Who'd you call?" Henry asked.

"The police," she replied.

"About what?" Henry was decidedly concerned, and the rest of their table listened with great interest.

"The security camera pointed at the kitchen."

"There's a camera there?" he said in a low voice. Sharon interrupted.

"Does this mean there's footage of… the accident?" She looked understandably uncomfortable.

"The police no longer think it was an accident," Steph confessed.

"What?!" Sharon's parents were flabbergasted.

"It's true, and they're coming to review the evidence tomorrow," Steph answered.

"Oh." Sharon was taken aback.

People filtered in and out of chairs, going back for seconds and thirds. Steph made her rounds around the different tables. She came to one where Greg, Rachel, and Dennis were seated.

"Hey." Steph stood by them, glass in hand. "*So*, I just heard the police are coming tomorrow to review security footage." Wavering, she pointed to a small, inconspicuous lens in the corner over the door overlooking the register and kitchen.

"Really? So they're going to catch who… killed Sameed?" Rachel whispered the last two words.

"The police think so," Steph replied.

"Did you hear anything that night?" Dennis asked.

"Noo, only Madeline. You?"

"No," Dennis answered. "What about you, Greg? Hear anything?"

"Nope," Greg answered. "Seemed like a normal Monday night."

"Whoops." Steph tripped over her own feet, spilling a little bit of her drink.

"Have you had a little too much, Steph?" Henry asked, coming up beside his wife.

"I'm fiiine. Really." Steph waved the question off with a swish of her hand. "Maybe just a *little* drunk. It's just been a while, ya know? See you all tomorrow," she added brightly, waving.

The party dispersed not long after. Steph went upstairs to change Madeline's diaper and get ready for bed, struggling a little, while Henry stayed downstairs, enjoying the party. The other guests trickled out the door, most grabbing a few desserts to go.

"Here, let me help you with that," Henry offered, taking a heavy trash bag from Leyla, who had started cleaning up. Ayman and his family were the last group to leave. His mother followed.

"I'll see you tomorrow, Charlotte," Leyla said.

"Bye." Charlotte waved. "Thanks for helping clean up, Henry. Do you want to take anything up with you," Charlotte asked.

"Anything you don't want, we'll eat," he answered honestly.

"Great." Charlotte bagged the remaining rolls and pieces of baklava, then handed them to Henry. He walked with her as she turned off the lights and, lastly, locked the front door. They parted ways.

Back in their apartment, Henry followed Steph's example and changed out of his clothes. He wished her a good night. The hours ticked by.

Downstairs, a hooded figure quietly approached The Likable Daisy, checking over each shoulder for any possible passersby or nosy parkers across the street. There was no one in sight. Fingers trembled with nervous energy.

Starting around the back, the hidden individual slinked from one entry to another. A few hours prior, a tour of the bakery gave no indication that the new partners had installed an alarm system. There was little reason to. No one had broken in the last time.

Furtive hands worked quickly and quietly, first trying every door and window obscured by night. None would oblige. Risking exposure to greater light on Greenway Avenue, the front door was next, but it too was locked. Desperate, the left hand wrapped the right in cloth, retreated, and let the other fly toward glass.

CHAPTER 19

Detective Harris sweated beneath his bulletproof vest in a windowless van. The two pounds of armor felt like twenty and constricted his torso. Heat radiated from the squad of bodies crowding him, and the thought of being shot at sent his blood racing.

The drive was painfully slow, but Harris perspired as if it were a high-speed chase. They could have been a courier service, but the only thing they were delivering was a warrant and eight men in tactical gear.

They pulled up beside their target. Harris and the other officers in black poured out of a sliding side door before the unmarked vehicle even fully stopped. Harris found his footing and led the men to the front entrance.

The team slipped across the concrete sidewalk in formation, signaling with their hands. Harris knocked on the door, announcing their presence, and waited for a response. None came. He gave the sign to force their way through the front door, and his men acted in tandem.

Across the street, sparrows greeted the sunrise with chirps, emerging from their dewy hiding places. Rustling leaves danced across the street, and early birds gaped over their morning coffee and newspapers.

Heavy boots tread as lightly and quickly as possible up the stairwell to avoid waking any sleeping inhabitants. Harris lumbered to the landing, swearing he'd start exercising more.

"Police! Drop your weapon!" he warned before a numbered oak door crashed open and splintered. Harris' heart threatened to leap out of its bulletproof cage, and he resisted the urge to clutch at it. The team followed him around every corner of the dwelling, shouting warnings to anyone who might be hiding. They came to a second door.

"Police! Drop your weapon!" he repeated. The next door came off its hinges, revealing another room devoid of people, as well as an unlocked window leading to the fire escape. Harris radioed to check if anyone had escaped out the back when they entered, but the squad car positioned behind the building responded in the negative.

The team quickly established that all rooms were in fact empty of occupants, but full of incriminating evidence. Harris' heart slowed its pounding. He radioed back again, saying, "Clear," and waited for orders.

Behind the closed bedroom door, he heard, "Hey, you here?"

Harris gave a muffled "Yeah." His hearted started thumping in his chest again, and he aimed his gun at the door.

"Awesome. It's only been two weeks, but I already sold…" The door opened and revealed eight police officers, weapons all pointed in his direction. "…everything."

Steph returned early in the morning despite Jane's protests.

"You better call me later," Jane threatened in faked sternness. She drove off. Jane had a shift at the hospital that day and couldn't wait around to find out.

Steph went up the stairs with a huge grin on her face and knocked a little too loudly on her door. A weary Henry answered, but his face brightened upon seeing his wife and daughter.

"I thought you were the police," he said in crumpled clothes.

"Were you here all night?" Steph asked, concerned. That hadn't been the plan.

"No, I spent a few hours at Jason's place, then camped out at Black Coffee Bistro when it opened. I came back when the police said it was okay to, but I'm pretty tired. Jason has a pretty nice apartment, actually. Maybe he'll be willing to trade since ours is famous now."

"I'll glad you're okay." Steph kissed him on the cheek. "I couldn't wait to be home again either. Now, go and get some sleep."

Henry walked back to their bedroom and closed the door. Steph situated herself and Madeline on the couch. She offered Madeline a glimpse of food to see if she were interested. That would help keep her quiet, but the baby just snuggled her. Madeline's tiny fist ever so gently pressed against her mother's chest. The littleness of her proportions and her tiny body curled up on Steph reminded her of their former oneness, and for the first time in weeks, she was fully at peace.

When Henry reawakened, he was surprised to see the remote untouched and the television off. He had been expecting expertly landscaped gardens, but instead stumbled across the sweetly slumbering duo. He took a picture, then nudged Steph's shoulder.

"I think the police are here," he whispered. She nodded and carefully walked over to the window to take a peak at the police cruiser parked below, while Henry walked into the kitchen and grabbed a roll. "You want one?" he mouthed, raising a roll to her eye level.

Her lips silently confirmed, "Yes." Steph returned to her warm spot on the couch, and Henry sat down next to her. Once Madeline reawakened, the pair decided to descend together to check out what was happening.

Nearly everyone who had attended the party had gathered once again, having been alerted by the police or by the commotion downstairs.

"Steph, someone tried to break in last night!" Charlotte informed her. "I think they were after the footage you mentioned. Thanks for letting me know not to say anything."

"Steph, I spent the night at a friend's like you suggested. Did you know this was going to happen?" Rachel exclaimed.

Detective Harris walked into to bakery and headed straight for Steph and Henry.

"Mr. and Mrs. Wu?"

"Yes?" Steph and Henry replied together.

"I would like to have a word with you privately for a moment." They drew aside for a few minutes, then returned, and Harris addressed everyone else gathered.

"Thanks to the Wus, the police have apprehended a potential burglar, murderer, and meth dealer, as well as an accomplice."

"Murderer?! Meth dealer?!" several shouted, incredulous.

"Can someone please explain?" Dennis requested.

"Last night, Mrs. Wu called us saying she believed there was a lab of some kind in the building."

"What? Where?" Dennis interrupted the detective. It was his building, and he wanted to know.

"She also suspected that the owner of the lab was responsible for the murder of Sameed Haddad," Detective Harris continued. "Later, we received a call from Henry informing us that a break-in was taking place, and that the reason for it was the suspect's belief that there was incriminating footage."

"So, there are no tapes?" This time it was Sharon sporting a brand new apron with the bakery's name and logo. Today had been her first day at the register, but there were no customers around now, as onlookers observed the police tape.

"Not that we know of, but we will be checking with neighboring buildings just in case."

"Is it safe to stay here?" Charlotte asked, more immediately concerned about the building itself and the lab's impact on their reopening.

"Yes, a hazmat team has already removed any dangerous materials. You probably don't want to thank your neighbor, but he kept a pretty tidy operation. However, please call if you have any concerns." Another policeman was flagging Detective Harris down. "I need to discuss something with my colleagues. Excuse me."

"I still have so many questions," Charlotte said after he left. Sharon concurred.

"Me too. Who did it, and how do we know if there's no proof?"

"Steph, you're the one who figured it out," Henry prompted. Steph handed Madeline to Henry. It would be easier to talk if she had full use of her hands. She started with an apology.

"I'm sorry I lied about the security tapes, but I thought it was the only way to catch Greg." Several voices chimed in simultaneously.

"Greg?!"

"Yes, Greg Novak killed Sameed, and it was Greg who had a secret meth lab in his apartment. Pretending the camera was old and the police were coming to review tapes was a bold lie, but Greg proved he was willing to take risks on more than one occasion if the payout was big enough, in this case, getting away with murder."

"How did you figure that all out?" Rachel asked. "Everyone thought it was an accident until yesterday."

"After Sameed's death, I felt really unsettled, not just that he had died, but that his death didn't make any sense to me. He was a capable baker, so why was he killed by his own mixer? Why wasn't his tie tucked into an apron, like he normally did? Later I found out that he had a date that night, so baking after work didn't make any sense. Then Charlotte told me he wasn't even wearing an apron and the ovens weren't on when she found him. Sameed always kept his clothes neat, and what baker doesn't preheat their oven? More and more it seemed to me like someone was trying to make everyone believe he had died in an accident." Heads nodded.

"I got stuck though. It wasn't enough to convince the police. Sharon happened to come by. She had Sameed's old watch and mentioned that Leyla had taken it in to fix some cosmetic damage before giving it to her. That to me seemed suspicious. I went back to Charlotte. I asked if she had noticed anything else the night she found him or if there was anything unusual about the kitchen. She recalled what looked like a reddish brown spice on the back of his shirt, but the kitchen had been immaculate. *It didn't look like anyone had been working in there.* A busted watch and spice on the *back* of his shirt? Sameed would have never taken such poor care of that watch or himself. I suspected he had been pushed against a wall and the latter was brick dust, but there was only one way to find out if there had been a struggle." Steph looked at Leyla to watch her expression.

"I talked to Ayman. There was a chance he had noticed something that the coroner might have missed. Sure enough, there were bruises that didn't appear until after the initial examination. When Ayman described them, I knew it had been no accident, and the police were convinced too."

"But how did you connect his death to Greg?" Sharon asked.

"When Sameed first died, I asked myself how well I really knew him, but every story we heard confirmed that he was the wonderful man we had found him to be. But then I started to think, how well did I know the other people in the building? Anyone who was here often would have had the opportunity. One by one, nearly everyone revealed themselves to be the person I thought they were, except Greg. Greg was the 'photographer–'" Steph used finger quotation marks. "–who used his bedroom as a dark room, or so we all thought, but he never showed anyone his work or carried a camera. Then, I found it curious how he was only ever busy with other projects whenever I asked him to schedule a portrait session with us. You'd think he'd have wanted the work and tried to find the time to do it, or at least suggested another photographer. And when I did get him to take a picture on my phone, it was completely blown out, the sun was so bright behind us."

"Finally, I got a glimpse into his apartment, where there were no signs of photographs or photography equipment anywhere, but an impressive liquor collection. After picking up a bottle for Henry's poker night, I could guess at what his home bar was worth. That's when it clicked for me. When I stopped thinking of Greg as a photographer, the other pieces started to come together, the mounds of trash, the abundance of paint thinner, the splotches on the grass and concrete, Rachel's headaches, the homeless woman who overdosed behind the building… even Alaska probably got sick from the meth lab fumes. I saw Greg when he was allegedly developing photos, and he was wearing a heavy-duty mask. Moreover, his hair was pulled back, and for the first time I noticed an ear was pierced."

"So, what happened that night?" Everyone was waiting for Steph to fill them in.

"This is what I think happened. Sameed stayed late after closing to organize his office before his date instead of leaving the downtown area. He went to throw out some trash, propping the door, so he could get back in. Unfortunately, Greg wasn't expecting anyone to be out back after closing, and Sameed witnessed Greg in the middle of a drug deal. Greg couldn't afford to be snitched on, and Sameed wasn't someone who could be bribed. So,

Greg rushed him, slamming him into the side of the building, hence the dust and damaged watch. Likely dazed if not unconscious, Sameed was unable to defend himself, and Greg strangled him. Seeing the door propped open, Greg got the idea to make it look like an accident happened inside the bakery. He didn't want police to suspect foul play and start sniffing around. He saw the mixer, tossed in some ingredients, and made sure the tie was twisted tightly enough to be believable, then he let the door close and lock on its own. But he forgot to put an apron on Sameed or turn on the oven. Maybe it was an oversight, or maybe he didn't want to leave any more traces of himself. Either way, the scene was incomplete."

"Greg had said he was home all night, but I remember hearing Alaska barking around the time Henry came back from work, which she only did when Greg was out. In addition, two whole weeks *after* Sameed's death, racist, amateur graffiti shows up immediately following the police interviews, which I found suspicious. Not only that, but Dennis struggled to reach parts of it, so the perp was probably tall. Sure enough, Detective Harris has since informed me that they discovered red spray paint in Greg's apartment. He had probably hoped to lead them in the wrong direction." Stunned silence followed. Steph looked around. A few people were holding back tears.

"Thank you," Leyla offered, lifting her glasses to wipe at the corner of her eye. "Thank you for getting my son justice."

"Yes, thank you," Sharon added with a sniffle, followed by Charlotte and the others. Once she had a moment of privacy with Steph, she said. "I had no idea. Did you suspect all along?"

"Not Greg, but I suspected it wasn't an accident right away." Steph had one last unanswered question. "Sharon? Why'd you lie about how long you'd dated Sameed?"

"I was embarrassed," she confessed. "We hadn't dated long, and I was already pregnant. I was afraid you'd judge me."

"Of course not." Steph gave her a big hug. Dennis came up to her next.

"Thank you, Steph," he said. "I thought the police suspected me. The interrogation was... horrible, but Sameed had been my friend, one of my only friends."

"Well, you're always welcome at poker night," Steph replied, to which Dennis smiled.

After receiving a multitude of thank-you's, Steph and her little family headed back upstairs to their apartment. Steph settled Madeline down for a nap, texted Jane, then walked back into the living room.

"Remember when you asked me why this case was so important? I think it's because, like Sharon's baby, I never knew my father," Steph reflected. "My mother was also taken from me at young age, and I never got a satisfying answer as to why."

"Well, because of you, we all know the truth of what really happened here." Henry paused. "And, you're really sexy when you solve crime," he declared, grabbing her butt.

"You know I don't see my OB for another three weeks," she replied, but when she saw his face deflate added, "but I'm sure I can think of something."

A minute later, her phone buzzed. It was Jane.

"You almost set me up with a murderer!"

CHAPTER 20

Four months later…

Once again celebration filled The Likable Daisy with joy and laughter, but this time there were no awkward, drunken interludes. Sharon was glowing and showing. She had planned to surprise everyone, herself included, with the baby's gender. Charlotte baked the cupcakes for her, having received an envelope with the results. Except for the sonogram technician, no one else was privy.

"Steph, this is beautiful! Thank you!" Sharon said, hugging her friend. Pink and blue balloons and streamers lined the walls and windows. Even the displays were festive. Instead of macarons and other sweet treats, the gleaming tiers held diapers, bottles, baby books, and stuffed animals.

"My pleasure," Steph replied, satisfied with the results.

Friends and family mingled happily in the seating area. Along the far wall where Sameed had previously stacked sumptuous pastries and Lebanese dishes for his Ramadan parties were towers of gifts in a rainbow of pastel wrapping paper and bags. Five-month-old Madeline was wide-eyed in wonder at the explosion of color and movement in the bakery, and wriggled with excitement in an exersaucer.

Steph and Leyla greeted and directed additional guests coming in through the front entrance. Powdery white snow gathered on the mat.

"Thank you for coming," they welcomed.

"Where can I put this?" Sharon's roommate held up a large, wrapped box. Based on the size and her struggle to carry it, Steph guessed it was a car seat, perfect for the newer, working vehicle the Haddads had gifted Sharon.

"Presents on the left." Steph directed her toward a long white table.

"You can put your coats on the back of a chair," Sharon told a friend of her mother's. "Pick any table. There's no assigned seating."

"Bathroom straight back across from the kitchen," Steph informed one of Ayman's sons. Ayman himself approached her next.

"Hi, Steph," he said. "I wanted to thank you again for planning the interfaith charity auction last weekend."

"I was happy to," Steph replied.

"I know you had to leave early for Madeline, so no one may have told you yet, but we raised more than $10,000 for the women's shelter, and your painting alone sold for over $1,000."

"What?" Steph was incredulous. "That's wonderful news! Who bought the painting?"

"Abila," Ayman replied. Steph looked over to where she was sitting.

"Oh, I need to go thank her."

Steph walked over to Abila radiating gratitude.

"I can't thank you enough for your generous

donation."

"I wouldn't call it generous. I got caught in a bidding war. Didn't Ayman tell you?"

"No," Steph replied. "Well, I hope you like the painting."

"Of course, I do. I wouldn't have bid on it if I didn't. You have an eye for color."

"Thank you." Steph was warmed by the compliment.

A moment later, she went back to helping seat everyone. After they all had settled, Sharon, the luminous mom-to-be, stood in front of everyone cupcake in hand.

"Everyone, please take a cupcake," she instructed. "One. Two. Three. Eat!" Sharon quickly took a big bite before holding up the center of the cupcake for all to see. "It's a GIRL!" She squealed with glee.

"I KNEW it," Steph declared. Leyla smiled broadly, as did Ayman and Abila. Ayman's sons buzzed with sugar and excitement at the prospect of a little girl cousin.

"Congratulations!" many exclaimed.

"Do you have a named picked out," someone asked.

"I was thinking about naming her Daisy," Sharon answered. "After her great-grandmother."

"She will love that," Leyla said, grinning again. Steph came up to Sharon to offer her personal congratulations and a gift.

"I'm so excited for you. A little girl. I had a

feeling. Here," she said, offering a small box tied with a pink ribbon. "I think Sameed would have wanted his daughter to have one." Sharon opened the box. Inside was a gold bracelet identical to the one he had once given to baby Madeline.

"Oh, Steph. Thank you so much." Sharon hugged her.

"Absolutely. And one day soon our baby girls can play together."

"That sounds wonderful." Sharon smiled, the two women separated, and Steph opened her mouth again for another announcement.

"Okay, ladies and gents. It's time for our first shower game. Now grab a baby bottle, fill it with milk, juice, or tea," she gestured toward the table with refreshments. "And went I say, 'Go,' start chugging! Whoever sucks the most in one minute wins!" Several attendees already started laughing before the countdown. The baby shower had officially commenced.

In a residential neighborhood not far away, Detective Harris sweated bullets trying to maintain his composure. He felt several pairs of eyes watching him, waiting to see what he'd do.

The slimmer father of four dropped his second foot after wobbling in tree pose beside his wife and daughters. Clarence, his son, stifled a laugh as his mother Florence whipped her head around to wordlessly correct him. Yoga was good for regulating his father's stress, and Bert needed all the encouragement he could get.

"I feel ridiculous," he complained for the umpteenth time, but if he were honest, he'd also say he was feeling better.

"Trust us, dad," Tiffany said.

"This is good for you," Monique finished, as the girls transitioned into another pose.

"Wanna join, Clarence?" Patricia offered.

"Not in a million years," he replied.

"Laugh again, and I'll sign you up for classes," his mother warned.

Clarence decided now was a good time to practice his layup outside.

Across town, Jane and David met up for a lunch date after the shower finished, celebrating their four months together.

"I had a feeling on our first date," Jane admitted. "Anyone who's willing to go to such lengths for a bear must be a keeper."

"Really? Well, I had a feeling when I first met you, but I knew for sure when you leaned in and told me I smelled nice."

"What? How? I thought maybe…" Jane realized she had not been as composed as she had hoped, but, on the plus side, David hadn't dumped her thinking she was a lush.

"Don't worry. For the record, I think you smell nice too."

Jane burned with embarrassment, turning her face aside for a moment. When she did, she noticed Ayman and Abila alone at another table holding hands.

"Well, would you look at that?" Her fingers itched for her phone, but she resisted the urge to pull away from David's hand. She could keep quiet, for a little while at least.

Later than evening, Henry and the guys gathered once again for their biweekly poker night. Dennis, David, Jason, and Richard all still attended, and this night Henry's father joined, as he made it a monthly habit.

"Hey, Dad! Good to see you! What did you bring this time?" Wu Peng walked in wearing his favorite Syracuse sweatshirt and held a bottle of something in one hand.

"I brought *baijiu* for a change."

"Rice wine? Are you trying to kill the competition?" The men seated looked on with interest.

"You still have the cups we bought, don't you?"

"Yes," Henry replied grabbing them from a high shelf.

"Peng, why are the cups so small?" Richard asked.

"Because it packs a huge punch," Henry explained. "Careful, my dad could drink all of you under the table."

"I'd like to see him try," David challenged. "Bring it on" was the general spirit. Even Dennis raised his glass. Happy to be with her new owner, Alaska stood guard at his side, wagging her tail.

Instead of in the nursery, Steph sat down across town. Though she took taekwondo classes with Rachel every other Monday, when her father-in-law came to their apartment, she traded places with him.

Steph and Madeline bundled up and drove to her in-laws' house for a few hours of tea, sesame cookies, and serious mahjong playing. Her sister-in-law Catherine and their Lao Lao, Li Ming's elderly but wicked sharp mother, joined them to make a party of four at the table, as the baby watched the flipping tiles with fascination.

Li Ming's Chow Chow Mei Mei quietly chewed on a dog toy under the table, while her mistress executed another brilliant play. Though she was still learning the strategy, Steph found the game beautiful. Each tile was a small work of art with vibrant illustrations and charismatic brushstrokes.

"She's got one!" Catherine warned. Sure enough, Madeline, who had been sitting on her grandmother's lap, had managed to grab a tile. Steph quickly ripped it away from her and substituted her panda lovey.

"*Sorry,*" Li Ming apologized reflexively in Chinese.

A few turns later, Steph drew the winning tile for the first time. She revealed her hand.

"Mahjong!"

The End

Get the first chapter of the next Likable Daisy Mystery for free by subscribing to my mailing list at:
www.hannahrkurz.com

Follow me for updates on new releases:
Facebook @hannahrkurz
Twitter @hannahrkurz
Instagram @hannahrkurz

Printed in Great Britain
by Amazon